LITTLE,
BROWN

LB

LARGE
PRINT

LESS IS LOST

ANDREW SEAN GREER

LITTLE, BROWN AND COMPANY

LARGE PRINT EDITION

The author would like to thank Lynn Nesbit, Judy Clain, Anna de la Rosa, Reagan Arthur, Nia Howard, Stacey Parshall Jensen, Shadae Mallory, Tracy Roe, Lee Boudreaux, Daniel Handler, Julie Orringer, Ayelet Waldman, the Westleys, David Ross, Priscilla Gillman, and Claudia Fieger, as well as his family, including Elagene Trostle and nephews Arlo and Mack, who he thinks will enjoy being in a book. Thanks to the Guggenheim Foundation for the grant that allowed for all the RV rentals. This novel was begun at the MacDowell Colony, written at the Santa Maddalena Foundation, and finished at Civitella Ranieri. Special thanks to Quo the dog, who was steadfast, and to Enrico Rotelli, who always is. In memory of beloved Olive the pug (2006–2022).

The characters and events in this book are fictitious. Any similarity to real persons, living or dead, is coincidental and not intended by the author.

Little, Brown and Company
Hachette Book Group
1290 Avenue of the Americas, New York, NY 10104
littlebrown.com

First Edition: September 2022

Little, Brown and Company is a division of Hachette Book Group, Inc. The Little, Brown name and logo are trademarks of Hachette Book Group, Inc.

The publisher is not responsible for websites (or their content) that are not owned by the publisher.

The Hachette Speakers Bureau provides a wide range of authors for speaking events. To find out more, go to hachettespeakersbureau.com or call (866) 376-6591.

Illustrations by Lilli Carré

ISBN 9780316498906 (hc) / 9780316301398 (large print) / 9780316509978 (international)
LCCN 2021952281

Printing 1, 2022

LSC-C

Printed in the United States of America

For William Greer, my wonderful father

And the man that has anything bountifully laughable about him, be sure there is more in that man than you perhaps think for.

—Herman Melville, *Moby-Dick*

LESS
IS
LOST

SUNSET

LESS should have known, at the clinic a few weeks before, that his relationship was in some trouble. It was an ordinary blood draw for an ordinary medical checkup, the kind a man over fifty must submit to once a year in America. The bell jingled as he opened the clinic door, then jingled again as he failed to close it, then jingled again. And again. "Sorry!" he shouted to the empty waiting room, its only inhabitants a clipboard, a watercooler, and a fan of gossip magazines in absurd hues. But look at Less: A sweatshirt as bright as a highlighter, a little Marseillais fisherman's hat. Let's not anyone here call anyone else absurd.

In the exam room, the phlebotomist (bald, Taiwanese, heavily tattooed, suffering a fresh heartbreak that has no bearing on our story) arrived with a clipboard, which he handed to Arthur Less.

"Please write your full name at the top," the phlebotomist said, preparing an intriguing tray of vials.

The patient wrote the name *Arthur Less*.

"Please write down the name of your emergency contact," the phlebotomist said, preparing the inflatable cuff.

The patient wrote the name *Freddy Pelu*.

"Please write down the nature of your relationship," the phlebotomist said.

The patient looked up with surprise. Our lovelorn phlebotomist glanced at the questionnaire and replaced the blood pressure cuff, with its kelp-like tubing and bulb, on the tray beside him (such a device is called, by the way, a manometer).

"The nature of your relationship, Mr. Less," he said brusquely.

"It's a tough question," said the patient. Pausing for a moment, misunderstanding the universe, he finally wrote:

Uncertain.

This clumsiness of the heart also became apparent on a certain California road trip: Less was equipped only with his lover, an old Saab, and some hastily purchased camping equipment consisting of two intra-zipping sleeping bags and a large nylon disk. This disk, of Swiss manufacture, unfolded into a tent whose vast interior defied belief; Less was fascinated by its pockets, air vents, rain flies; its stitching, netting, and circular Guggenheim ceiling. But, like the Swiss, it was neutral; it did not love him back. Sure of his infallibility, he unzipped the insect mesh and let in a rowdy bachelorette party of mosquitoes that raided the human open bar; he even zipped the sleeping bags to the ceiling. And on the final day, when a wild downpour arrived at lunchtime, it was decided that, while the tent could be trusted, Less himself could not. A hotel must be booked. The nearest was something called the Hotel d'Amour. This turned out to be a cream-colored cake in a rain-drenched forest, decorated inside with white roses and gilt furniture, and the desk clerk greeted them with surprise and delight; there were no guests at the hotel due to the last-minute cancellation of a wedding. "We've got a rose altar, and a priest, and a wedding dinner and cake and champagne and a DJ and everything!" She sighed, and her fellow staff members looked upon their new guests expectantly. Doves within a cage cooed romantically. The stout priest, her vestments dark with rain, smiled hopefully. A string quartet was playing "Anything Goes." Outside, the storm shut the door and blocked the escape. It seemed there was no dodging destiny.

"What do you think?" I said to Arthur Less.

That's me. I am Freddy Pelu. I am the emergency contact (who picked up Less at the blood-draw clinic shortly after he fainted). I am a short and slight man approaching forty, the age at which the charming eccentricities of one's twenties (sleeping in a silk bonnet to save my curls and wearing rabbit-eared slippers) become the zaniness of middle age. My curls have patinaed like scallops on old silver; my red glasses magnify my myopia; I am winded after chasing my dog one time around the park. But I am as yet unwrinkled; I am no Arthur Less. Rather, I am what I would call an alloy (and my grand-mother would call a pasticcio) of Italian, Spanish, and Mexican heritages—mere nationalities, being themselves mixtures of Iberian, Indigenous, African, Arab, and Frankish migrations, breaking down further until we get to the elemental humans from whom we all descend.

For the past nine months, I have lived with this troubled patient, this Arthur Less, novelist and traveler, in San Francisco in an almost-but-not-quite-waterproof one-bedroom bungalow on the Vulcan Steps that we tenderly call "the Shack," a house belonging to his old lover Robert Brown-burn that Less has called home for a decade without paying rent. Sharing in this good fortune is a bulldog named Tomboy, whom people assume is a boy, although, as Less takes pains to point out, tomboys are, by definition, girls. It is a chore and an honor and a comedy to live with them both. Nine months of un-marital bliss. But we have been linked for far longer.

We got together, quite casually, when I was twenty-seven and he forty-one, and "quite casu-ally" is how I kept things for nine years. Staying with my grouchy uncle Carlos, unsettled in my adopted home (while living and breathing through the bulky apparatus of a second language), I found the Shack a cozy place to flop. Less never pressed for more than a kiss goodbye; I assumed he was caught up in his work or whatever engaged men of his age. Nine years of assuming these things—it feels cruel to admit, but those years are among my most treasured. The only time in my life when I was a prince. Walking in and out, chided and adored. At the time, I did not know what to call "love."

I had to learn the hard way. I awoke one morning across the world from Arthur Less and saw nothing but the bright blue of his signature suit. I understood that happiness is within our grasp if we reach for it. And so I traveled the world to win him back...

But he did not marry me that day at the Hotel d'Amour. Even with the doves and caterers as witnesses, the skylights above us drumming from the pounding rain. On his face was written a single word: *uncertain*. "I have to think about it," he said.

This is the story of a crisis in our lives. Not at the clinic or at the Hotel d'Amour (or on other ill-fated trips), but during a journey alone. It begins in San Francisco and it ends in San Francisco. In between: a donkey, a pug, a whale, and a moose. For now, let us pivot away from me, Freddy Pelu. For I do not appear in this story until much later.

(To be clear: At the clinic, he should have written *partner*.)

Look at Arthur Less today:

Standing on the deck of a San Francisco ferry-boat, in a gray suit so precisely the same color as the fog that he seems (as in a not particularly scary movie) to be a ghostly floating head. Look at his thinning hair wind-whipped into the stiff peak of a blond meringue, his delicate lips, sharpened nose, and elongated chin recalling Viking invaders from the Bayeux Tapestry, as white as a white man can get, colored only by the pink tips of his nose and ears and the blown-glass blue of his eyes. Look at Arthur Less. Somewhere past fifty, indeed a ghost of his former self, but as the sky begins to darken, he fully materializes into a tall middle-aged man shivering in the cold. Here he stands, our hero, looking around like a man who has grown a mustache and is waiting for someone to notice.

He has, in fact, grown a mustache. He is, in fact, waiting for someone to notice.

On this foggy October morning, our Minor

American Novelist is making his way to a small gold-rush town in the Sierra Nevadas to give a lecture in their Significant Speakers series. For anyone else, it would be a mere three-hour journey, but our Arthur Less has to do things the hard way; he has chosen to take a ferry and a train. This should land him in the townlet in about five hours, and along the way he expects to take in the view gold miners must have had climbing from bawdy San Francisco up to the barren mountain of their fortunes.

Oh, to have a manometer that truly measures the essence of man! What would it show of our protagonist, smiling gently on his city as it fades into the fog like a photograph too long exposed? Perhaps the restlessness of a heart swimming inside a fiftyish rib cage. But also, I think: the seeping pleasure of recognition, which, though writers claim to desire only for their ink to dry before they leave the planet, must be what warms this sole occupant of the upper decks on this cold, foggy Sunday. For is he not a Significant Speaker? Traveling even now to be applauded by gold miners, much like Oscar Wilde on his tour of the Wild West (such are his delusions that Less imagines miners and not marijuana farmers)? And more: Arthur Less has received more invitations in recent days than in all the past year put together. A major Prize has asked him to be on its jury; a theater company has requested permission to perform one of his stories. Could there be some silent audience eagerly awaiting his new novel? Some hidden force unrecognized by the publishing and critical world of New York City, which, like an orbiting space station, looks upon the rest of America without ever interacting with it?

Ignore all that, the poet Robert Brownburn says to him in memory. *The point of writing is the page.* The famous poet Robert Brownburn; easy for him to say, *Turn away from love.*

The poet Robert Brownburn—my predecessor. They were together fifteen years and lived in the Shack for most of those. They met when Less was only twenty-one, on Baker Beach in San Francisco. Less had struck up a conversation with a woman in sunglasses smoking a cigarette who said her name was Marian, advised him to use his youth well, to waste it, and then asked him a favor: Could he accompany her husband into the dangerous surf? He did; the man turned out to be Robert Brownburn. He left Marian to live with Less; he brought Less to the Pulitzer ceremony when he won the prize; he brought him to Paris and Berlin and Italy. When they parted, Arthur Less was in his mid-thirties. You could say Robert Brownburn was his youth. I have been his middle age. Is there yet another, unmet, to be Arthur Less's dotage? It is possible that he would have married Robert Brownburn if he could have. But times were different, laws were different. And I have never asked.

Back to the chill of San Francisco as Less, aboard the ferry, receives the first of three calls this morning:

"Hello-I-have-Peter-Hunt-on-the-line-please-hold."

Less listens as Céline Dion performs the entirety of AC/DC's "You Shook Me All Night Long," followed by an interlude of silence, followed by the voice of Peter Hunt, his literary agent: "Arthur, let me get right to it." He delivers news, good or bad, in a jolting way, like the electric shock used to prod cattle.

"Peter!"

"You're on the jury for this Prize," Peter says in a terse voice; one can picture him swinging his stallion's tail of white hair behind him. "I wish you hadn't agreed to it, because I thought you had a chance this year—"

"Peter, don't be ridiculous—"

"My advice is not to bother reading anything. The winner will come to you, like a divination. Your time is better spent on other things."

"Thank you, Peter, but my duty—"

"Speaking of other things," Peter barges through, "good news! I've got you an exclusive profile of H. H. H. Mandern, a big ten-page profile, glossy with photos and everything. And he asked specifically for you."

"Who?"

"You, Arthur."

"No, I mean who asked?"

"Mandern asked. He was confused; I cleared things up. He's heading out on tour for his latest book."

"I'm not up for a road trip."

"No road, no trip. You go to Palm Springs and Santa Fe. Interview him onstage. Talk with him after. Put together a profile for the magazine. Only catch is you fly out in two days."

"Then it's a no," Less says firmly. "I'm going to Maine."

"Working on something?"

"Peter, I just finished a book!"

"So Palm Springs—"

"Peter, it's a no."

"Starts Tuesday, think about it, enjoy the Prize Committee, welcome home—" And the line goes dead.

From the waters of the San Francisco Bay, a face appears: a seal, staring fixedly at Arthur Less, who stands alone in the chill wind of the ferry's deck. Less stares back. Who knows of what it is trying to warn him? The seal (or selkie?) vanishes into the water and Less is left alone.

Welcome home indeed, for this Minor American Novelist has been gone a long time from his native land. So long that he now thinks of it, as the salmon must think of the streamlet of her parents when returning to it, as yet another foreign country. After a zigzagging itinerary around the world—six thousand miles as the albatross flies (and a story for another time)—he landed home in San Francisco . . . only to launch himself up again for three more America-free months finishing his novel. Our thrifty author booked himself a hut on a beach in Oaxaca, a solar-powered one that forced him to rise at dawn and work until the power failed at sunset. He was a wreck when he returned to me, but I could see he had never been more content in his life.

What is it like to return to your country after so long? Less assumed it would be like picking up a novel you had put aside some time ago; perhaps you'll need to reread a little, remind yourself of who Janie is, and Butch, and Jack, and why everyone in Newtown-on-Tippet is so upset about the castle. But no, no, no. It is far stranger. More like picking up a novel only to discover the novel has been writing itself while you were away. No Janie, no Butch, no Jack. No Newtown. No castle. For some reason, you are in outer space, orbiting Saturn. Worse, the previous pages have been torn out; there is no rereading. You have to start from where you are—where your country is—and simply plod ahead. You may think: *What's happened? Good God, are they kidding?*

But it is a rule of life, alas, that nobody is kidding.

The second call is from me, Freddy Pelu.

"Ladder down!" (a private joke).

"Freddy, good news!"

"You sound happy!"

"Peter just called and apparently H. H. H. Mandern asked for me to do a profile."

I ask, "Who?"

"H. H. H. Mandern!" says Less. "One of the
most famous writers of our time. It's money. And
I said no!"

"That's the good news?"

Less is jubilant: "I said no! Because tomorrow I'll
be with you in Maine! I don't know what's going
on, I don't know why I'm on this Prize Committee, I don't know why I'm speaking today, I don't
know why Mandern asked for me, but Freddy, it's
just nice! It's nice to be wanted! But really, who
wants a middle-aged gay white novelist nobody's
ever heard of?"

"Me," I say. "I do."

I am not in the chill of San Francisco; I am in the
chill of the Northeast. I am in a small Maine college
town for the three months of my sabbatical, taking
a course in narrative form.

"Well, you're in luck," he says. "My flight is
tomorrow at noon."

"You really turned it down?"

"Of course I did! I'm joining you in Maine, that's
our plan. I don't want to be apart for months."

"You do love to travel."

"I don't love to travel, I love to travel to you,"

Less says as a foghorn sounds. "I'm going to a mining town and then I'm coming to see you in Maine."

"You know what I like in a middle-aged gay white novelist nobody's ever heard of? A little confidence. Maybe you're getting these invitations because you really are a great writer."

"You know what?" Less says. "Today I feel like maybe I am!"

"Of course you are!" I say.

"Sorry, Freddy, I'm getting another call. I love you!"

"Take it! Maybe it's the Nobel Committee!"

"Maybe it is!" he says. I tell him I love him. The seals or selkies seem to wave to Less from the water, a final warning; he waves back and merrily answers his ringing phone for the third call this morning. Things are going so well today that it feels not impossible it is the Nobel Committee.

But, friends, it is not the Nobel Committee. It is a rule of life, alas, that it is never the Nobel Committee.

A somber voice comes on the line: "Arthur, it's Marian..."

Be strong, Arthur Less. Do you remember we made a deal? Not long after I moved into the Shack? It was a Sunday, and I had spent the entire day in that white bed (below the trumpet-vine window) correcting student papers; I had not moved since breakfast, and it had been dark a long time. You came in with a pizza and a bottle of red wine. You, too, had spent the day in your bathrobe. You sat down on the bed and poured me a glass of wine and said, "Freddy, now that we're living together, I have a proposal." Your hair was a blondish mess, your cheeks in "high color," as they say in English novels; perhaps you had already gone through the remains of another bottle. "Neither of us is strong. We can't put up a shelf or fix the sink and neither of us can catch a mouse." You put your hand on my arm. "But somebody has to catch the mouse. So here's my proposal. You be the strong one Mondays, Wednesdays, and Fridays. And I'll be the strong one Tuesdays, Thursdays, and Saturdays."

I paused, suspicious. "What about Sundays?"

You patted me on the arm with reassurance. "On Sundays, Freddy, nobody's the strong one."

I receive a voice mail in Maine: "Freddy. Robert's ex-wife, Marian, called." And then a pause. "Robert died a few hours ago. Multi-organ failure. I canceled my event. I have to head back. Marian says she's already on her way here from Sonoma, she's staying the night at the Shack, we have to plan the funeral, which is tomorrow, so don't try to fly home. It will be something small, just a few people.

I'll figure it out and let you know. I'll call you later. I love you."

Today is Sunday.

★ ★ ★ ★ ★ ★

  ★ ★ ★ ★ ★

★ ★ ★ ★ ★ ★

The first person not to notice his mustache is the ex-wife of Robert Brownburn.

"I'm so sorry, I shouldn't be smoking in here," says Marian. He has found her already waiting for him in the bedroom of the Shack. From the other room comes the hurricane of a vacuum cleaner; our hippie cleaning lady, Lydia, has sprinkled white powder all over the carpets. Less closes the door behind him and sighs.

Small and solid and beautiful, nearly eighty now, Marian still gives off the aroma of vitality Less remembers from their first meeting on a beach. Her hair—in his memory brown and curly, perhaps permed—has become a chin-length bob of white steel, framing her face as severely as a Greek helmet. Less's, of course, has faded to an abbot's tonsure.

Seated on the bed, she wears a long purple cotton poncho or chasuble and a large pebble on a cord around her neck. Marian is smiling, though her face is dark and smudged from crying.

"I'm indulging in all my vices," she says, throwing her cigarette out the window. She struggles to stand; both her hips, so sumptuous in the sand that day they met, have had their bones replaced, also with white steel. "I only have two vices left. The other one is optimism. Same vice, in fact." She and Less embrace.

"Oh, Marian, it's awful, just awful."

"You look different, Arthur."

"Do I?" he asks, touching his mustache.

"Thinner," she says. "I wish grief could do that to me."

"Thinner, huh? You look wonderful, Marian."

She seats herself again and laughs, wiping her face with the heel of her hand.

Is it easier to bear an old lover's death when you're eighty or when you're fifty? Hard to say, seeing these old enemies and their fading grins. Marian looks still lively but despairing, like a plant that has been torn up at the roots; there is no help for what she is suffering, and her eyes keep going to the window as if it opens onto another plane on which none of this has happened. And Arthur Less. Arthur Less looks like a magician's assistant without a magician. Now who will saw him in half?

Less joins her on the bed. "Marian, how have you been?" They have sensitively avoided each other these last months at Robert's hospice.

"Well, you know I've been weaving rugs," she says, grabbing the stone that lies on her breast, perhaps reflexively, for comfort. "Weaving all the rugs in a rich woman's mansion, up in Montana. A dozen rooms. Now I'm almost done and, Arthur, I'm slowing down; it feels like I've cast a spell and that when I finish that last rug...I'll fall down dead."

"You sound like a novelist," he says ruefully.

She shrugs and looks out the window. "I told the woman I was afraid of finishing, so she went and built a guesthouse. Just so I'd have another rug to make."

Less looks around. "There's a dog here somewhere..."

"I met the dog; that nice woman has him trapped in the bathroom. Apparently *we're* trapped in *here* while the magic powder does its work on the rugs. Thank you for putting me up."

Less does not correct her about Tomboy's gender. "It's good to see you, Marian. Even if it's so sad."

She looks directly at him and continues not to notice his mustache. They can hear the vacuum in the other room coming closer. They sit without speaking until the hurricane passes.

"And you, Arthur? You said you were traveling somewhere."

"Oh, just north of here," he says. "I canceled."

"I always picture you traveling."

"Not anymore," Less says. "I have a lot of invitations. And I'm on a Prize Committee. But I don't travel since Freddy moved in."

"You know," Marian says, "I don't think of Robert as dead. Isn't that silly? I think of him like Merlin, wandered off and sealed in the trunk of a hawthorn tree. For a thousand years."

Less finds himself smiling. "Really? That's funny. He used to talk about that story. I thought he was talking about me. Saying that I was the tree."

"No, Arthur, no."

"That I'd lured him away," he says. "Like a fairy. Stolen his powers."

"No, Arthur, nobody ever thought that. If anything, I was the tree." Marian rests her hands on her thighs and then suddenly exhales. "This is the most ridiculous conversation anybody ever had. We are the most ridiculous creatures."

"Robert would be proud of us."

Oh, Marian! Let us draw no boundaries around existence, which contains wonders unknown! For there is a creature more ridiculous still and here it comes, scrabbling across the floor, bewigged in white powder, snorting like a steam engine: a bulldog, Tomboy, losing her little mind with love.

Marian has retreated to the bedroom for the night, Less and I have talked, and now Less, having changed into pajamas and plugged in his special electric razor for his mustache, relaxes on the sofa bed listening to *Slow German News,* a program in which a woman reads aloud articles from *Die Welt* at the calm, unhurried pace of a Zugpferd pulling a wagon of manure. Less's German, practiced often in his youth, now comes out as seldom as a retired great lady of the stage, but *Slow German News* is one of his great comforts. *Monotonous German News,* I like to call it, and Less shyly hides his headphones as if caught listening to *Slow German Porn.* I believe, in his Lessian way, he is. "Die wachsende Kluft," she soothingly tells him, "zwischen dem amerikanischen Volk"—at which point he receives a call. Not his partner this time; it's his sister, Rebecca.

"Oh, Archie!" she sighs. She calls him Archie. She has always called him that and always will. "You holding up?"

"Not at all. Neither is Marian. And that's how it should be."

"This is so shocking."

"It's not shocking," Less admits. "I knew it was coming. I just didn't prepare myself properly."

"Archie, your only job for the next few days is to nod your head when people say they're sad and eat as much as possible. And remember to drink alcohol. That's important. Get some of those mini-bottles you like. Wait, is there a German woman there with you?"

"No, no," Less says, turning off his program. "No, it's just me."

"All right. When's the funeral?"

"Tomorrow," Less says. "At the Columbarium. It's just his ashes. Marian and I scrambled to put everything together. She asked some old friends. I hired a chorale."

"A what?"

"A chorale. Singers."

"Well done."

"And afterward there's a celebration of his life. At least, that's how they announced it. Robert would've hated that. And you?"

"Just me and the ocean."

He hears her sigh. She is in their home state of Delaware, three time zones away. Less's sister moved, in a simultaneous expansion and contraction of possibilities, from a Brooklyn one-bedroom with a husband to a small house on the Atlantic without one. The divorce went through a week ago.

"Are you doing okay, Bee?"

"As well as any of us." She is talking about divorce in their family as one talks about an ancestral scourge. And with Less, she is talking about his and Robert's breakup. "You went through it. Things are harder but better. I don't have to paw through someone else's junk drawer to find the scissors. Metaphorically speaking."

"Do you think it was harder but better for Mom?"

"I think Dad was crazy," his sister says. "What if you had to wake up every day with someone promising a miracle, and every day you believed it, and every day it didn't happen?"

"Bee, I did wake up with that."

"I'm so glad I was little when Dad left. Mostly what I remember is him calling me a Walloon."

Merry laughter from them both. She tells him to get some rest, and the call is over.

It is only later, after Less has made one last sentry round of his little house and carried Tomboy to the sofa bed, after he puts the headphones back on and the woman starts to speak in her fairy-tale voice—"Momentan unklar welche Richtung dieses Land..."—that Less begins the great heaving sobs that will last all night.

His sister used the word *Walloon,* and it is one full of meaning for me, because I always felt it said something about our mourner. I have mentioned my heritage, but it was some time before I bothered to ask about Less's. We were in the bedroom of the Shack, Less and I; this was in the early days, when I was very young and I suppose Less was too. He lay lazily in tousled white sheets below the window that trumpet vine had conquered long ago, and bright sunlight filtered through to cast a shadow of wrought-iron leaves upon my lover. I was standing before a mirror, wearing his tuxedo jacket and nothing else. Out-side the neighbor's cat could be heard saying, *Ciao . . . ciao . . . ciao.*

"Where are your ancestors from?" I asked.

He sat very still in the bed, observing me. "You promise you won't make fun of me?" he asked.

"Less, I promise."

"You have to really promise. I don't want to be teased for this." (I had recently teased him for the story of his first kiss.)

Half naked, I crossed myself. "I would never tease you about something like that."

He looked away, then said, "I'm a Walloon."

I considered this. "Say it again for me."

"I'm a Walloon," he said. "My ancestor Prudent Deless came here in 1638."

"From where?"

"Wallonia."

I burst into unruly laughter, doubling over before the mirror. He sipped his coffee silently. "I'm sorry, I'm sorry, I can't help it!" I pleaded, crawling onto the bed. "You're a Walloon from Wallonia?" He nodded solemnly. "Is that a Smurf or some-thing?"

"I knew you'd make fun of me. I knew it."

"Okay, okay, okay. I'm sorry." I crept toward him and frowned. "Tell me more about this . . . Prudent?"

He raised his eyebrows but went on: "Prudent Deless. My father told us all about it. Rebecca thinks it's the funniest thing in the world. Prudent Deless, that's a man, he was a rascal who came over in 1638 to found New Sweden."

"There's no New Sweden."

Less explained that, in addition to New France, New Spain, and New England, there was supposed to be a New Sweden. It lasted, however, only briefly; New Sweden was the first contestant sent home from the New World. And after traveling all that way!

"And Prudent?" I asked.

Less said, "He was the sole Walloon."

I sat up now and put his coffee on the little side table. "But...come on. You didn't all intermarry with other Walloons for four hundred years. You must be something else."

He spread his arms wide. "Obviously. The whole Walloon thing is nonsense."

"More like invention."

"You're still not allowed to make fun of me."

I found myself more annoyed than amused, though I did not then know why. Here I was, reciting my heritage to every American who asked, like those spies in war movies told to show their papers, and yet my lover could act as if he'd sprung from the brow of Zeus! But all I could say on that day was:

"I'm going to call you Prudent from now on." I got off the bed and looked at myself in the mirror and at him behind me. "I think that's a perfect name for you."

"Please, Freddy, don't..."

Prudent rises, removing his earplugs, to find Marian has already showered and made coffee. When she brings him a cup, he sees she is all in black, and Prudent remembers what they must do today.

The memorial is in the Columbarium—a beaux arts Bundt pan of a building tucked between a copy shop and a parking lot in the northwest region of the city—the repository for the cremated remains of many famous San Franciscans. As in most crematoria, nooks hold the ashes of the departed; unlike most, here, these nooks are glass. This affords the bereaved the opportunity to display not only the urn but anything the heart desires: dollhouse furniture, Mardi Gras beads, a box for Chinese takeout, and a jar of gefilte fish. It is edifying to see so many lives on display; Less would have thought, for instance, that surely nobody loved *Paint Your Wagon* enough to be entombed with its DVD, and yet here is irrefutable proof! And here is Madonna's *The Immaculate Collection*. And here is *Judy at Carnegie Hall*. Through these, another facet of San Francisco history is revealed: During the early years of AIDS, when many cemeteries refused to accept the bodies, this strange place offered niches for those dead gay men. And here they are, gaily decorating the solemn chamber, with years of death in 1992, 1993, 1994, and so on—the hardest years. Something like the old Mission Dolores graveyard, where so many of the death dates on gravestones read 1850 or 1851— a year or two after hundreds of thousands raced to San Francisco to dig for gold. They came and died here. Just like these young gay men. The barren mountain of their fortunes.

"Look at this," Marian says to Less. They are dressed in black, Marian in a kind of nightshirt and Less in his only black suit, in the breast pocket of which is folded a white linen handkerchief. He bought it with Robert in Paris twenty years ago. They stand beside a glass case containing two crystal images, each of a young mustached man. He assumes they were a couple but Marian points out the engravings: they were "beloved partners" of the same man, a man apparently still living. "He was with this one," Marian says, "until he died. And then he was with *this* one until *he* died."

"Oh my God."

"Imagine being the second man. He must have come here; he must have seen this memorial. And when he got sick, maybe the man promised him he'd have a memorial too. Imagine that. Turned to crystal."

"'Leonard LeDuke,'" Less says, reading the much-beloved's name carved there. "Unlucky man."

"Lucky man," Marian counters.

There is a sound outside, and here they come, in black suits and dresses—the old clothes they stumbled upon now and then in their closets and thought, *I never wear that, I should get rid of it,* and took out for a moment before noticing the color and remembering that death was near—here they come, in sunglasses and scuffed shoes, Kleenex in their pockets, chattering amiably, here they come through the Columbarium gates: the Americans in mourning.

And here they come: the Russian River School. At least, those who remain of that artistic movement from Robert's day, and how old they look! Less remembers evenings up in a cabin, card games and red wine and shouting, sitting back shyly as Robert argued meter with Stella Barry; they had seemed so old to him in those days, with their wrinkles and paunches, when of course they were younger then than he is now, and the time will come, inshallah, when Less will be older still than they are here (you can always count on time for a fancy prose style). Will he still feel as foolish? Here is Stella now, a great blue heron lifting each foot carefully along the gravel path; her hair is a white flame, her bearing gaunt and unsure, but her fine beak still darts back and forth as she speaks to the man on her arm. The man on her arm: Franklin Woodhouse, the famous artist who once painted a nude Arthur Less (now in a private collection).

So hunched over he seems to stare only at his shuffling feet, seeing nothing of the path ahead, as perhaps we all must. And others whose names Less cannot recall, the ones in the background of the photographs with him, now moving with canes and walkers and, for one, an electric wheelchair. All heading toward the place where Less and Marian have turned to crystal.

In the middle of their time together as a couple, when the hazy spell of early love had faded but the mist of disillusion had not yet settled over them, a romantic period whose ordinariness can sometimes overshadow its clarity, which has its own beauty, Robert took Less to Provincetown. He said Less had not seen enough of America. Each low tide, the couple strolled out across the cove, now miraculously drained of seawater, revealing the coarse dark sand of the seafloor and red caterpillars resembling editor's marks on a manuscript (*Cut this, and this, and this*), perhaps because to Less, almost everything resembled his continuing failure to get his dreams onto a page. The soft wool sky spread out in skeins of gray above the ambling men. They were still in love.

It was in Provincetown Less learned that his mother had cancer. He sat shaking at the rickety little table; a thunderstorm had driven them indoors. A fire crackled beside the captain's bed. Less said he was flying home to Delaware, and Robert said nothing. Less said he was giving up on the novel. It was all vanity anyway. How could he write while his mother was dying?

"I'm sorry you've become a writer," Robert said at last, kneeling beside him and taking his hand. "I'm sorry this disaster has come for you. I love you. But you have to pay attention. It won't help now, I don't know what will help now, but I promise it will help later. That's all you need to do. Pay attention."

Less said he would not use his mother's death as a writing exercise.

Robert stood up and got a bottle of wine, opened it, and poured two glasses. The fire ticked like a clock beside them; Robert's sandalwood cologne completed the sense of solace. "When I was teaching in Padua, my sister died. I've told you that. I went into the Scrovegni Chapel there to look at the Giottos and I felt nothing. But I made myself look. He painted that chapel in 1305. Dante visited him. And in the scene of the Slaughter of the Innocents is one of the first realistic depictions of human tears. How they leave a trail down the cheek and hang for a moment on the jaw before falling. Someone noticed, seven hundred years ago. Someone knew my pain." He put Less's glass on the table. "That's what you have to do. Pay attention. It's not for yourself. It's for someone seven hundred years from now." Less lifted his face, bright with rage at this, his first real encounter with death. Later, Robert said the tears had made their way into a poem, a detail he had noticed. Less asked what that was. "The tears were black."

The memorial opens with a chorale of varied homosexuals singing a Leonard Cohen song. Marian leans over and asks, softly, where Less found such an awful group, and Less says someone else found them but whispers, "They're okay, they're okay," to which Marian snorts and says: "It's the OK Chorale."

There is a violin piece inspired by a poem of Robert's. It is performed by a teenager with pink hair spiked like a sea urchin. Marian begins to cry, and though there are boxes of tissues placed on columns everywhere, Less hands her the linen handkerchief from his breast pocket, into which she blows her nose loudly.

Less watches as Marian stuffs his favorite handkerchief into her purse.

An elderly Black man in a beret tremblingly recites the final utterance of the Delphic Oracle: "All is ended!"

The OK Chorale sings another Leonard Cohen song.

Pay attention, Arthur Less. Here, as people walk upstairs to Robert Brownburn's niche. Try to shepherd your thoughts toward the body in ashes in that urn, now being placed within the little cove— for this is the moment, the chance to mourn—but as soon as you coax your mind through the narrow gate of sorrow . . . off they go, the thoughts, gamboling into some new field. Yes, you are thinking about your linen handkerchief, for instance, which Marian has put in her purse, and you realize that your gesture at a funeral means you have given the handkerchief to the weeping recipient forever. Because at funerals, forever is the theme of the day. That linen handkerchief will come no more. And you bought it specially in Paris. You are thinking about the ceremony and the stammering words people have said. You are thinking about the OK Chorale, and you had better not think about it because now you have fought back a little grin. And now you have caught Marian's eye. It is happening to her as well. Robert is being moved into his private grotto before this crowd of famous poets and artists who have come after him to join the famous poets and artists who went before him, a grand moment, and his ex-wife and ex-lover are about to lose it. Think about something else, Arthur Less. Anything else. Robert's face like a skull, for instance, his breathing, his awful final haircut, like a cartoon baby with one white forelock . . . not working. The OK Chorale starts to sing a hymn in Slow German. Marian is trying to hide her smile; she takes out of her purse the Handkerchief, and it happens: Arthur Less snorts with laughter.

The first time I met Robert Brownburn, I was twenty-seven and he was over sixty—an almost grandfatherly difference in age—and though I had no official association with Arthur Less at the time and was as free and unattached as a young bonobo, still, I thought of him as a rival. It was a small dinner party at the Shack, and when he rang the doorbell, I was a sight, my hands yellow from turmeric and my eyes red from chilies. Less was in the bedroom, and so, arms outstretched like a saint and weeping like one, I answered the door, and this is how I first met Robert—I got a wry smile and "You must be Carlos's son." The next hour is a blur of inexplicable rage, inexplicable because Robert was kind and gracious to me, as was everyone, but I could not shake the understanding that, though I knew he was my rival, Robert clearly did not think of me as his. Otherwise, why be kind and gracious?

Less informed the poet that I was a high-school teacher. I added: "We're reading Homer."

"Oh, lucky you!" Robert said brightly. "You know, I was thinking the other day, *The Odyssey* has the most amazing cameo in all of literature."

"My students always love it."

He smiled and turned to the rest of the table, spreading his arms wide. "When Telemachus gets to the court of Menelaus," he said, "we hear all about the silver and gold and electrum decorations, and they talk forever, and then, in the background, Helen walks by. Fucking Helen of Troy."

"'Out of her scented room,'" I quoted.

"Exactly. Here is the woman at the heart of his *last epic,* and Homer has her reappear, it must be twenty years later, just walking around the palace, and he never tells us what we're dying to know: *Is she beautiful?*"

I reached for the papaya salad. "My students don't accept the idea that Helen—"

He turned to the group: "Isn't it *fascinating?*"

Later, when the party was over, and I was cleaning up with Less and swooning with sugared gin and champagne, he asked me what I thought of Robert. I was too young to know what I thought of Robert; I only knew what I thought of myself, which was that I felt conquered. So I just repeated, "Isn't it *fascinating?* Isn't it *fascinating?* Isn't it *fascinating?*" until Less left the room. We argued and he broke a glass and wept over it and I stood there holding my own cocktail of triumph and shame.

The second time I met the poet Robert Brownburn was, as it happens, at a funeral. It was for Less's mother, whose cancer had returned after years in remission. Less was lost; his sister, Rebecca, equally so, and so it was left to me to plan the reception. I remember when the poet Robert Brownburn arrived to greet his old lover and then, in the midst of their sad embrace, how the eyes of the poet came to rest on me. The message they contained resisted my intelligence almost successfully. He mouthed the words *Hi, Freddy*. Then he moved on to Less's sister and out of my line of sight. A procession of ghosts followed. Later, I came upon the poet staring with uncertainty at the Mexican spread, and I suggested what to combine. He turned to me and said, "I was thinking about what you said, and Helen does do something in that scene, doesn't she?" As if years had not passed between our encounters. I said yes, she put an herb in their wine, a drug against penthos and kholon: sorrow and anger. "'None would shed a tear that day,'" I quoted to him. "So they can talk about the past without pain." He nodded and took another serving of beans. Then he said to me: "I hope you put some in the margaritas." He left soon afterward and I did not see him again for many years.

So that was the second time I met the late Robert Brownburn.

The "celebration of life" is in a Sea Cliff mansion. Less is handed a glass of bourbon—someone knows Robert's preferred tipple—and led into a great glass room with a view of the strait connecting the ocean and the Bay: the Golden Gate. The sunlight sparkles on its dark waters as it seems to exhale into the Pacific, rippling beneath the famous bridge.

"Excuse me, are you a friend of Mr. Brownburn?"

Less has been approached by a young man in an ill-fitting navy suit—how young, Less cannot tell you. His guess is somewhere between conception and thirty.

Less smiles and says, "I am."

"I'm sorry, I don't wanna intrude. I'm just such a fan." The young man has cut his hair very close and wears rimless glasses. "I read all his poetry, not just the Library of America stuff but the *old* stuff, the really juicy stuff. That sixties stuff that evades the intelligence almost successfully, as Stevens said, you know? I'm just such a fan. And he never traveled much and I live in Hollister, so I never got to see him read."

"That's a pity," Less says. "He did some incredible readings. I first saw him read at City Lights."

"Oh, man, what a dream!"

Less: "I didn't know anything about his poetry then. We'd just started dating. And seeing him read his work, it was like . . . finding out the person you're dating is Spider-Man." He laughs, but the young man does not. Instead, he seems shocked.

"Oh . . . are you . . . are you Arthur Less?"

"I am."

"*The* Arthur Less?"

Is there another Arthur Less? "I guess so," Less replies. "I was with Robert for fifteen years."

The young man's face seems to ripple with joy.

"Oh, I know," he says. "What an honor to be here, I can't tell you. And to talk with Arthur Less! One day you're gonna win one of those prizes! I have to admit, I'm gate-crashing here. I just saw a notice about a celebration of Robert Brownburn and I had to come. Sorry, I know it's not for the public."

"It's not my house. Robert never turned away fans of poetry."

"What was it like to live with him? To live with genius?"

Less sighs. He decides to speak honestly about Robert, because today is the day to speak honestly about the poet Robert Brownburn: "You didn't see it happening, because for a long time every morning, nothing was happening, which was very tense, and then out of nowhere it would be done. And when he was finished he'd call out, 'Champagne!'" Less is enjoying a memory of that happy shout, which of course did not actually mean for Less to open champagne (they were almost always broke). "Most days. Some days. It wasn't always easy. Robert was hard on himself. And hard on people around him."

"Was it worth it for you?"

Without knowing it, the young man has asked the toughest question of all. Less sees Marian across the room, moving slowly in her marionette walk toward an ornate sofa. Those years living on the Vulcan Steps in which he gave each hour to protecting the creativity of Robert, tiptoeing around the house, making lunch as quietly as possible and knocking gently on the door, only to see Robert lying on the daybed looking angrily at the ceiling; the years when he was twenty-one, twenty-two, twenty-three—are they to be savored or spent? "Waste your youth," Marian had told him on that beach thirty years ago, and at the time he said he was. But had he? He had invested it, perhaps, but certainly not in himself; one could not withdraw the days of one's youth in retirement and throw them on the fire to warm old bones. He had invested it in Robert.

Less answers: "It was my privilege."

Across the room, Marian seizes the sofa with a look of triumph and lowers herself onto it. She folds her hands on her dress; she closes her eyes. Where is she traveling to? From the locked door in Less's memory: *Champagne!*

"Do you think he's going to read something?"

Less has not been listening. "I'm sorry? Who?"

"Mr. Brownburn," the young man says, abashed. "I know it's a party for him, but I was hoping maybe he might read something."

Understanding comes to Arthur Less with a contraction of his breath.

The young man offers a shy smile. "Or maybe this is asking too much, but for a second, could you introduce me? It's okay if you can't. It's just...I came all the way from Hollister."

Less is not one to touch anyone he does not know, but he puts his hand on the young man's arm. He looks at the hopeful face and tries to think of how to tell someone he is too late.

I can tell you what it was like to live with genius.

It was as if we were a couple who had moved into a haunted house. At first, my life with Less was bliss. We painted the Shack all white within, and the paint stayed on our nails and hair as a reminder of our fresh life together. And then there began to be signs—a door that opened by itself; a shadow where no shadow should be. I mean these metaphorically, of course—what I saw out of the corner of my eye was in fact the phantom presence of Robert Brownburn (still alive in those days). Its first manifestation was an anxiety that seized the house each day at six; it took me a long time to realize this was the hour when Robert used to emerge from writing and demand a drink and dinner. And before my eyes, at six, Less would change from a dopey, smiling lover into a terrified domestic, each impressive dish seasoned with worry—"Do you like it? Is it overcooked?" I see now he was not asking me; he was asking Robert twenty years ago. Back when Less did not know if he deserved to be loved. I reassured him, and these tensions calmed. The Shack lost its shadows, its creaking doors. But then came the possession.

One day, I came home to find a poltergeist!—or evidence of one. Laundry was strewn eerily around the place; there were books in teetering piles, coffee cups where none had been that morning, and from the bedroom an unearthly voice was chanting: "No, no, no, no, no..." When I opened the door, I found, to my horror, a demon staring back at me with red-rimmed eyes and growling: "Freddy, I'm working!" I closed the door on this hellscape and stood a moment taking in the horror: my partner had begun a novel.

I had never thought the process would be so messy or demanding. For instance, Less wrote in the bedroom (the Shack's only other room), so if I wanted anything from in there, I had to set it out the night before, planning as carefully as for an Everest ascent. But even worse was when I began to suspect a transference, or spiritual possession, in which the soul of Robert Brownburn had moved into the body of Arthur Less. The screams of torture, the firing-squad sound of his typing; I shivered to think of what went on in that Gehenna. I think the turning point came when Arthur Less banged open the door, hitting me as I was washing dishes, and shouted: "Champagne!" He had become the Great Writer, the Robert Brownburn. And I'd become the devil's janissary. I told him this in so many words. His response? Less sat on the couch and wept. "I guess I was trying something on. I guess I was trying to feel confident."

"And that means treating me like a servant?"

"I only know Robert's way. I'm so sorry."

I explained that not every relationship had to have a Robert; it isn't *Antony and Cleopatra and Robert* or *Romeo and Juliet and Robert*. I said, "We can just be Freddy and Less."

Less said quietly, "Maybe I didn't know any other way."

I felt such pity for him then that I stroked his back as he shook his head and we sat in silence. And things were better. But every once in a while, at six precisely, I heard a phantom laughing from the fog.

As for Arthur Less, is there just one? Or perhaps another? It turns out there are hundreds. There is the Christian music star Arthur Less whose prayerful videos clog every internet search our hero performs; the organic farmer Arthur Less whose inedible squashes friends send on birthdays ("Get more with Less!"); the horror-movie actor Arthur Less, star of *Eel of Panic, Eel of Panic 2,* and *Eel of Panic 3: The Wriggler;* the South Carolinian real estate baron Arthur Less ("Get more with Less!"); the myriad of investment managers, managing editors, editing managers. And, yes, in fact, there is another novelist Arthur Less. The two are well aware of each other; there have been a few cordial forwardings of messages meant for the other and joking online comments when they are mistaken for each other, but nothing more than that. Once Less arrived at a literary event and was confronted with a poster of a brooding, bearded author in a velvet jacket—not himself (pity the overworked intern who'd done too brief a search). The two novelist Arthur Lesses do not even find themselves shelved together— our Arthur Less gets shelved in Queer Authors, the other in Black Authors; neither gets shelved in General Fiction. They are both too unknown for General Fiction. It goes without saying, the literary world being as it is, that they have never met.

Less excuses himself from the conversation with Robert's young man. He feels he has done something terrible, and he cannot bear the pain of witnessing the consequences; the young man now stands with his bourbon, staring around a room vacant of the one person he traveled all this way to meet.

But Arthur has nowhere to go; Marian is in communication with the past, or the future, or perhaps a state free of thought—and if so, good for her—and Stella has a crowd gathered around her, as always. So he migrates, over and over, to the bar. Another bourbon. Another. On his third terrified journey, he overhears an elderly man talking to one of the servers. His hair is long and Iron Curtain gray and so is his accent: "You know you have no talent, so what is the purpose of going on? Listen to me. Give up writing now." The woman bristles visibly but professionally and continues clearing wineglasses. The man seems not to notice, turns his eyes to other parts of the room, their periorbitals darkened perhaps by horrors unknown to Americans, then lands on Less and smiles: "Hello, Arthur, my darling."

"Hello."

"You do not remember me. I am Vit—" And here follows a surname from which all the vowels have been removed, like dissidents. "I was Bob's Czech editor. We meet once in Berlin but you were a very young and silly boy and I was a grown man. You are not changed at all!"

Less is no wiser but says, "Good to see you . . . Vit." He believes he has never come across this name before.

The man laughs. "And you spoke such terrible German!"

"Then it couldn't have been me," Less answers confidently. "Ich bin Deutschunterricht genommen, seit—"

Vit stops him with a flat palm. "Thank you, but this dish, as they say, I will not eat twice. I happen to be in town and I hear about Bob. So sad. I hear you have become a writer." Less fears the old vampire is going for blood, but he is saved some- what. "So have I. I suspect we are very different kinds of writers."

"I share your suspicions."

"To begin with the obvious, I am a European writer. You are an American one." Vit says this in such a way—much like *I am a man, you are a woman*—that Less believes he might be being hit on. But Vit varies from the formula: "Do you know the problem with American writers?"

"Commas."

A finger-wag from the Czech. "Your problem is you are all New Yorkers." Less has no idea anymore what they are talking about. His mind is making the pointless scribbles of a pen that has run out of ink. But the man goes on: "New York, Boston, San Francisco. You don't bother with the rest of the country. Have you seen the Mojave Desert? The Natchez Trace? The Appalachian Trail? No, you only know this city by the sea. No wonder you keep rewriting Fitzgerald!"

"Robert was an American writer."

"Bob was a European writer," Vit says. "He had that Beckett sensibility. That things are broken, in shards, that being human means *nothing,* that mem- ory is *nothing,* that love is *nothing.*" Each *nothing* sounds as if he were tearing a propaganda poster down its length.

"You didn't know Robert at all."

Vit produces a grin, and his teeth seem as crammed together as the consonants in his name. "You know the real problem with America?" He does not wait for Less to speak. "All of your elbowing, unblushing, 'can-do' achievements. And nobody ever says, 'Wait! What if we're wrong?'"

"I ask that all the time," Less replies.

"I don't mean you, my darling. I mean America. What if it's wrong? The whole idea?"

Less searches for an answer; the notion has never occurred to him.

"What if the whole idea of America is wrong?"

What should he do with this man? Strangle him? Salute him? Put him in a novel? *You are seeing suffering,* Robert used to say when confronted with a horrible person. *You are seeing someone in pain.* But Vit has prepared his own exit, literal and cosmic: Nodding to Less, he brings out a pack of cigarettes, and now the Czech writer passes through French doors to an Italian loggia, joining a European Union of smokers. Only the cologne of the man remains, and Less says to it, "What do you know about America?" The cologne has no reply, and Less grins in triumph; after all, he has been to Provincetown.

"Well, it's over," Marian says. Not another final utterance of the Delphic Oracle; Marian is merely stating the obvious, taking off her shoes after a long, wearying day. She is sitting in the wine-dark living room of the Shack, beside the old ship's clock as it marks six bells. The reception has ended, the Russian River School has disbanded, perhaps for the final time; there were whispers that Franklin Woodhouse had refused another round of cancer treatment. He gave Less a dry kiss on each cheek before bidding him goodbye, and Less watched the old man struggle down the walk, again on the arm of Stella Barry. Once, Less remembered, he had jumped from stone to stone across a river. Today— placed into a waiting taxi like a piece of luggage.

"Marian, did you meet that young man?" Less asks, going over the day in his head. He is sitting on the rocking chair across from her, Tomboy asleep in his lap. He tells her about the young man who had come all the way from Hollister. He gives her every detail: His close-cropped hair, his ill-fitting suit. How he had heard it was a party for Robert. How he somehow misunderstood . . .

"Oh no," Marian gasps.

"He was waiting for Robert to do a reading," Less says. "He is an avid reader of poetry."

"Oh no, oh no!" Her hand is in front of her mouth, her eyes wide.

Less adds, shrugging: "I guess he's not an avid reader of obituaries."

They both break into wild laughter. It has been a long and painful day. She is weeping with mirth now, and the Handkerchief comes out again, and the OK Chorale seems to sing off-key in his head, and he cannot help joining her, for a moment, in reckless abandonment of grief.

Had he ever thought he would share these days with Marian? These last days, this shared mourning, with Marian Brownburn, the woman who hated him for years, for decades, for stealing her husband from her? Who wove her shroud each day and unraveled it at night? It hardly seems worth contemplating; it is only to be grateful for.

"Stay for dinner," he says.

She removes the Handkerchief and he sees her mascara has begun to run. "I can't. I can't drive after dark anymore. I'm old, Arthur." Her tears are black.

"Then stay the night."

"I can't," Marian says, pulling her shawl around her. "In fact...Arthur, did you take one of your anxiety pills?"

"Yes," he says, thinking of the Czech writer's words. "Do you need one?"

"No, honey," she says. "But I have something very hard to tell you."

"Oh no."

She raises her chin and takes a deep breath. "Something that will make things even more difficult. I heard from the executor. Is this a good time to tell you?"

Through the window, piano music steals in softly and, finding nothing worth taking, steals back out again and goes silent.

"Tell me," he says.

So she tells him.

"Say that again, Less, I couldn't hear you."

Less sits on the white bed beside a sleeping Tomboy; his voice squeaks with worry like the bed itself. It is a reasonable hour for him but far past midnight for me in Maine.

"We don't...we don't...we don't have a home."

"Did you flood everything again?"

"No, no, no." Less speaks in the rat-a-tat manner of a submarine captain ordering, *Dive! Dive! Dive!* "We have to leave the Shack, it's in something called probate—"

"Slow down, Less. You don't have to leave a property in probate—"

Breathing heavily now: "I owe. Back rent. To the. Estate." He says it as if he has indeed flooded everything.

"Rent?" I say in shock. "I thought the Shack was yours!"

"Robert never asked for anything. It was just sort of...understood."

"Understood?"

Silence.

"Less," I say, exasperated, "you just thought it

would go on forever? And you never told me? And now we owe rent?"

"Freddy, after Robert and I split up, I . . . just didn't think about it."

"How much back rent do we owe?"

"Ten years," Less says. "It will cover the reverse mortgage or something—I don't understand—and then the Shack is ours. But I only have a month."

This time, the silence is mine.

"So I can't come to Maine just yet. I'm going to Palm Springs. Then Santa Fe."

"You're doing the profile?"

"I'm doing the profile," he says, a bank robber agreeing to one last heist. "And whatever else comes along. I'll make everything okay. Mandern is money, and I'm on the Prize Committee, that's money. I'll make everything okay. I have one month. I'll call you from Palm Springs."

"Palm Springs," I say as if it were an abracadabra that might make all our cares vanish.

"And I'll plan a new book," he says. "I'll sell it. You'll see, Freddy, I'll make everything okay!"

A cool silence greets this assertion, like a bartender's to a stranger come to town.

"You could get a job," I say.

"I've tried that," he tells me. "Remember Wichita?" A pause as we both recall his disastrous stay as Distinguished Visiting Chair. "But yes, if I have to, I'll get a job. Let me try this first."

"All this time," I say, "the Shack wasn't even ours?"

"I have one month. This Prize and this profile get us a third of the way—"

"My hero," I say, somewhat cruelly.

"And after that I'm coming to Maine—"

"I'm sorry, I know, I'm sorry," I say, snapping out of it. "This is all awful for you, I know. And you were going to start your novel—"

"It will have to wait."

"It's all so awful."

"Freddy, we'll have our home. I'll make everything okay."

"I know you will, my love."

"I'll make everything okay and then I'll come to you in Maine."

I tell him I love him and I let him go.

And yet... now it is my turn to be *uncertain*. What other infelicities has my Prudent hidden, forgotten, mislaid? Should I start calling him *Imprudent*?

I think often of Lewis and Clark. Not the young explorers President Jefferson sent out into the Northwest Territory. No—Less's friends Lewis and Clark. Twenty years a couple, they suddenly announced they were splitting up. It turned out they had a date every ten years to reconsider their contract, and at the last appointment, the contract was not renewed. They drank champagne and parted. "We took each other as far as we could," Clark reported, smiling, to a stunned Arthur Less, who reported it to me. Just like that, the love was over. And after traveling all that way! Not so different after all from the explorers Lewis and Clark, who drank eighteen toasts at the end of their journey. But the story fills me with worry. "We took each other as far as we could." Is this how couples talk? Does ten years signal some contractual formality— like a starlet with her studio—engendering this *uncertain* feeling? Panicked phone calls? Panicked travel to Palm Springs? For soon it will be ten years since our first kiss. On a porch, at a party, a candle in a mason jar...

A dramatic reaction, I know, to such Walloonery; his innocence about rent and probate and the passage of time is, of course, part of Arthur Less's charm. He thinks each day will be better than the next; he is wrong. He awakens the next morning and thinks it again; he is wrong. He thinks we are free to become our true selves, that we are free to love as we choose. A mindset so UnitedStatesian, you could serve it with ketchup.

But, friends, you cannot live on ketchup.

Another story comes to mind. It was in the time between Robert and me; Less was doing a travel piece in the Northwest and, for detail and local color, headed to a hot springs recommended by his lodge. As Less tells it, he followed a trail along a noisy creek that clattered like a short-order kitchen.

He came upon the springs, peeled off his clothes, and settled naked into the pool. Mist haunted the surface of the water. Above him, the stern mountains folded their violet hands, looking down like chess players upon a castled king. That was when, very quietly but startlingly, stepping gingerly among the stones, out of the forest came an enormous moose.

It walked over to Arthur Less and sat beside him in the pool. A moment of silence. Less urinated freely in pure terror.

As he tells it, however, in those few minutes as, man and moose, they watched the setting sun, Arthur Less felt chosen. Struggling for years in Robert's shadow, then a castaway in the wide ocean of possibility, and suddenly this great creature had chosen him! Less felt a metamorphosis beside this massive moose—his muse. And when it left him, headed back into the woods, when the moose-moment had passed and Less had survived it, he accepted he could survive anything. He could survive without Robert; he could survive any change, any moose that came his way. He would be a writer, and to hell with worry and doubt.

That is what I want. I want to be chosen. Chosen as Arthur Less, bumbling among the larches, was chosen. Where is my moose? Isn't that promised in the Constitution, somewhere between quartering of soldiers and foreign emoluments? It is a country

of grand injustice. Less blunders and fails and is rewarded with a moose, rewarded with Palm Springs,
rewarded with me, Freddy Pelu. And I sit here at
my conference in Maine and wonder: *Where is my
moose? Where is my moose?*

The last time I met the poet Robert Brownburn was
in hospice. Less and I drove up to Sonoma County
to meet Marian at the care facility. She was waiting
patiently in the glass and sunlight of the lobby and
walked us to Robert's room: bright yellow, perfumed
by a laurel tree outside the open window. A curtain,
also yellow, patterned with circling swallows, was
drawn aside to reveal the poet on his deathbed.
Less went to him at once and sat on a plastic chair,
also yellow. Less took his also yellow hand. But the
poet's eyes were on me: "Hello, Freddy." Robert's
eyes were deeply sunk in dark circles, as if absorbing
all available light; his lips were pressed tight, and his
chin was wavering, not from any palsy but from the
simple fact that he was suffering and did not wish
to show it. "You've grown!" he said through the
grin. "Welcome to the middle part of life, Freddy.
I warn you: you won't like the last part." He and
Less talked about his food, his medicine, dramas
with the nursing team, and the curtain pattern,
which the poet claimed was not swallows at all but
circling vultures. Less called him Tiresias, a private
joke. Then it was time to go. His eyes turned to me

again. "You know the worst thing an Italian woman can be called? A Trojan, meaning Helen of Troy! Isn't that something? Ancient grudges, Freddy." I kissed him goodbye on his cheek. That was the last time I saw the poet Robert Brownburn.

But not the last time Arthur Less saw him. He visited his Tiresias two weeks later. Less told me that he held his hand, again, and that Robert complained again about the food and the nurses and the circling vultures all around him. He was being fed nothing but honey and milk, he said. They gave him water from a tainted spring and so on; he was agitated and confused. Then the old man turned to face the middle-aged one: "Arthur. Go get lost somewhere, it always does you good. But not yet. Don't leave me just yet."

Arthur Less said to his lover: "What are you talking about? I'm not going to leave you!"

In the end, as you know, it was Robert Brownburn who left.

"An end everything has," our hero might say in his Lessian German, "except the sausage, which two has." Is this his last night in the Shack? After all these not-quite-watertight years? Our hero packs his pink sweater, his special electric razor, his gray silk suit, and sets an alarm. He crawls into our bed alone; a neighbor has already taken Tomboy.

What ghost will visit our Hamlet tonight on

the castle walls of his dreams? Surely not Robert Brownburn; even if there is a heaven where all animals and men are brought together in a mad re-union, atheists such as Robert will not return to us in phantom form—not because they reside in some celestial detention but out of pure stubbornness. Surely not Less's mother; she would never want to frighten him. She is omnipresent, in any case, within Less's nervous system, calling out every dangerous power outlet and slippery shower floor, an anxious phantom-in-residence. Surely not old friends hid in death's dateless night; those plague victims went on to better parties long ago. Not grandmothers or grandfathers; could even a voluble afterlife make up for so much unsaid? Not his father, Lawrence Less, the other man who left our hero, if only because he is still alive somewhere...

And yet—is that shadow not in the wrong place, there beside Woodhouse's portrait of Less? Is it not now moving toward the bed?

Go get lost somewhere, it seems to whisper.

Less hears another sound: a snap. A clumsy ghost? He recognizes it, of course; it is the sound Robert made many times during the night: a popping of his jaw. He used to awaken in a muscle spasm and, to make himself go back to sleep, would imagine relax-ing each part of his body, starting at his toes, until he stretched his jaw with a *pop.* It often awakened Less beside him. Of course Robert has not made it;

of course there is no ghost. Less realizes he has made the sound himself. For the dead live only in us.

Less blinks his eyes to wipe away the film of sleep; all has vanished. The room is dark and quiet, and the shadows are in their proper places. He touches his nightstand to be sure his lucky charm is there: his mother's antique pen. Its cool cylinder gives him comfort. Then the headlights of a car shine brightly through the window, casting the shadow of trumpet vine across the bed, evoking a memory to anyone watching... but Less is already unconscious, already halfway to Palm Springs.

Sleep well, my love. More than a continent lies between us tonight.

SOUTHWEST

[THE *following interview is translated from the German.*]

"Mr. Less, thank you for coming on the program. And for joining us from the United States."

"Here is my thanks."

"I'm sure our audience is delighted you could do this interview in German. So few Americans speak our language."

"Here is my German. AH-ah-ah."

"We only have a minute, but I wanted to ask about your upcoming travel. I hear you're going on a tour with the writer H. H. H. Mandern, who is quite famous here in Germany."

"It seems a mental illness Mr. Mandern me asked to with him go, but he has, yes!"

"Mental illness indeed. You seem to be very different sorts of writers. We hear your next book, *Swift,* is a comedy. And Mr. Mandern is known for his science fiction, not for his comedy."

"There is a well-known robot detective."

"Yes, yes, Peabody. Why do you think Mr. Mandern asked for you in particular?"

"We had an interview. He liked my interrogation of him. Have you interrogated him?"

"I have, in fact. It was difficult. I think it's not unfair to say he's famous for being a little touchy. Some say he is not mentally stable. Are you nervous?"

"I do not understand."

"Are you nervous to be intimately entangled with such an erratic companion?"

"I do not understand."

"Are you nervous?"

"We are not to share a hotel room, AH-ah-ah."

"Well, Mr. Less, with your new book and with your tour, we in Germany wish you the best of luck."

"AH-ah-ah."

Less flies from San Francisco to Palm Springs, a city located in the lower left-hand coin pocket of America. Less places his bag (with special electric razor, books, and favorite pink sweater) in the overhead compartment and seats himself beside the window. He looks out at the wing. In his panicked state, he wonders whether man can really fly. And then the attendant wearily offers him peanuts. Less giggles at the very notion. Peanuts! At thirty thousand feet! To Arthur Less, anything at high altitude feels miraculous; he simply cannot believe it's happening. Perhaps it correlates in his system with quasi-forbidden boyhood delights such as flashlight-reading under the covers and smuggling chocolate into a treehouse. An offer of wine and Less shivers at the impossibility. How did they get wine up here? To him, it is as delicious as a cup of lemonade bought from a five-year-old's stand, which is to say, always delicious. The same goes for the food; when he unwraps the foil to expose microwaved chicken or curdled lasagna, you would think he had found a golden ticket to a chocolate factory. His joy seems endless.

But an end everything has; not long after takeoff, other passengers become alarmed about a persistent buzzing. Less joins in the speculation—is a piece of the plane loose? Something wrong with the pressurization? Soon the attendants are involved. The captain is summoned; he attunes himself to the sound, then vanishes. "Passengers, we are cleared for an emergency descent into Palm Springs ahead of other aircraft. The plane needs minor repairs, but it will not affect this short flight." They begin their emergency descent. Less is terrified; what minor repairs? What crucial device has come fatally and noisily undone? It does not take long, of course, for him to realize the source of the threat: It is his special electric razor. It has somehow turned on by itself in the overhead storage. He says nothing; the special electric razor (a skilled ventriloquist) throws its noise everywhere in the cabin, so he remains unincriminated. Less's plan is to wait for landing, dash for the razor, and defuse it before anyone gets wise. All goes well at first; his glass of water is collected, his minor trash, and then they have arrived in Palm Springs. A bell of freedom goes off, and Less leaps to unzip his bag—only to be confettied with pink fluff. All through the flight, the razor has not merely been alarming the crew; it has decided to devour a companion: his sweater. Such is love.

Arthur Less (still decorated with pink fluff) is picked up at the Palm Springs airport by a publicist named Eleanor and taken into Palm Springs proper, where he experiences, in the sudden transition from Northern to Southern California, a shock similar to a diver's on rising too fast from the depths. Oh, California! The statistically impossible blondness; the ubiquity of sunglasses, as if everyone has just been to the ophthalmologist; the non-native date palms that, like many non-natives, seem positively patriotic about their newfound country; the

pretense of sun and warmth in chill October, such
as here, in Eleanor's convertible, where, to counter-
act the cold, she has turned the heat up high. It
feels to Less like the kind of deep act of denial seen
only at family holidays.

Let us be honest: He is afraid. Afraid of money
and travel and humiliations yet unmet. For rather
than enter the warm embrace of a beloved in a cold
northeastern state, Arthur Less has entered some
ultraviolet nightmare for which no Walloon could
be prepared. Not even with sun protection. And
what new loneliness is in store? For surely he will
barely meet this famous author with his famous
fedora and famous pug. Less will be alone in a hotel
room attending meetings for the Prize before they
fly to Santa Fe. And more: he has traveled even
farther away from me, Freddy Pelu.

Eleanor takes Less to a building that looks like a
giant metal avocado but is in fact an auditorium,
leads him to the avocado's greenroom (avocado
green; nobody is kidding), and abandons him beside
a fruit plate and a minibar. Less manages to make
himself a mini-cocktail but sips it cautiously; he does
not want to be drunk onstage. His job is to evade
attention almost entirely; it is to let the great author
shine; it is to be as well remembered as the onstage
chair and table, the glass of water, the spotlight,
which is to say, not at all. Less feels highly qualified
for this position. He is considering whether the

time has arrived to eat his mini-cocktail's cherry when a serious-looking man enters but does not glance at Arthur Less. He wears a headset over his gray curly hair and carries a clipboard, a sign he is in charge.

"Excuse me," Less says. "Excuse me. When is Mr. Mandern arriving? I have a quick phone meeting. For a literary prize."

The man looks at him impatiently, taking in the bits of pink fluff. "Mr. Mandern will arrive shortly."

"So I have some time?"

The man has one of those dividing scars on his left eyebrow, like a dueling scar; he frowns. "Mr. Mandern's schedule is his own, Mr. Yes."

"It's Less," says Less. "Arthur Less. Not Yes." Has he become a James Bond villain?

The man looks at his clipboard. "I have *Yes* written here." He crosses it out neatly.

"Can you let me know when Mr. Mandern arrives?"

The man briefly considers Less. "When Mr. Mandern arrives," he says, *"you'll know."*

A bestselling author since his first book, *Incubus,* came out in 1978, followed by the controversial movie version, H. H. H. Mandern instantly became a towering figure in the world of books, with his trademark fedora and pipe, his striped Vincent Price beard, drawing thousands of fans to his events and making headlines with rock-star behavior such as trashing hotel rooms, setting money on fire, and trying to hijack a commercial plane to take him to Puerto Rico (where it was already headed). He later blamed it on prescription medicine. But nothing stopped his output: a novel, sometimes two, a year, and not just any novels but six-hundred-page portraits of interstellar war and alien empire-building that would take a normal human being a year just to *type*. Mandern has never broken a sweat. One critic recently called him "America's Dickens." Another: a "crap factory." None of it has dulled his productivity, though he is now in his eighties.

Arthur Less has met H. H. H. Mandern before. It was in New York City, two years ago or so, when he interviewed the great man in public—nearly a disaster, as Mandern had food poisoning and had to be guided onstage under the trance of various drugs. And while he gamely answered Less's questions for an hour, when the time came for questions from the audience, Mandern turned his lonely eyes to Arthur Less. Less saw there the fluttering candle stub of despair. And then it went out. "Well, Mr. Mandern, you answer that fairly well in book five when you..." Less went on, speaking Mandernian as if possessed by his holy spirit. He saved the day. When the time was up, poor Mandern could only whisper, "Is it over?" and Less led him offstage to thunderous applause. Mandern vanished to a hotel sickbed, and Less expected never to hear from the great man again.

But he did hear from the great man again, because we find ourselves in a greenroom in Palm Springs, where Arthur Less has his first meeting as a juror of the Prize Committee.

"Hello, everybody!"

The Prize Committee is never to meet in person; their meetings are incorporeal, like those of the angels. Arthur Less has often been close to prizes— once, in Italy, he even won one. But now he has the chance to enter the star-chamber world of being a judge.

The chair begins their phone call with a challenge: "I think we should state what we feel this Prize is *for*."

Besides himself, there are three others, all of whom Less has heard of but none of whom Less has ever read. There is the African American writer Alcofribas ("Freebie") Nasier, the historical novelist Vivian Lee, and, finally, Edgar Box, whose grand triumph—*Stairway,* said to be the last word in "hallucinogenic Mormon literature"—lies twenty years in the past. Less can only tell his colleagues apart by their distinctive tones of voice and, for Edgar Box, by his almost complete silence on the phone.

Wait, I'm sorry, not *finally* at all; there is another. The chair of the committee. How could I forget?

Just when we lose hope and believe life to be chaos, Fate provides a pattern, for it is none other than his old nemesis Finley Dwyer.

For decades, the two white gay male writers followed similar publication paths, sometimes reading on adjoining nights at the same queer bookstore, but because Less lived in San Francisco and Finley Dwyer in New York, they had never met. But there was a party (in Paris) where Finley buttonholed Less in a private library and offered to tell him what no one else had dared. How could Less resist this devil's bargain? To hear what no one dares to say? Here is what it turned out to be:

Arthur Less was a "bad gay."

Less has been turning that over in his mind for two solid years now.

"Arthur," Finley Dwyer says over the phone, "you know I'm such a fan of your work, you're my first choice, but alas, and lucky us, you're on the jury! Tell us what you think the Prize is for."

"Someone extraordinary," Less finds himself blurting out as he roams the greenroom. "A new way of telling a story, a new use of language, you know? I think we could give it to a new voice or reclaim one of our greats. We should keep open minds and we'll find them."

"Thank you, Arthur. Vivian?"

Vivian Lee has the elegant voice of an elocution professor: "I can tell you what it's not for. It's not for writers already in the literary canon. We have the chance to change someone's life. Let us not waste it."

"Wonderful, Vivian," Finley Dwyer says. "How about you, Freebie?"

Freebie's voice is that of an eager debater: "Finley, I think it's not for Canadians! They win too many of these!"

"Well, okay, okay, Freebie, that's interesting. Edgar, would you like to add something?" Silence of contemplation follows. "Edgar, are you there?"

"I'm here."

"Would you like to add something?"

More silence, and then at last a sigh: "This Prize is not for those kids who win everything just for putting *pussy* in the first paragraph."

"Whom do you mean?" Vivian asks.

"I thought we were saying what it was *for,*" Arthur interjects, sounding very much like the teacher's-pet self of his youth.

"You know," Edgar says. "The ones with *pussy* in the first paragraph."

Freebie puts in: "Arthur thinks we should read with open minds, Edgar."

Finley's melodic voice now arrives, like a hostess with a tray of cocktails: "Well, it's good to have our personalities out in the open. I think we all agree this Prize is not for the ones we all know are bad writers. Lauded, famed, but bad. The mimics, the frauds, the lazy copyists or, as Truman would have put it, the *typers*. Enough of them. It is not for those without talent. I know that's unpopular."

"Hear, hear!" Freebie says, then enters a round of coughing.

Arthur again: "I thought we were saying—"

"I have no problem with *pussy* in the first paragraph," Vivian adds pointedly.

"Fine," says Edgar, "I take it back. They can have *pussy*."

Finley: "We are given the chance to survey the breadth of American literature. This is going to be an exciting month! Remember to clear your calendar for the ceremony in New York. And let's see if the rest of us can live up to Arthur's exacting parameters!"

Arthur: "I just meant that—"

"Until next time, then! Au réécouter!"

Is Arthur Less a "bad gay"? He's certainly bad at it. Let us examine this more closely; there is plenty of time while we wait for H. H. H. Mandern to arrive...

When he moved to New York after college, in the eighties, Arthur Less tried his hardest to be a good gay. He joined a gym that turned out to be a sex dungeon. He joined a political party that turned out to believe a conspiracy theory about government health clinics. He joined a German-language society that turned out to be a sex dungeon. He joined a book group that turned out to be only for a political party. He joined a role-playing game club that turned out to be a sex dungeon. He joined a sex dungeon that turned out to be a government health clinic. It was all so confusing.

But what confused him most was how sexually free every man was. Over and over, Less was told that he needed to "loosen up." He was certain this was true. But how had *absolutely everybody else* loosened up and not him? It seemed statistically impossible that so many men, particularly so many ordinary, clean-cut *American* men, could feel so carefree about sex. You couldn't shake your past just like that, could you? An Amish farmer, for instance, could not wake up one morning as a creditable NASCAR driver. That would take years, if it was even possible. And it was not as if these men were carefree across the board; quite the opposite. They remained uptight in so many other, familiar ways— about music, dry cleaning, cheese spreads, place settings, skin care—ways that would have pleased their mothers or even grandmothers. But when it came to sex—well, welcome to the Monkey House! Less could not believe it. Had they all taken some drug his doctor would not prescribe? Were there free night classes he had not attended? Were the other unliberated men all trapped on a boat offshore? In a sex dungeon? Slowly, the impossible dawned on him, and with terror he was forced to look deep within himself, as we all someday must, and ask: *Am I the only frigid homosexual in New York?*

It turned out he was. So he left.

So: Bad gay?

"Mr. Yes?"

"Yes."

The man in the headset is not looking at Less; he is looking at his clipboard. He is also not listening to Less; he is listening to his headset. But he is indeed talking to Less: "There seems to be a little problem. A problem with Mr. Mandern."

"He's sick again?"

"Sick?" The man finally meets Less's eyes in concern. "Why would you say that? No, he's not sick. It's just that Mr. Mandern has yet to arrive."

"That's clear."

"So we're going to have to start without him. The audience can't wait any longer."

"But...but it's an interview with Mr. Mandern."

"Do you think you could read something of yours? As a kind of opening act."

"I think the audience wants Mr. Mandern, not me."

"They're very unhappy," the man says. "They're starting to chant things. Do you, perhaps, have a piece that's long enough it can cover us in case Mr.

Mandern doesn't show up and yet short enough that if he arrives, you can stop instantly?"

"Both long and short?"

"Maybe an hour but also as little as five minutes? Something for the science fiction crowd but also not science fiction, because of course that's for Mr. Mandern, if you see what I mean."

"Both science fiction and not science fiction?"

"Yes."

"I can be both old and young, if you like. Tall and short."

"I leave it to you. We have to get you onstage before there is a riot. Follow me, Mr. Yes."

Arthur Less hears his name (or something similar) announced and stumbles onto a stage that has been painted white, under bright white lights, so that he stands dazzled by a whiteness that offers him confused, sporadic applause, something like the last kernels bursting in a popcorn maker. The chanting has stopped for the moment. He clears his throat before the microphone; he can sense, in his blindness, the mass of humanity already electric with disappointment. And from the darkness comes a call: "Who the hell are you?" From the same darkness: a shudder of laughter.

Less answers: "I'm Arthur Less."

"Where's H.H.H.?"

"Mr. Mandern is getting ready. I'm the interviewer,

so they've sent me out here to read something."
How can it be that he has been persuaded, like
those prisoners forced to saw and sand their own
coffins, into fitting his own mad humiliation? He
begins to sweat. All his handkerchiefs are in the
greenroom covered in pink fluff. How happy they
must be there.

"I promise you we're not hiding Mr. Mandern
backstage somewhere," he says with a maddened
grin. "He's on his way. In the meantime, they've
asked me to read from my novel *Dark Matter*—"

The crowd begins to chant again—"H.H.H.!
H.H.H.!"—and he feels it jackhammering his bones.
Freddy, he thinks, *you don't know what I go through.*

Perhaps it is the snow-blinding effect of the auditorium lights or the high-wind sound of the crowd,
but the scene shakes and blurs in Less's vision. He is
standing on another stage, forty years ago or more.
The venue is smaller, the lights dimmer, but again a
man is shouting to a packed house; it is his father,
Lawrence Less. Bristling with sweat and decorated
in fringed denim, his father moves around the stage
like an earthbound anemone. He is yelling into a
microphone. Less's mother is not present in this
memory; there is only himself, his father, the lights,
and the applause. People are being charmed; something is being sold. What Less is doing onstage is a
mystery as well; surely he is part of his father's act,
but all that remains is his father's flailing form. This

is probably six months before the police begin their investigations and the anemone vanishes from the scene, and from Less's life, on the lam from the law: public anemone number one.

"We find our narrator," Less bellows into the microphone, and the audience quiets immediately, as if he has uttered a malediction. They are listening; who knows why? Best not to ask. He is back in control. A tremor has taken hold of his right hand and makes the pages shake; there is no choice but to go on.

"We find our narrator," he repeats and his voice booms through the hall, "already in motion—"

The interrupting roar stops him mid-sentence; it is the audience on its feet. Beside him, Less sees a shadow that appears to be of a tall man with a helmet and a lance. But of course he knows exactly who it is. H. H. H. Mandern has appeared to save the day.

An hour later, it is over. Less can hardly remember any of it; it is so utterly unlike his prior event with Mandern as to persuade him someone hired an impersonator. Previously, Less had cared for a weak, elderly writer who could barely walk onstage. Here: Some great god in a fedora strode forth, carrying a silver cane, leading the audience in a religious revival of chants and slogans. When it was finished, the roar was Tyrannosaurian. Mandern held out his arms to embrace the sound's monstrous shape, and Arthur could only stand in awe.

They are driven back from the event in Mandern's car. The great author does not look at Less; he looks out the window at the smear of lights going by. He wears sunglasses, his trademark fedora, a bloodred corduroy blazer, a striped badger of a beard, and (below his hat) a shag of hair not unsatisfyingly dyed the color of eggplant. The deep-grooved planes of his face like chain-saw art; the ears projecting from his skull like the garitas of a Spanish fortress; his growl of a voice; and, above all, his size, his majesty—these elements have combined in many a mesmerist before (Henry VIII comes to mind, and Orson Welles) and turn their menace now on Arthur Less. From behind sunglasses, he says:

"So *you're* who they sent to profile me? Not what I expected."

Less says, "You probably don't remember but we met before..."

Our hero waits expectantly for the fairy of memory to touch the scene with color. But Mandern does not speak or stir.

"In New York," Less clarifies. "You were ill."

Still no movement from the famous writer. Palm Springs rolls by behind smoked windows, a kind of day-for-night, and the palms and neon signs seem illuminated by moonlight. At last the great man takes a lozenge out of a small tin, then offers it to Less with a grunt.

"What is it?" Less asks.

"Magic mushroom."

Less is startled. "Really?"

A frown beneath the sunglasses. "It's a breath mint, man. I'm fucking eighty-four."

Arthur demurs and asks where they are going.

Mandern leans toward him. Less can see himself reflected in the dark glasses, diminished. Mandern answers with a non sequitur, which is perhaps the right of eighty-four-year-olds. "I have a very important question for you, Mr. Yes."

"It's Less."

"What's that?" Mandern seems a little deaf, as is also the right of eighty-four-year-olds.

"It's *Less*. L-e-s-s."

"Less."

"Yes."

Mandern shakes off this irritation and continues: "Mr. Less or Yes, we have a problem. I'm very late on a book and my publisher has imprisoned me. I'm under house arrest. Marco here is only allowed to drive me to events and to the airport. I am a literary prisoner."

"We can just do the profile at—"

"There is no profile," Mandern says, waving a lion's paw and looking out the window. "I'm canceling the whole fucking thing."

Panic siroccos through Less's mind. Canceled? He has come all this way and lost a sweater only to be thrown once more into financial ruin? He feels uncomfortably like New Sweden. "What's...what? But we have a flight to Santa Fe—"

"I don't fly. I started to have these spins, this vertigo. Like I'm a whirling dervish. So it's fucking canceled," Mandern states, then adds: "Unless..."

"Unless what?" Less asks. "Unless what?"

The old man sighs. "There is someone I need to find."

"Okay."

Mandern turns to him. "We stop tonight in the desert. And tomorrow in an oasis where she was last seen. And then if we find her, we arrive in Santa Fe for our event."

"We? Are you asking if I'm willing to go?"

"No, Mr. Less, I'm asking..." the great author says. His sunglasses are directed at Less, the large, chatoyant, emotionless eyes of an octopus drifting slowly toward Less in the murk of the car. "I'm asking: Do you have a driver's license?"

This purely practical query, coming like the check after an evening of strong liquor, brings Less out of his panic. And with his fear of things falling apart, his desire and need, his pathological tendency to answer every question directly and honestly—and other rules of the cosmos—Mr. Yes can only answer:

"Yes!"

How long can a gay man survive in a desert?

We are about to find out, for, from our buzzard's-eye view of California, we see an old conversion van painted a pristine shade of green tottering through the night toward the Mojave Desert. Through its windshield, we can make out three passengers: an elderly man in a fedora, a black pug dog, and a Minor American Novelist at the wheel. Start your timers now.

It all happened so quickly; Less was taken to a garage where awaited two "beauties," as Mandern put it. The first was named Dolly: a glossy black dog, a pug, that fixed our hero with an almost human gaze. By which I mean one of garrulous idiocy. "Dolly, meet our friend Arthur." Dolly cocked her head, as if Less might make more sense sideways.

The second was named Rosina: a camper van, one of those antique, live-in conversions you see all over the West Coast, with granny-glasses headlights, a wrapped spare tire for a nose, and a tight-lipped front bumper to complete the absurd, blank expression of a bauta mask. Bright green and, he will later learn, equipped with a roof that pops up like the expanding pouch of a frigate bird. Apparently Mandern bought it from an ophthalmologist who never drove it, as Mandern never has himself ("An ophthalmologist at heart," Mandern added with a sigh). He tossed Less the keys; they climbed inside. Less did not know what he was doing.

"So are we taking this to Santa Fe tonight?" he

asked. "What about the limousine? Are we going to sleep in this thing? What if it breaks down?"

"Just drive," he was told. And he did.

Less and the van have taken a while to get to know each other; he is certainly used to old cars, but not to something that feels so human. Every time he moves, it moves with him, like a drunken dance partner. And the reverse is true; since it vibrates dramatically, and he is clenched to its controls, he finds himself vibrating right along. Like driving a martini shaker. After almost two hours of being shaken, driving along back roads as dark as a haunted house, the headlights peering around each terrifying turn like the flashlight of a ghost hunter, they head southward to an inland sea.

The "stop tonight in the desert" is called Bombay Beach (no beach) and the bar is called Ski Inn (no skiing), but its bland, intimidating exterior opens to a warm, paneled room whose ceiling and walls are almost entirely covered in dollar bills. It is hard to picture our hero in these carriage-wheel-chandeliered, sawdust-floored, spittooned surroundings. He seems to shimmer like a hologram projection. To be honest, it is hard to picture Arthur Less in America at all. His awkwardness abroad seems natural; here, it seems vexing. In thoroughly American settings—a football stadium, a beer-and-television bar, a railroad-car diner— where most citizens relax among their own kind, finally free of foreign entanglements, Less sits bolt upright, looking as if he were not actually there. Place him in a wheat field, for instance, and he seems to be added in postproduction. Or, worst of all, a church—he wears the bewildered expression of a man who has arrived expecting a performance of *Godspell*. Which expression he wears today. Perhaps expecting *Paint Your Wagon*.

"Is this a saloon?" Less asks.

"I think you've been in a bar before," Mandern replies curtly, sitting himself on a stool.

Less looks around. The place is decorated with street signs and antique photographs of trick riders and an iron whatsit perhaps belonging to a horse; the bar is worn so smooth, you could certainly sail a pint of beer from one end to the other. It is a cartoon of itself, but then, in his trim gray suit, so is Arthur Less. So are we all.

"What'll it be?" asks the bartender, his white hair pulled into a small ponytail; he looks like Thomas Jefferson.

"Two martinis," Mandern says in a gentle voice. "Very cold."

Arthur Less is staring up at the ceiling. "How do you get the dollars up there?"

"Use a quarter and a tack," says Jefferson, setting up their drinks. "To give it weight. Gotta practice the throw. Unfolds after a bit and the quarter falls."

Mandern asks, "May I try?" and Jefferson jerks his

head toward a bowl of thumbtacks. "Got a pen?" Mandern asks of Less, who produces his mother's antique one, and the old man brings out a dollar and deftly signs it before inserting a tack through the middle, covering the tack with a quarter, and twisting the dollar closed like a dumpling.

Jefferson: "Give it all you got."

Mandern does; miraculously, it sticks. Less laughs in surprise but the old man merely looks up at the ceiling.

"So," Less says, taking a sip from his martini. "What I think everyone wants to know about, Mr. Mandern, is what's—"

"Is this your awkward way of beginning this profile?" Mandern says, pivoting his sunglasses to Less.

"We have a bargain, Mr. Mandern."

"I'll trade a question for a question." Mandern now brings out a pipe and, without lighting it, puts the end in his mouth. "My question first. My family used to come here back when this was a resort. It was our ritual. Salton Sea, they call it. It wasn't even a real sea, just a break in an irrigation canal that filled up a dry lake bed. For a while there were houses and motels and swimming and waterskiing. Long gone now, of course."

That would account for the Ski Inn. "Where did the water go?"

Mandern seems to be staring at his reflection in

the mirror, framed by dollars. He shrugs. "Now tell me a family ritual."

"Ritual?"

"You know, like you always had to hide the gin when Grandma was coming."

"My grandmother was a Southern Baptist," Less says, still fascinated by the empty pipe.

"A question for a question."

Less looks at the old man and tries to imagine him as a boy, splashing in a vanished sea. "My father left when I was young," Less says. "My mother's second husband was a chemist. So he always celebrated birthdays from the periodic table. According to the atomic number. Ruthenium, rhodium, like that."

Mandern laughs and others turn to look. "That's ridiculous."

This seems a strong statement from a man with a pug, a pipe, and a conversion van. Less goes on: "When he turned silver, that was a big deal, because she could finally buy him a present. You can't buy ruthenium cuff links, can you?"

"I don't see why not. What did she get him for silver?"

"Silver cuff links." Less hears a sigh. "And there was the gold birthday. His last birthday," Less says, trying to remember, "his last birthday was . . . thallium."

"Thallium," Mandern repeats solemnly.

"That's eighty-one," Less says, staring up at the

constellation of dollar bills. "He never made it to lead."

There is a sound that cannot possibly be laughter. When Less looks over at Mandern, he is surprised; the man has removed his sunglasses. His eyes are golden, leonine, somehow smaller than expected in the dry lake bed of his face—little Salton Seas.

"Mr. Less," Mandern says, "when was the last time you saw your father? I mean your real father."

Less examines the old man carefully. Is he a mind reader as well as a maniac? He watches as the bartender who looks like Jefferson is approached by an old woman with white hair curled above her ears like James Madison. The two confer in whispers. Less seems to be in the middle of the Continental Congress. "I think it's my turn for a question."

Mandern sighs, replacing his sunglasses.

Less: "Who are we trying to find?"

The old man says not a word.

Less is about to speak but instead lets out a sudden yelp; something has hit him on the head.

Jefferson wipes the bar, nodding. "That'll be the quarter."

A call made from an antique phone booth in an inn that is not an inn by a beach that is not a beach:

"Ladder down!" Less says to me.

"Less! What happened to you? You were supposed to call from—"

"Plans changed. Mandern wouldn't do the profile unless I drove him out here, so—"

"So you're in Santa Fe?"

"Not yet. We're in . . . I don't know exactly where. We're in a camper van."

"Is everything okay? Is this some kind of seduction?"

"No! He . . . he was going to cancel the whole thing. No profile, no money, Freddy."

"You could call Wichita—"

"Stop bringing that up! I've got this."

"Take notes, is all I can say." *Pay attention.*

"I will. I promise."

We say we love each other. But during our traditional goodbye, there is worry beneath the words.

Mandern directs him away from Bombay Beach and into the desert for their lodgings, down a dirt road between creosote bushes. At last they come to a stop where two canvas tents glow like lanterns on the tabletop of the night. Between: a fire blazing in a barrel. A woman wrapped in a sheepskin approaches, a Black woman with gray dreadlocks and sculpted round cheeks that catch the firelight; she must own the property. "Dolly!" the woman shouts, and Mandern gets out of the van. Less watches as he puts the dog on the ground and she scrabbles over to the woman. What he is supposed to do now is a mystery. Is this what it is like to be a character in someone's novel?

"Don't leave out any food," the woman warns Less sternly. "Or clothing." He wants to tell her he has no clothing. He is shown to his tent, which is one of those miracles of humanity: a big brass bed, covered in Serrano tribal blankets and fur throws, that someone has been kind enough to drag all the way out here to the middle of nowhere. Less bows his head in gratitude and climbs into the bed.

He is just on the edge of sleep when he hears a voice from beyond the canvas wall; it is Mandern's deep growl: "I was thinking about your stepfather."

"Yes?"

"I think it would be fitting to die at plutonium. Pluto the god of death."

Less searches the table he was made to memorize. "But that's like ninety-four or ninety-five!"

"You're right," the great man mutters. "Too young, too young." Less assumes Mandern falls asleep with that thought in his head because afterward Less can hear only his heavy breathing until one last sentence comes out of the darkness: "We're looking for my daughter."

As our hero huddles in his counterpane against the cold desert night, I am reminded of times I have spent "camping" with Arthur Less. There was, of course, the ill-fated Hotel d'Amour. But before that came my own proposal of a trip. I believed I had not seen enough of America: "There's a train that goes from here straight up to Portland and then over to Boston. We go through Oregon, Idaho, Montana, one of the Dakotas . . . it's four days and we can have a little room all our own and . . ."

He stared at me as at a lover proposing a peculiar sexual act. I thought at first he did not deem me suitable for travel, but after some heated discussion it turned out it was not this at all. It was that he had already planned a trip. He had meant it to be a surprise for my school break but now was forced to reveal all.

Our first stop was what Less referred to as an "exclusive waterfront hotel," which turned out to be an artist's project: a single room floating on a California lake. It was nothing but a bobbing out-house with a submarine's hatch that led down to an underwater Plexiglas bedroom. We arrived after dark, a teenager took us out on a speedboat, and we were informed that, as in a submarine, we should call out "Ladder up!" or "Ladder down!" to avoid collisions. It was a hard night's sleep, but the tides rocked us like an underwater cradle, and I awoke to a scream: Arthur Less, sitting straight up in bed. I saw what had alarmed him: we lay in a cube of morning light with perhaps a hundred fish staring in at us, arranged like magic daggers in the glow.

The second part of the "water" trip was far more

involved than the "Ladder down!" incident, for the task he fancifully signed us up for was to make a raft and float it two nights down the American River. Perhaps Less had a Huck Finn fantasy, common to many writers; perhaps Californians harbor gold-rush dreams; perhaps the lumberjackery of it all held an erotic charge. What we found dispelled any fantasy: a muddy shore with piles of bare logs, coils of rope, two other couples, and a broad-shouldered woman from Stockholm presiding over our manual labor. Let me add: it was raining. Each couple's job (as she commanded from beneath her olive rain slicker) was to turn the logs into a seaworthy vessel, including an A-frame shelter, securing them with a variety of knots that she demonstrated. This was all to be done, of course, hip-deep in the river. Having not been raised by longshoremen, I found the knots impossible, but Less had an even harder time; our leader savaged my Walloon ruthlessly, as if seeking redress for the failures of New Sweden, and more than once, Less slipped into the currents of the American and had to pull himself to shore. We finished far behind the other two couples, setting off late in the day but relieved to be free of our ogre master. We floated lazily, poling our way along the river, quite pleased that our relationship had survived this colossal macramé project. The banks rose above us in white stone and pines; sunlight re-placed the rain, and the forest preened in the river's looking glass. We had, however, left one essential item ashore: our food.

This came to light almost immediately; I heard a yelp from the shelter, and Less appeared wide-eyed, holding out two cans of beer. We had apparently brought with us only the case of Dewey beer (from Delaware) and camping equipment; the food lay far behind us, like so many fond memories. Blame was passed hot-potato back and forth; anxiety's moon was full in Less's brain, that toothless werewolf; and the threat of cannibalism was in the air.

"I'm going to invent a time machine!" I shouted furiously, and he said, Oh, really? "I'm going to invent a time machine and *never choose you!*" He was visibly hurt by this, perhaps the worst thing I ever said to him.

Ah, but fast turns fortune's wheel! An hour later, we found one of the other couples stuck on a sandbar (the river was unseasonably low). So we resorted to that most ancient of solutions: piracy.

For four cans of Dewey beer and assistance in their release, we received half a bag of sliced bread, a tomato, and some cheese. This held us until early evening, when we came across the other couple trapped on some rocks; they gave us a box of gluten-free pasta and more tomatoes. We all camped ashore at a scrubby place called Lotus (hardly Homeric), where I am ashamed to say I stole eggs from some very loud snorers. We slept well, as villains do. The next day was sunny and equally profitable; our unlucky companions needed our assistance thrice more. It was with poignancy we reached our final encampment at Folsom Lake, where at sunset the low water revealed a former mining town flooded long ago by a dam. We shared our final Deweys among the weary travelers and stuffed ourselves beside the fire with our plunder. The next morning, the Swede shouted us awake, insisting we scupper our vessel and return it to mere wood and sodden hemp. It was a sad farewell; our charmed voyage had come to an end and along with it our wicked ways.

When we arrived, bruised and weary, back in the Shack, Less sat on the couch with his head in his hands; nothing had gone according to plan, and he felt it was all his doing.

"Of course it's your doing," I said to him.

He said he was so sorry he always made a mess of things.

"Less," I said to my poor Walloon.

He said I was going to invent a time machine and never choose him.

"Less!" I said, squatting on the floor before him. "I loved it!"

A desert sound. This time it is almost certainly a wolf's howl. Instantly Less is outside the tent, wrapped in a Serrano blanket.

The landscape is reversed; the desert is now in the sky, streaked with heliotrope and tawny gold as if along the crests of sand dunes, and below it spreads a dark galaxy of spiny plants: the Joshua trees. They lie out to the horizon in clumps, Holy Rollers at a revival, lifting their heavy arms. How long has this been going on? For all time? Why did no one tell him? The stars are being extinguished one by one, as if by a lamplighter, as the horizon begins to whiten in expectation. And he notices, out there among the Joshua trees, almost of them, silhouetted against the sky, the shape of an old man in a robe regarding the sunrise. His little dog begins to bay.

To tell the truth, America looks fine from here.

"Arise and shine, for thy light has come," Less's mother used to say each morning when she let the sunlight in through the plastic blinds. She always gave chapter and verse: "Isaiah, sixty, one." Then she would hand little Archie a handkerchief in which to blow his nose.

Dawn arrives (along with Less's matinal nose-blowing) and he emerges again from his tent to find Mandern thoughtful by the morning fire. Less is left alone with his coffee, looking around at this foreign world, his own country. He looks over at Mandern: When will this gruff old man reveal even deeper instability? Today, at this supposed oasis? He watched Mandern easily put down two martinis last night; will it be something stronger tonight? Were those, in fact, breath mints? Is that pipe, in fact, empty? Less girds himself against chaos, but then again, he girds himself against everything.

They hit the road, which now has become perfectly ordinary, even bland, as the Joshua trees begin to be replaced by comic-book saguaros. Less wonders how far it is to the OK Corral.

Mandern growls: "Another question, Arthur Less."

Less clears his throat: "Why are you—"

"I meant mine. Is your father alive?"

Our author steers himself back into the right lane. A pause, a panic, thinking to himself that if he wants the money, he must play by the rules. "He left when I was young," Less says. "An early motivational-speaker kind of guy, part of a Ponzi scheme, all that crap. He left us just before the police came for him. The night of the school play."

"A criminal!" Mandern exclaims. "What had he done?"

"You know, I have no idea. I never heard from him again, not really. I got a call—" And he suddenly sighs. "I got a call from a sheriff in White Sands, New Mexico. He'd arrested my father for indecent congress with a satellite dish."

For the second time, Less hears the old writer laugh. A real laugh, and his ears turn red. "That is the best fucking thing I've heard in a year," he says. "Granted, it's been a shitty year."

Less: "Now me. Why are you taking so long with this novel?"

Mandern pulls the pipe out of his mouth. "You know Penelope, who said she would marry when she finished weaving her father-in-law's shroud? And every night she unraveled what she'd made? That's me."

Oddly, Less smiles. "You remind me of a woman in California."

"Will she marry when she finishes?"

"I don't think so."

"Neither will I," says Mandern, tapping his empty pipe into his palm. "I'm going to die."

After spending a foolish half hour trapped in an abandoned town seemingly run (as if in a folktale) by donkeys, they cross the Colorado River and enter Arizona, which announces itself with signs of mineral extraction: towns named Quartzsite and Bauxite and Perlite teetering on the edges of quarries, and signs for failed mines rebranded as "ghost towns" in the way rickety old hotels, with faulty electricity, will call themselves "haunted" and add an extra fee. Gravel pits abound; ugliness is everywhere; one begins to despair for mankind. Far away, red rock mounds cast blue-black shadows, and in the spot beneath these splendors where, in other states, might sit a grand "haunted" hotel lie always a trailer and a satellite dish. Otherwise, the land is flat and bare of life—so flat that it is hours before the road even ventures a turn, and then Less sees, lining the road, some seemingly immortal acacias that somebody has decorated (why this sudden feeling of joy?) for Christmas. Miles of tinsel and ornaments. The desert glitters in beauty. Mankind: Make up your mind.

AMBROGIO—THE LAST FREE PLACE—ALMOST THERE! reads graffiti sprayed on the side of a rock. And *almost there* about describes it . . .

Arthur Less has been out of place many times in his life. I would guess he has been out of place almost everywhere except that bedroom with the trumpet vine (as perhaps have I). He has been at Cub Scout meetings where every boy has been asked to tie his favorite knot, gay parties where he has had to write on his name tag his sexual kink (long underwear), bars where he has had to pick songs from the jukebox, yoga classes where he has had to imitate the pose of a contortionist, and every morning of his life when he has had to decide whether it could be done today. He has done them all. So being in a place of utter misrule and chaos is no problem for him. In some way, that is the comfort zone of Arthur Less. He knows, in such places, where he stands.

At first, a mirage, shimmering at the rim of the desert like something you cannot get out of your eye, resolving into the pinkish cupola of a

long-buried temple that at the next turn reveals itself to be hollow: a half shell trimmed in gleaming
metal. Beside and below it, down into the gorge,
are scattered crude concrete cubes; they all face the
shell, as if (trapped in their rectilinearity) they are
kneeling in worship. A wall surrounds it all, with a
set of gates. The gorge is touched with green where
a river, miraculously, runs. Dusty, surrounded by
wild acacias and mesquite, it seems like something
abandoned a century ago; there is not a single sign
of life. But along the wall there is a name carved
into the rock: AMBROGIO.

(Where he stands is: he will fail.)

"The last of the old-fashioned pirate bays," Mandern explains. "No police, no rules. Man on his
own, more or less."

"Your daughter is here?"

"Was here."

"And then on to Santa Fe? We have to get you
to Santa Fe!" No profile, no money. Brief vision
of the trumpet vine ripped down, the window
boarded over, the wrecking ball beginning its crush-
ing swing...

Mandern exits the van without a response.

For a place in so much disarray, Ambrogio's gates
are surprisingly sturdy: cast iron set into apricot-
colored brick. All along the gate dangle bronze
bells, swinging in the wind. With his broad hand
(and flinching a little from the effort), Mandern

makes them clangor all at once. A sturdy young man arrives in a sheepskin vest and suede pants; his hair is sugared in pink dust.

"We have some iced tea!" Mandern shouts. This seems to be a code of some kind, because the young man readily unlocks the gate—a combination, like you use on a locker—and lets them in. The walkway is concrete blocks inlaid with glass in which can be seen skeletal fish and, in one, a human skull. The man does not lead them into the dome but behind the pinkish walls onto a dusted mesa, where four great telephone poles have been driven into the ground. Planks have been nailed between them as a makeshift ladder and two other men are up there attaching a pulley system. Less is ashamed to admit he finds it all shabby and impoverished and unfriendly, possibly criminal, and he feels afraid.

Mandern laughs. "Baloo's made some great improvements!"

"I guess," the young man says. His noble features imply a mestizo heritage accompanied by a distinctly California mumble: "They're building a Universe Appreciation Platform."

"Say again?" Less asks.

Louder mumble: "A Universe Appreciation Platform." It is still nonsense. This reminds Less of a college roommate, a posh Pakistani who always claimed he could not understand Americans when they spoke. To him, everything sounded like "Hamburger-hamburger-hamburger."

Mandern turns with a wide grin. "Arthur," he says, "we're in for a magnificent sight." If he means the view from the platform, he is in for a surprise. Less is not going up that hamburger for love or money.

A woman comes around the corner all in turquoise gauze with a big sun hat. She is beautiful, in her forties or fifties, with long kinky auburn hair—a pasticcio like myself—and she moves with the lightness of a Persian peri. "H.!" she yells and runs to embrace H. H. H. Mandern. The way she caresses his cheeks and kisses them seems to imply the improbable.

"You haven't changed a bit," she exclaims.

"You're not a blonde anymore," Mandern says.

"I've gone vegan," she says gravely. Less cannot see the connection.

"Arathusa, this is my colleague Arthur Less. Or Yes."

It is as if a host of turquoise spirits descends upon him, combines with his soul, and then drifts away; she has that kind of touch. She leaves behind the scent of orange and sesame, as might a vegan ghost.

"It's wonderful to meet you, Art. I'm Council Leader Arathusa."

So now he's "Art"? "How's it going?"

She pouts. "Well, Art, this morning my dog ate half my boomerang." She pulls a chewed piece of wood from a pocket.

"Does it still work?"

Arathusa considers this question and throws the object across the yard with surprising skill. It whistles through the air and lands in the dust a few feet from the latrine. They both stare at it for a moment. "Well," she says with delight, "I guess it half works! Art, what's your philosophy?"

A few axioms come to mind—*Don't buy tomatoes in winter; men over forty should not dye their hair; expensive underwear is worth it*—but no philosophies. Less demurs: "Um, I don't think I have one."

"Everybody has one; you just have to discover it. Mine is about embracing the affirmative. It goes like this: Know no *no*."

"No, no, no," Less parrots.

"You're mishearing me," she says, smiling. "Now, listen: Know no *no*."

"No, no, no."

Arathusa's smile sharpens. "No, no, no!" she says, then starts again: "Know. No. *No*."

"No," Less begins slowly. "No. No."

A sigh. "No."

Apparently he is to be housed in a tepee, whereas Mandern, in the settlement below, will be "left to the wolves," as the chortling old writer puts it. For

Less, nothing in the word *tepee* precludes the presence of wolves, especially since the tepee he sees
ahead is painted all over with wolves (in fact not a
tepee but a lavvu, also unindigenous to the region,
but who or what here is not?). There is the creeping
feeling that he has made a terrible mistake. How is
this getting him any closer to a profile, a payment
on the Shack? Or to his lover in faraway Maine—
me, Freddy Pelu?

Less turns and finds Dolly and Mandern gone;
only his shadow is visible, descending into the valley
below. "Wait!" Less cries out without thinking.
"Don't leave me!"

But the old man's shadow vanishes below the edge.

"Sunset is fabulous here," says Arathusa, oblivious
to wolves and disappearing profile subjects. She
points toward the concrete cubes already in shadow.
"Dinner is down that way in an hour or so, bring
something if you can, but everyone is welcome! And
you should hit the hot springs, right near you—
follow the hose. Yes, that hose there. Don't touch
the valve, though! You'll flood Ambrogio, ha-ha!
The hot springs is great for sunset. Which is about
now, I guess. Check out the sign. Here we are."

She means his lavvu, but here we are indeed:
the sun, monarch of the Southwest, has been
exiled behind the peaks, and the whole valley can
now relax into this cantaloupe horizontal glow,
which brings out the intricate tooled leatherwork

of the mountainside, below which a concatenation of surfaces (windows, puddles, chromed vehicles) reflect this afterlight, one after the other, like the final notes of a symphony repeated in each section of the orchestra, until the rim of the half shell lets off one last flare and the event is concluded. Only connoisseurs remain after the sun has set, to enjoy the varying bars of tangerine and coral that linger in the sky, and it is against this gaudy afterthought that a dove, in silhouette, flies across Less's vision to land on a somewhat slack electric line, where it begins an inelegant high-wire act, bobbing and lurching, its tail feathers toggling up and down until it gains its balance. It reaches equilibrium, looks around with satisfaction—and is of course immediately joined by another dove, who monkeys everything up. The toggling dance begins again, complexity doubled, tail feathers alternating madly. Who would play such a trick? The birds do not seem to mind, however; their composure is part of the comedy and part of the astonishing scene before him, which must play out every evening in this way. Such is love.

Less watches them and wonders how such simple beings could master higher-level physics when he himself received only a B minus until the doves (in truth just ordinary pigeons) give up on the whole damn thing and take off, together, into the murky shadows of the canyon. That is when

Arthur Less, finding himself alone, at last reads the sign that stands directly between him and his lavvu:

CLOTHING OPTIONAL BEYOND THIS POINT

"Archie."

His sister's face is on the screen before him. The advanced technology required for this feat is at odds with his wolf-painted background but totally appropriate for the austere metal-and-white of her setting; while he seems to be in the eighteenth century, she could be orbiting Jupiter.

"How's it going out east, Rebecca?"

She closes her eyes and sighs. "How's it going in the Wild West?"

"I'm in a commune with a naked hot springs. I'm feeling lonely."

Rebecca studies him with care. She does not look much like Arthur Less, but when you see them together, there is something unmistakable—like the "hand" of a master in late and early periods. The hard line of the nose, the plump lower lip compensating for the thin upper one, the eerily tiny ears, the ghostly pallor, and the hair so thin it seems more like a low cloud. Until last year, Rebecca was blond. Now she is completely gray. Less has never asked her if it was previously dyed or went all at once, like a maple in autumn. With her tangle of gray curls, her black leotard top, her concerned expression, she looks like a French ballet instructor.

"I'm sorry, Archie," his sister says. "Did you forget this is what travel is like?"

"I guess I did."

Rebecca: "It isn't all camels and elephants."

"I wouldn't rule it out—"

"Archie, I have something serious to talk about." Her expression rearranges itself into a solemn one; Less comes to attention. The ballet instructor is beginning class. "It's Dad. He called."

Less is startled. "He called?"

"He called."

"From where?" he asks, feeling a fresh new panic. "New Mexico?"

"No, somewhere in Georgia. He said he was on an island."

Less: "What did he want?"

"He wanted to know about you," she says. "Has he called you? Written you?"

What is this sensation? Of being free of something you thought you had conquered, only to have it lash out with a tentacle to draw you back? "No. No, I haven't heard anything. What is he up to?"

Rebecca: "He says he's running a nonprofit for the arts."

Less laughs. "Whatever that means!"

"Archie, he sounded . . ." The pause is of someone

searching for the right knife in a drawer, the right word to do a hard job quickly. "He sounded old."

Less is not buying it. "Did he turn on the charm?"

"No, he was…contrite," she says. "Like something wore him down."

"Probably the White Sands sheriff."

Her face is all sorrow now. "Archie. If he calls you…"

"Rebecca."

"Don't hang up," she says. "I think he's dying."

He can see the gravity in his sister's face. He wants to tell her that she never really knew their father, she was too young, that he is as much a phantom as her imaginary friend when she was three: a purple goat named Speckles. Speckles has called. Speckles is living on an island. Speckles is dying. Speckles had indecent congress with a satellite dish. Though, as he knows, Rebecca does not remember Speckles at all and she only vaguely remembers their father vanishing on the night of her elementary-school performance as one-half of a whole-wheat sandwich and, months later, breaking into the house to take things he'd left behind. None of it, for her, will ever be as real as it was for Less.

Less says, "If he wanted to call me, he would have called me. But he called you."

"I think he's afraid of you."

He laughs. "Nobody's afraid of me."

"I've been afraid of you," Rebecca says.

Less starts back, blinking. This feels true, if previously unknown. Perhaps because he never thought about it. If so, how awful! Four years older, surely he transferred some of his own terror onto her over the years, terror hidden by the arrogance and pomposity of adolescence or even more recently than he realizes.

Rebecca must see all this in his face; she knows him well. "Don't worry," she says. "You were a good big brother. The best. I'm sorry to lay this on you so soon after Robert."

"I don't understand why Robert's death is hitting me so hard."

She says, "It's death, Archie. When Mom died, we—"

"But it's something else," he says. "Not existential. Not grief. It's something selfish, so selfish." He pauses. "I can't say it."

A sigh. "Archie."

"It's . . . I'm a fool, Bee. I break things and forget things and put off things until it's too late, but I always knew somebody was there to . . . fix things. To be the grown-up. To buy the tickets or find a ride or repair whatever I had screwed up."

"Robert."

"When I fell apart, he always had advice. Even after we broke up. He was bossy and impossible, but he held me up."

"Archie."

"I don't know if I can do it without him, Bee. I don't know if I can do it without Robert somewhere."

The glasses magnify her startled expression. "You don't know if you can go through Robert's death without Robert's help?"

Less grimaces. "Well, when *you* say it, it sounds *crazy*."

Her face becomes stern. "You're very lucky, Archie. You have Freddy."

"Freddy..." Imagine one's name said with a combination of tenderness and impossibility, the same tone in which Less's mother used to sigh the word *France*.

Rebecca asks, "You don't think Freddy can hold you up?"

"I don't know. I don't know. But if he can't, then what?"

"Then you hold yourself up."

"No," Less says. "Then I fall apart. I won't survive it."

She says, "You will survive it. Go get in that hot springs."

No one is more surprised than your narrator to find Arthur Less, wearing nothing but a towel over his arm, wandering through the dusk until he reaches the "hot springs" the signs portend. It is no more than a muddy pondlet and lying in it

are two women and a man, all white, all young.
From some invisible quadrant, a man is singing the
Beatles' "Hey Jude" accompanied by guitar and lots
of *na-na-na*s. The bathers turn to look at nude,
middle-aged Arthur Less.

None of them are naked.

A quite cold breeze begins to blow. The universe
holds its breath for a moment. And then he hears
one of the women talking to the man beside her:

"Wer ist dieser alte Mann?"

Arthur Less is saved; they are Germans! Noncha-
lantly, he throws his towel on a nearby mesquite
and smiles.

[*The following is translated from the German.*]

"Hello," he says. "I am name Arthur."

"Oh, you speak some German!" says the man.
He is long and lanky, blond, with a newish-looking
brown beard; his round, handsome face seems
to have never been hardened by care. "I'm glad
to see someone naked. The women are making
me shy."

"Also shy I am!" Less answers brightly.

"Come on in, Arthur. This is Helga and Greta
and I am Felix. We were just talking about break-
ups." Helga is slim and smiley, her hair knotted into
a blond pretzel; Greta, a substantial green-haired
mermaid, seems mute and stunned.

"Here is a sad conversation," Less says.

"Helga just found out her boyfriend was cheating

on her!" says Felix, and Helga nods. "Well. Big trouble. Want a blueberry?"

Less takes the bag from him, then looks over at the blond girl. "I am sorry, Helga," he says. "This is a raisin."

"No, it's a blueberry," she replies.

Less frowns. "Not raisin," he says, thinking over his words. "*Surprise*. It is a surprise, your boyfriend finding."

She opens her arms to the dimming sky. "I just think it's all for a reason, you know? Oh, don't take more than two of those blueberries! Oh well, too late. And the universe is guiding me somewhere else, you know?"

"I know," Less replies. And he does know. The blueberries turn out to be chocolate-covered, which suits him fine. How wonderful to believe in a universe that holds, for you, a special plan! Only the very young, Less observes, could think so. Only those still at the beginning of this novel would trust the Author knows what He is doing. While Less, being an author himself, knows that no authors know what they are doing. That is what the drink and drugs and madness are about (we have two authors in a van as evidence). And, having seen twice as much of life as anyone here, he knows the Author has long ago lost the plot.

From behind a hill, someone is still singing the

chorus to "Hey Jude": *Na na na na-na-na na, na-na-na na . . .*

"Thank you for the very few blueberries," Less says. "Water warm."

Felix explains: "A pipe broke a few kilometers back, I don't think the authorities even know about it, almost flooded the whole compound. We redirected the flow and made our hot springs! Make sure you don't touch the valve, it'll flood again."

Less, merrily: "It is a lucky Pan flute!"

They all look at him strangely.

"Pan flute! Pan flute!" he repeats with frustration. "Noah and the Pan flute!"

Recognition on their faces. Felix says, "Ahh! Flood! It is Noah and the *flood*."

"Ah, yes, flood. Pan flute. I make a stupid mistake."

Helga turns to him: "Arthur, when did you first kiss a girl? Sorry, I'm really high. But tell us."

"By me this is never done."

"What? You've never kissed a girl?"

Felix: "He's gay, Helga."

How do they *know*?

Helga shakes her pretzel as if she cannot believe it, but she means something else. "But everybody's kissed a girl!" she says. "Never, Arthur, not even when you were young?"

"Once, perhaps. When I was young," Less relates.

"In a play a girl I kissed. I was very scared. What play I do not remember." (My dear partner, it was *Oklahoma!* and you know it.)

She shakes her pretzel again. "Oh, that's not a real kiss! How about a boy, then?"

"I had nineteen years."

"Nineteen!" Felix interjects, grinning salaciously. "Come on! I hear gay guys get way more sex than us. And you didn't even kiss a boy until you were nineteen? I don't believe it. I thought you guys all messed around in youth camp or something."

"Not I," Less says with a poignant smile. "Remember how old me am. High school the early 1980s was. I finally kissed a boy..." Naked in the hot springs, in the Arizona twilight, Arthur Less tells the story in a condensed, bowdlerized, and broken-German version—but I will spare him that humiliation in these pages.

"This is not a very funny story," Felix states.

Helga smiles consolingly and rests the back of her hand on his cheek. "What's your full name, Arthur?"

"Arthur Less."

"Do you have a boy now, Arthur Less?"

"Yes."

"What's his name?"

"Name Freddy is. Across the world to choose me traveled he."

Greta frowns and asks him to repeat this.

"Across the world he traveled. To me choose."

"To choose you?"

"To choose me."

Less looks down. The twilight seems almost like the morning light as it falls across his naked skin, and the fallen leaves could be the shadow of a trumpet vine. From somewhere in the valley comes a faint, metallic sound—

"Would you like to kiss me, Arthur Less?"

What fresh moose is this? For who could have expected such a question? Arthur Less has had this kind of offer before, of course, but not often from a woman. When their chaste kiss is over, he leans back in the muddy pool. Helga laughs and turns to her friends. "Gay men are such good kissers!" But Less is not thinking of the kiss, particularly. For him, it was not a kiss. It was a transfusion, briefly, of her carefree existence, her simple world of blueberries and hot springs, a transfusion directly into his blood. The pale horizon trembles as if coming to a simmer. He looks up: the stars. "The universe is big train," Less announces.

Felix nods. "It is indeed, my friend."

"Not big train," Less says, correcting himself. "*Generous.* The universe is very generous." He sits very still and looks up again at the stars. "But maybe also big train."

Felix smiles. "You're on a wild ride, my friend."

"Big generous train."

The sigh in the wind goes on and on, for as long as someone singing the Beatles' "Hey Jude," which is to say: Forever.

There is now a gap of almost ten hours in the chronicle, and surely some future Lessologists, studying this lacuna in the Lessiana, will conjecture it is during this time that our author begins to make notes for his next novel, that somewhere in the weeds of the preceding hours lie the seeds of art. And perhaps these poor devils will fritter away their lives combing over each blade of memory—each Jeffersonian martini, each vegan ghost, each Pan flute and blueberry—working on the vast desert of time like archaeologists who are certain a great Tyrannosaurus lies fossilized below them and yet have come equipped with mere toothbrushes. Perhaps great works will spring from their toil.

My thinking, however, is more straightforward:

Those were not blueberries.

And, since we have some time, it looks like I won't spare him after all . . .

Arthur Less finally kissed a boy in his penultimate year in college. For about six months, Arthur Less led a virginal existence, and a sad one. And then, one fine spring day while crossing the magnolia-blooming "Quad," where well-adjusted young men threw and caught plastic disks, stealing glances at well-adjusted young women who giggled back, yes, while heading toward his dormitory on Damascus (oh, coincidence!), young Arthur Less came to a sudden stop. The dappled tree light effulged upon the lawn, a heart-shaped flock of pigeons rose from the chapel, and the bronze Revolutionary War statue seemed to be pointing directly at Less. Our hero took three stunned steps forward. He looked at the light, the birds, the bronze. He looked at the disk-throwers. He looked at the girls. He saw that he was not part of this performance and never would be. He realized, at last, what absolutely everybody else already knew.

An empty set of months went by—like those accidentally blank slides in the projector—in which he chatted with timid "questioning" newcomers like himself (all doughy and pimply, none of them his "type"), but his celibacy overwintered hardily until, in March, the Queer Dance Party.

Let us savor the scene in all its details: The

wood-paneled basement room where young Less and two "questioning" newcomers would meet and embolden themselves with drink. One of the "questioning" newcomers failed to show. The other arrived late, in a light blue sweater, with only bottles of Fanta and Drambuie. They put on George Michael and the "questioning" newcomer said they should dance. Let's call him Reilly O'Shaunessy. Because that was his name. Younger than Less by a year (adolescence still blurring his blondish-pinkish looks), he was more experienced, having been taken up and discarded by a married dentist back in Amarillo, Texas. Picture the two white boys dancing like debutantes, Less with his arms around Reilly's shoulders. They were quite drunk. I imagine it was a surprise for both of them when they kissed—a rusty cocktail of Drambuie, George Michael, and a suffocating desire to be touched. Was the kiss any good? As with every first kiss: good enough. This led to Reilly unpantsed on the couch and Less kneeling prayerfully before him. Reilly, immersed in his pleasure, eventually leaned forward, quite naturally, and, preceded by a little sigh, such as babies give after a full breast of milk, vomited his rusty cocktail onto Less's bowed head.

Later, after our protagonist led the staggering Reilly back to his dormitory, after he spent a lonely hour in the laundry room erasing all trace of the evening from his and Reilly's sweaters, Less crept into his dormitory room and tried to sleep. But he was overwhelmed. So he wrote a few versions of a note to leave on Reilly's door in the morning. He has one still; I found it among his papers. I give it to you unabridged:

Reilly

Good morning! How you feeling? I'd like if possible to talk about what happened. We were very drunk, but I don't regret anything. In fact, I think it was funny. Ha-ha! And I like you very much. Let's talk sometime today. I also have your sweater, which I cleaned. Ha-ha! I'll return it to you.

A

He was mistaken; he never returned it. Reilly never spoke to him again. He avoided Less on campus and in the dining hall and shunned Questioning Men's Group. For Arthur: Bouts of sobbing, sessions of terrible poetry writing, afternoons listening to Leonard Cohen, and private moments bringing Reilly's light blue sweater to his face, trying to recapture some lost molecule, some leftover scent, which he himself, of course, had washed away. Months of this. It is possible, in some way, he never got over it. And all for a boy who wasn't even his type.

Which is my purpose in telling of his first kiss—in

a way, it opened the path that led to Robert. And, afterward, to me.

Less used to call his sister after every dating disaster. "I just want to be young together and in love," he would tell her. She would listen and sigh. All he wanted was to be young together and in love. Too much to ask? "Nobody gets that," she would say. "Nobody. Your problem is you're convinced you have a type." He would say of course he had a type, and she would say: "Give that up. Find someone who treats you decently."

Some scenes of romance still run through his mind, even at the age of fiftyish, like a cinema that plays the same four or five old movies. There is his first time with another man, a sour-faced German who afterward commented, upon learning of his virginity: "Well, this explains a lot!" There is the short Italian who, asked weeks later why he vanished when Less was in the bathroom, explained, "I decided you weren't attractive enough." And the Portuguese grad student who, in the blissful moments after the act, looked over at Less and said, "You know, your eyes aren't the right color blue." And so on. From the distance of decades, the diagnosis is simple: These men had their own heartbreaks. Their own cold-shoulderings, spurnings, senseless silences from a man they loved. How could they know how to handle another's heart? They were, after all, mere novices at dark magic. Gay Sex, already an advanced course of study, was nothing compared to that higher-level curriculum for which nothing in life in the 1970s—not high school or television or movies or library books or even gropings with girls or boys or themselves—had prepared these poor young men: mastery of Gay Love. Let me now admit the hard truth: Robert Brownburn was the first man to treat Less decently.

After moving from New York to San Francisco, years after that first kiss, Less met Robert and Marian Brownburn and not much later found himself in an Italian restaurant in North Beach where the poet took young Arthur Less's hand and wept from love. I believe that Less sat stunned before this display. For here it was: What he always wanted. Here was a man who loved him and was willing to sacrifice marriage and friends and an untroubled life for Arthur Less. Arthur Less! Here was a decent man. And more: Here was a way to be done with care—the risks Less had been talked into taking, his blood tested every six months, the agonizing two-week wait for results, the visions of AIDS dancing in his dreams. Here was a man who would stop the door against Death.

Did he love Robert? Of course he did. But Robert was not young. And by the time the relationship was over, fifteen years later, neither was Arthur Less. Let us admit Less never had what he wanted—will never have what he wanted. Will never be young with someone and in love.

As for his type (according to his sister), it was perfectly simple: a short, curly-haired man with glasses who would tease and love him endlessly.

I blush to write those words.

Arthur Less awakens to darkness. Or not quite darkness: above him, with remarkable clarity, he can see the twinkling star cluster of the Pleiades. Is he back in the lavvu? No; the lavvu may be cornerless, but not as cornerless as this, for the big train of the universe runs all around. One by one his senses come to him: the weight of the cowhide covering him, the sound of water running, the scent of a night-blooming flower. He shivers beneath his cowhide; he is naked on a makeshift bed. Less has missed the dinner, missed paying attention, and missed the promised phone call to his partner: me, Freddy Pelu. He closes his eyes and opens them. Cold, cold, cold. The world is so cold and quiet, and the Milky Way spreads above him like smoke from some Great Fire burned out billions of years ago, and our Walloon smiles in amazement at the sky. Who knows what constellation rises there, shaped like a question mark? The Question Mark, perhaps. Coming at the end of an ever-expanding cosmic doubt begun at the first keystroke of Time. If only there were another constellation: The Answer.

Perhaps we do have a provisional answer, for do we not have among us a Mr. Yes?

Less sits up, alert to some flaw in his pleasure. Are the stars perhaps too clear? The horizon too far below? Must he doubt each sweet sensation? But a new sensation comes to him: not that of floating on a starry sea but of floating in midair. He shifts his weight slightly, experimenting, and, alarmingly, the world shifts with him. With a shiver of terror, he peers to his left; there, far below, lies the wolf-painted lavvu where a Minor American Novelist should be sleeping. From the desert, some creature howls to an absent moon, and Less feels like howling too: he has awakened atop the Universe Appreciation Platform.

He interrogates his memory under the bare bulb of panic, but it reveals only flashes of water, a tube that he followed, and more water. Perhaps a valve of some kind, then stars. How did he end up here, so precariously perched below the sky? How did he end up safe? Well, my darling, the world is so constructed that men like you will always end up safe. Almost always.

Arthur Less, naked, wrapped in his cowhide, shakily stands up on the rather splintery Universal Appreciation Platform. Miraculously alive, hardly appreciating the universe, he looks down to the settlement below, where a lake shimmers darkly in the starlight. Less tries, despite poor night vision, to look more closely at the lake. That wasn't there before, was it? A lake? Water is definitely flowing somewhere. He looks far below: a hose, gushing freely down the hillside to Ambrogio. It takes a moment for his frozen mind to understand, to remember a warning, to remember a valve, and then he drops the cowhide and yells, in German:

"Pan flute! Pan flute! Pan flute!"

"I, Council Leader Arathusa, bring this meeting to order. You, Art Yes, have been summoned this morning under accusations of tampering with the water system of Ambrogio, flooding the compound, and entering a restricted platform. German witnesses saw you at midnight at the water valve. The council has voted to expel you permanently from Ambrogio. Do you have anything to say in your defense?"

A pause, and then the voice of our dear protagonist: "Know no *no*?"

Hours later, Rosina trembles her way down the road beneath a gray congealed sky. Roadside stands, all closed at this early hour, mark the miles. In California they would advertise avocados, almonds, and artichokes, but here it is geodes and gems; one in particular shouts FOSSILS! in a font of pure amazement. Who would not visit? But Rosina drives on; in any case, the promise of dinosaurs surely yields to a reality of ammonites. Such are dreams in morning light.

Mandern, somehow showered and groomed, perfumed in sandalwood, and dressed in another corduroy blazer, is quiet behind his sunglasses. At last he takes a deep breath and says: "Well, that was certainly interesting!"

"Let's just get to Santa Fe" is Less's grumbled response.

"I didn't know I was in the hands of a madman."

"I'm fine now."

Mandern laughs. "Pan flute! Pan flute!"

"The Germans misheard me. I said *flood*."

"Well, to be honest, it needed a cleaning." Mandern seems amused and, strangely, impressed by his companion. His companion, however, wants to discuss it no further. He says he hopes Mandern found what he had come for because they have to hightail it to Santa Fe.

"We have about eight hours before the event—"

"We're not going to Santa Fe," says Mandern. "We're leaving the United States."

Panic. "I am *not* driving to Mexico—"

"The Navajo Nation," Mandern replies. "The home of the Spider Grandmother. Follow my directions. Up ahead, we'll—"

"I have to get you to Santa Fe."

Mandern: "Don't you want this profile?"

"A question," Less says.

Mandern clears his throat. "If your father showed up out of nowhere asking for forgiveness, what would you do? Take this next right to Flagstaff."

"You mean would I forgive him?"

"I suppose so."

"I really don't know," Less says. "My turn."

"That wasn't an answer."

Less asks, "What did you do that your daughter has to forgive you for?"

Mandern clears his throat, and Dolly harrumphingly rearranges herself in his lap.

"I thought you knew," the old man says. "I became a writer."

From Flagstaff, two roads head north.

One leads to the Grand Canyon, which Less visited once on a chance southwest trip in his early forties. He arrived before dawn and hiked out onto a promontory—utterly alone—to watch one of the wonders of America. Each level of the canyon began to be slowly colored in, as by a paint-by-numbers virtuoso, and quickly became saturated in sepias, umbers, buffs, fawns, coppers, and bronzes. The whole thing seemed queerly flat. He felt like he was looking at a mural in a high-school gymnasium. But he sipped from his water bottle and began a hike down into the canyon. Birds awakened and twattled, the mists receded in a geological striptease, and still he was alone, enjoying the crisp scent of nature, when, about half an hour into his hike, he came across a ranger standing under a pine tree. "Hey there!" she said, waving to him. "How's it going?" She was young, chipper, wearing a hijab beneath her cap and a uniform as sharply creased and clean as an envelope; she munched on a cereal bar. He said he was fine, thanks. "Got enough water?" she asked, and he held up his bottle, grinning and moving forward. "You know," she said, stepping out of the shadow to block him, "it's a saddle for the next hour, the view's just the same. Might just enjoy it here and head back up!" Her smile was bright and grim. He wondered if her job was to turn back middle-aged gay writers trying to hike the Grand Canyon in designer shoes. He asked her as much. She answered, essentially, yes. He thought he heard a chipmunk gasp from its rock enclosure. Then Less turned around and headed back up to the rim. He swore never to return to the Grand Canyon.

And he will not on this journey. The other road north from Flagstaff leads elsewhere, not to the Grand Canyon at all, and tourists never take it. This is, of course, the route our two novelists choose.

They enter the Navajo Nation and wind along the Grand Canyon's humbler cousin—the Little Colorado River Gorge—whose narrower chasm reveals, at this angle and this hour, only tenebrous hints of wonder, as might the notes of a Minor American Novelist (pay attention, Arthur Less). Out of a mute gray sky comes a confectioners' sugaring of snow, revealing massive Kaibab Plateau outcroppings: frosted towers above some unseeable abyss. The snow, at first just handfuls of flour thrown by playful gods in their divine kitchen, grows in intensity until it becomes a cream-pie food fight: one of those whiteout storms common to high desert plains. The gorge vanishes; the towers vanish; Rosina plunges through a world troubled by this whiteness, this blind danger, and while Less (perhaps still blueberried) is enchanted by what feels like an entrance to some fairy kingdom, Mandern's wizardly advice is to stop.

They sit out the worst of the storm in a roadside gift shop run by an elderly Navajo woman along the Little Colorado River Gorge, which Less watches, during the hour or so of their stay, as its depths fill with indigo and its pinnacles become topped with whipped snow like so many sundaes. How much more magical than its beastly quarterback cousin to the west. When the owner hears Less is from Delaware, she tells him she once visited her sister there. "It was a miracle!" She describes it, spreading her hands wide. "The water was coming out of the rocks!" Less cannot imagine Delaware being a miracle to anyone.

Later, while Mandern is examining a ceramic depiction of housing indigenous to the region, Less turns to him and asks: "What does H.H.H. stand for?"

A harrumph from Mandern. "Don't be so obvious. Look at these wonderful ponchos. I'm going to get you one—"

"I won't put it in the profile," Less says. "I just want to know."

Mandern turns, holding a poncho on its hanger. "Well, Arthur Less, I made it up."

"Really?"

"And I made up Mandern. I wanted something...aggressive. Those were the days of the great manly writers, remember." He smiles as he looks at the woolen poncho. "Who would read something by Parley Cant?"

"Parley Cant?"

"Mormon name," Mandern says, putting the item on the counter. "I left the church and the name. Where does Less come from?"

Our hero relates the story of the great Walloon Prudent Deless.

To Less's surprise, the old man seems intrigued. "Funny, I have a similar story. Not the Walloon part, that's ridiculous. But I was told Alistair Cant got kicked out of New Sweden for being a rascal. In 1654. Isn't that something?"

"It does seem like a funny coincidence."

"Maybe we both got told the same bullshit, Prudent Deless."

"Could be, Parley."

Soon after, a jangling phone is answered in the one corner of the gift shop with cell service:

"Hello-I-have-Peter-Hunt-on-the-line-please-hold..."

Céline Dion, Black Sabbath's "Children of the Grave." Silence. Then a voice: "Arthur, let me get right to it—"

"Peter!"

"How's the profile going?"

Arthur looks around at Mandern examining yet another dream catcher. "Not as expected—"

"Good news! This theater group in the South that's performing your story—"

It seems like something he heard about years before. "'Nutrition Play.' I remember."

"You get to be there."

"What?"

"They're desperate to be in contact," Peter says. "But I know you're hard at work on your profile, so I intervened. Just be in Breaux Bridge, Louisiana, on Tuesday."

"I didn't agree to that!" Less says in a panic. "I have to write this—"

"You said you needed money, Arthur. An

anonymous donor has reached out to the theater group..."

"You should do it, Less," I tell him.

"Freddy, it's a lot of travel."

I laugh. "It's not like there's a home to go back to."

"I could go to Maine," he tells me.

"Are we moving to Maine? Am I going to teach Longfellow and Hawthorne in a log cabin?"

"It does get us over halfway to paying our debt. My debt."

"You're doing what you promised," I say. "You're fixing things. Thank you."

"I miss you."

"I think what you mean by that is you're sorry. I miss you too."

It is only as the blizzard begins to wane and Mandern has bought more than the wise amount of dream catchers and heard the old woman's stories that Less notices her grand-nephew at a sewing machine in the corner. The young man, somewhere near twenty, burly but delicate, his long black hair draped over one shoulder like a satin shawl, works on a red sequined dress. How did Less not notice before? It seems the only light in the room, sparkling on the ceiling. "Who's that for?" Less asks, and the young man looks at him. "I have clients in Flag-staff," he says quietly. A mole on the left side of his lip bounces as he talks. In the pause, the snowdrifts move outside in their white desert. Then the young man smiles, seemingly having decided something. "Drag queens," he says, laughing a little. "They all come to me." Less, astonished, asks for more details. "I do dresses but I specialize in shoes. Beadwork. I learned it from my grandmother. I do all the shoes in Flagstaff. This is for Rachel N. Justice. You can catch her show this Saturday." Less asks if he ever performs himself. The young man glances at his "auntie" at the cash register. "When she lets me," he whispers before returning to his work. The blizzard subsides, and, like the stage lights coming up after an ingenious set change, the sun appears and shines upon this new moonscape. And so our writers move on.

Of many equines, it is said they "have a mind of their own," but the opposite is true of the donkey Less is currently riding; her mind is diligently at-tuned to our hero's, and she moves precisely as Less does not wish her to. And yet he and Dapple (for so is she named) manage to serpentine down the long slope from the canyon rim into the valley, not far behind Mandern (managing an old swaybacked mare; Dolly has been left in the van) and Delbert, their tribal guide, riding his proud, shining steed. The Canyon de Chelly (from Canyon de Tséyi', meaning "behind the rock") is part of the Navajo

Nation and accessible only to residents, who can hire themselves out as guides for such tourists as our distinctly non-Navajo writers. Delbert wears a green camouflage hat and jacket and rectangular wire glasses and makes no direct eye contact with his clients; he looks only at his horse and at the damask-rose canyon walls rising above them. He is hardly a font of information; when Less asks whether the peach crop was good this year, Delbert answers: "No." Questioned about whether the Navajo built the adobe ruins high on the sandstone walls, Delbert answers: "No." The same with the drawings on the smoky walls. He seems to know no *yes*.

The descent from barren snow-swept desert to the valley below would be represented, in the analog cinema beloved by Less, by a shift from black-and-white to color stock or, more synesthetically, from silence to sound: the sensation of going from winter deafness into perception, gradually, of murmuring willows and scraping peach boughs above a flowing river. Dapple chooses the river, of course, against all of Less's desires, and manages to muddy the gray-suited man from the waist down. And then Delbert points to a small trailer alongside a hexagonal stone house. They approach the trailer, the first two horses quietly and Dapple splashing haphazardly along the river, and from the little house a woman emerges. She wears a denim skirt, and her silver hair is braided and coiled on her head. As Mandern dismounts, the woman does not smile.

"Parley Cant."

Mandern grins nervously. "Hello, Lacey. You look beautiful."

"Baloo said you were coming."

The two stand regarding each other for a moment, then Mandern turns to Arthur and says, "Lacey once climbed down twenty stories in a blackout in Havana. Total chaos and darkness. When she got to the bottom, the military were there. And the capitán went up to her and said, 'Señora, you are a hero of the revolution.'"

The woman smiles thoughtfully. "That was Mother."

"You were there too."

"I was five."

Lacey turns to Less at last and looks him up and down. Our hero is covered in mud and looks dipped in chocolate. She moves on to his guide. "Hi, Delbert, you finished your fence?"

"No."

"This is Arthur Less," Mandern tells Lacey, then says to Less, "I need to be alone with my daughter for a little bit. Back in a moment."

"Mr. Mandern, Santa Fe—"

"Delbert will keep you company."

Less says, "Don't leave—"

But father and daughter vanish into the mobile

home; Less and Delbert are left with the stamping horses and the donkey. Snow blows down from the high cliffs, making a whistling sound. The creek clatters along. Somewhere high above, on her slender limestone pillar, the Spider Grandmother must be chuckling.

Less turns to Delbert. "Lacey a relative of yours?"

"No."

What I would give for a portrait of this moment! To frame forever in my mind and bring out for comfort when the old goblins come at night: Arthur Less, like some poor dude fresh off the plane, half in mud and half in Italian gray silk and a wool poncho, sitting astride a donkey while his guide, Delbert, perhaps to dismiss this vision from his retinas, turns to remove his glasses and wipe them with a piece of chamois. A turkey has somehow entered the background, looking like an old woman who has wandered into a bordello. Around them, as indifferent to comedy as they have been to life's abundant tragedy, the canyon walls—which began as sand dunes, were sifted, compressed, and baked over millennia into hard rock, then carved by this river into jagged slices of cake—rise almost infinitely into a blue sky, marked by a buzzard's silhouette and a few small clouds. Snow is drifting down from the cliffs onto the peach trees, miraculously in bud. America looks fine from here.

There is not a sound from the trailer. Arthur Less decides to strike up a conversation: "Delbert. What are those patches on your jacket?"

"Rodeo."

Less asks, "You're with the rodeo?"

This does not come out quite right (he says it the way one might say, "You're with the circus?") and Less is expecting another *No,* but something in the man has shifted; he nods. "The payout is good. I qualified once all the way to Albuquerque. I brought my son."

"You have a son?"

Another nod. A pause. Then Delbert looks Less in the eye. "I have two families. My clan here in the canyon and my rodeo family. They're good people. With them, you always have a place to stay."

"I thought you lived here."

"Sometimes. My auntie had some land she wasn't using; I asked if I could have it. In summer I sleep out under a big elm tree. You heard I haven't finished the fence. Not a lot of free time."

"You must work like this all year."

"Sometimes. Fact is, we do a lot of search and rescue. Folks don't want to hire a guide, or don't want to hire a Navajo, so they park up there on the rim and hike down. Harder than they think. Those are sheer cliffs. We bring them food and water,

blankets, till the Park Service gets them out. Last
year helped out some gay guy trying to hike it in
designer shoes."

Silence follows this disquisition. The only movement is the turkey, seemingly baffled by the yard
(where it has surely spent its life). Then from the
trailer comes the sound of laughter. It is at this
moment that Arthur Less receives a message (impossible in this remote canyon; is Spider Grandmother
a celestial transmitter?), which he assumes is from
the Prize Committee. After all, he has managed to
miss another meeting. But it is not; Less stares at it,
trying to decipher what to any other reader would
be unambiguous.

"What's that?" Delbert asks. Apparently Less's
surprise has been audible.

"Nothing. Just a message."

"Bad news?"

"Well, maybe."

Delbert asks, at last, what must have been on
his mind for some time: "What's Lacey's father
here for?"

Less looks up. The sun is released from behind
a cloud and throws a strip of gold in front of the
turkey, which yelps in panic and retreats behind
the trailer.

"Forgiveness," Less says.

Delbert nods one final time; he knows all about
search and rescue. He looks up to a smoke-blackened

outcropping nearby and, from his pack, pulls out a piece of broken mirror. He holds it to reflect an oblong of sunlight onto the rock, where Less can make out, in the soot, an ancient drawing of men on horseback. Delbert returns the mirror to his pack without explanation. I hope Arthur Less realizes he knows nothing, nothing at all, about the people who once lived here, or those who live here now. He shivers in his poncho. I suppose I do have a portrait after all; I have just made it.

A message on a phone in the Southwest:

> *Archie, I will see you in the South. I am delighted to support your literary efforts at last. Wir sehen uns im Süden.*
>
> *Dad*

A panic. What could this possibly mean? That his father, Lawrence Less, plans to ambush him some-where in the South? And *support your literary efforts*? Another question might also occur to readers: Why this sudden German? We must travel back in time, for it takes us to the root of things. Picture a sanctuary zebra'd by venetian blinds and aglow with a small gosling-necked lamp under which, minutely adjusting a small contraption, is lit a familiar face—

that of his father, Lawrence Less. "What are you boys up to?" he's asking, and little Archie Less stands in the doorway with Jeff Cooper, both around seven years old and in their pajamas, only that is not what his father is saying; he is saying, "Was habt ihr Jungs vor?" "That's German," Less explains to his friend. "It's another language." Jeff Cooper nods, in a trance. Lawrence Less is lit from one side as in a Caravaggio painting, and his wedding ring gleams for a moment and is gone.

In this moment, his father—already magical with his pipe, his contraptions, his promises, his fantasies—takes on a shape-shifting quality. It seems to little Archie that a person could have two selves, could exist equally in two worlds, thus doubling one's existence, and Archie is like that sorcerer's apprentice staring at the pages of the book of magic. Why did his father never tell him it was so simple?

"Gute Nacht, Jungs," his father says and closes the magic door.

Today our Less, standing in the shadow of Spider Grandmother, sees young Archie visiting his local library and taking a set of cassettes up to the stern librarian to check out. He can see them so clearly in their plastic case. The title? *Lessons in Slow German*.

His mind closes its own magic door as Mandern steps out of the house, looking grim, and motions to Delbert to prepare for their departure. The rest is a lesson in slow donkeys.

Despite Less's attempts to pursue his questioning, Mandern remains sunglassed and silent for most of their five-hour race to Santa Fe. Another snowstorm forces them into a diner famous for something called a "pie shake": an elderly woman bakes home-made pies—apple, cherry, peach—and hands them to her husband, who humorlessly destroys them in a blender with ice cream and then sells the concoction to customers. Such is love. When Mandern and Less get on the road again, the sunset turns the falling snow into a lavender mist. Mandern seems to be sleeping behind his sunglasses; Dolly, snoring, certainly is. Their arrival in Santa Fe is slowed only by a traffic-stopping silent march: a procession of women in purple robes heading into the falling darkness. As they are marching away from Less, he does not manage to read the signs they hold aloft or learn what they are marching against or for.

At last, the passenger speaks: "So you're going to see your father in the South?"

Less turns to look at his companion, but with his sunglasses, it is impossible to see how awake he really is. Dream catchers swing from the rearview mirror.

"I think so, yes."

"After all these years," the man says quietly. Less

is unsure of what happened in Canyon de Chelly, whether he and his daughter reconciled; he presumes not.

"We're almost at the venue," Less replies.

"Is it worth it, Arthur?"

"What?"

"Last question. Being a writer. Is it worth it?"

Less is stunned into silence. To him, it's impossible to answer because it is all he knows. It's like asking a dung beetle if it's worth it. Of course there's a better way to be, of course there's an easier life— one could be a leopard or a crocodile! But a dung beetle does do one thing well.

"It is," says Arthur Less.

"Good."

"My turn, Mr. Mandern."

"Of course."

"Is it worth it for you?"

Out of the lavender mist comes a sign: SOON TO BE PORTER'S; the sign and the store beneath it are weather-beaten and long abandoned, like many old ambitions. Mandern, only his hand moving to caress his sleeping pug, pronounces:

"You know, we live in the Age of Iron." Less has no idea what he is talking about, but Mandern goes on: "Hesiod says there are five ages of man. Ovid says only four. So do the Vedic texts. All of them, all of them tell us we're in the lowest age of all."

The darkening landscape passes: cars abandoned

by the side of the road, and sagebrush, and distant lightning.

"An Age of Iron," Mandern says, chuckling, "in which man has forsaken the gods! Only a fraction of the old magic remains, and impostors are everywhere!" The old man looks out at the smears of rain vibrating on the window glass. His smile fades. "But Arthur, there is hope." The great author quietly says: "*We* are that fraction of old magic that remains."

I know this face, as Less himself might have if a flourish of trumpeting eighteen-wheelers did not focus him back on the road. It is the expression of vanity, heartache, and ecstasy; genesis, joy, and destruction. I know it precisely. Talking to people and listening to nothing they utter, noticing just how they touch the small scar on the temple. Hearing only the Michigan accent they're trying to hide. Shaking with sobs in the morning and pouring the wine, with a smile, over dinner. Robbery: friends mined for stories; lovers for sentiment; history for structure; family for secrets; small talk for sorrow; sorrow for comedy; comedy for gold. Then triumph. A satisfied curl of the lip that is not for work done, and well done, but for doing a thing that has never been done.

I know this face, even though no one has ever asked the partner: *Freddy, is it worth it?*

★   ★   ★

The Santa Fe convention center is itself a kind of dream catcher: dreams of the ancient but still-vibrant Taos Pueblo culture, of the deadly regime of colonial Spain, and of the bohemian arts-colony life of O'Keeffe and Stieglitz, all of the architectural features of which (the baked-earth tower, wooden beam, roaring fire, and framed abstraction) have been captured from the past to serve this latest dream—the capitalist corporate gathering. As well as the rare book event, for here is the sign for all to see: TONIGHT! AN EVENING WITH H. H. H. MANDERN. There is no mention of an evening with another author. But our hero walks into the main hall in his mud-spattered poncho and approaches a woman at the front desk.

"Hello, I'm Arthur Less. I'm appearing tonight with Mr. Mandern."

"Who?"

"H. H. H. Mandern, the writer."

She smiles as if he has told a joke. "No, I mean who are *you*?"

He repeats his name and adds, "Do you have someplace I can keep a dog?"

"I decided to go," Less says to me. He is calling from outside the greenroom of the Santa Fe convention center.

"To Maine?"

"No, to the South," he says. "For this theater

thing. We only have three weeks left to pay back the estate, and I'm only halfway there. And I have this crazy idea about my dad—"

"I think you should go too."

"I think the donor money's his. I think he's trying to see me again."

"What makes you say that?"

"A message. He runs an arts foundation. Rebecca says he's ill. I have to go."

"My only worry is Alabama. I heard they kill queers there."

"Freddy. Freddy, I'll be perfectly safe."

"Being white might not be enough."

"Sorry, this connection isn't great. I wish you were here, Freddy. I flooded a commune and slept in a tepee and rode a horse into"—the connection briefly vanishes, then returns—"there is no winter."

"I'm glad you're having an adventure."

"I'm sorry, I have to go, I left Mandern alone in the greenroom—"

"I understand."

"Freddy, are you okay? Do you want me to—"

The connection fails and the call is over.

Let me present some family wisdom. I brought Less to my great aunt and uncle's anniversary in Florida, where, after being pampered and adored and served much grappa, he was taken aside by my elderly great-uncle Enrico. Enrico would later tell me the same thing he told Arthur, which is why I can repeat his advice word for word.

[*The following is translated from the Italian.*]

"I want to talk with you, Arthur. You understand Italian well, yes?"

"Little."

"Good. I want to talk with you about you and Federico. I want to talk about love. I have been with my wife, Federico's great-aunt, for a long time. I want to tell you it isn't something you celebrate every ten years. Or every five years. It's every day. You understand me? I believe in a Supreme Being. I don't know who God is, I don't know anything about God, but I know Maria is here because of God. The problem in the world is that we aren't kind to one another. It's kindness and human spirit that drives us. We have one another. That's all we have. We must celebrate them. Remember that. I don't care who you love, but if you love someone . . . if you love someone, you have to love them every day. You have to choose them every day."

They grasped hands; tears were streaming down my great-uncle's face. Afterward, I found Less standing looking slightly stunned in a hallway.

"What did my uncle say to you?" I asked.

Perhaps still hungover, perhaps in a linguistic daze, he answered in his honest Lessian manner: "Freddy, I have no idea."

So much for advice from our elders.

Here in Santa Fe, Arthur Less sits nodding off in another greenroom beside another fruit plate. In his weariness, Less wonders whether any of the past few days in the desert happened at all or if his adventures have not been the mere dream of a man nodding off in a greenroom. But he is starting to put the profile together in his mind, the act of distilling the toxins of chaos and disorder into the restorative tonic of a funny tale . . .

A low growl from the man beside him. Less asks, "Are you feeling all right, Mr. Mandern?"

The great writer is sitting in a folding chair with Dolly on his lap; his pipe is between his lips and he still wears his sunglasses. He speaks: "How are you heading to the South?"

Less provides his plan to fly to New Orleans.

"Don't give in to the prosaic so soon," says the great author. "Take Rosina. For your further travels. I can't imagine I'll ever need her again. After this, I go home to Palm Springs and finish."

"The book?"

"That too." Mandern looks at him again with those octopus eyes. "In exchange, a favor. Take

Dolly with you. I want her to see a little more than just a dying man."

"Take Dolly? I don't know—"

"She needs adventure."

"Well, you've picked the wrong guy."

"You may not know it, Arthur Less, but you're full of adventure. You're a reckless man."

Who has ever spoken of Arthur Less this way? Who has ever so misunderstood him? Or is it the rest of us who have been wrong, who have ignored all the signs and portents, that this slapstick, ridiculous, zigzagging queer is in fact a reckless man? Capable of anything? For in his way, he *is* reckless, as any cornered animal is reckless, and for Arthur Less, the world is all corners. Like a lavvu.

But I can tell you, he will miss his next Prize meeting. He will be busy writing Mandern's profile outside Muleshoe, Texas. He will edit it while parked in Waxahachie and submit it near Nacogdoches, after which he will call I-Have-Peter-Hunt-on-the-Line-Please-Hold to get his fee. He will be halfway to saving our home.

The title of the piece? "America Looks Fine from Here."

A ghostly whisper beside him:

"Arthur."

H. H. H. Mandern has collapsed in his chair, his mouth hanging open. His hands grip the armrests. Dolly sits asnore in his lap, but his sunglasses and fedora have fallen to the floor, revealing that the great man's hair dye goes only to his hat line; above, it is white as a cloud. Mandern is colored like an Easter egg. Whirling dervish.

Less panics and kneels before him: "Are you all right?"

"Is it over?" the old man whispers, just as he did years ago in New York. The gold has gone from his eyes, perhaps panned out at last. Less thinks of a father with cancer, of a poet drinking from a tainted spring: *Don't leave me just yet.*

"I'll get somebody. Hello!" Less shouts out into the hall, seeking someone with a clipboard. He gets up and goes to the door. "Hello!"

"I can't go on," comes the helpless voice of the writer.

"Hello!" Less shouts, now leaving Mandern alone and running down the hall. "We need a doctor!" He can almost read the headlines now: *America's Dickens Killed by Utterly Unknown Author.* He is determined for this not to be how this chapter ends. *Killer Previously Flooded Southwest Architectural Treasure.* It is moments until showtime, and the hallway seems almost delinquently absent of people with clipboards (though the auditorium is crowded with fans). *Blueberries Found in Killer's Blood.* The backstage is a labyrinth of passageways and storage rooms, but the inhabitants seem to have been taken by some municipal minotaur. *Pug to Take the Stand.*

Less, sweating now, returns to the greenroom. Dolly stares up at him with disdain. Less is panicked by the total absence of famous writers in the room. Has Mandern simply been assimilated into the universe? Has yet another old man abandoned Arthur Less?

Then Less hears an enormous noise, as of a dam bursting—he looks to the stage entrance, and there, standing upright in the spotlight, as if he needed nothing more than the crowd roar to animate him, is the famous writer. Hand raised in greeting and lit blindingly white, H. H. H. Mandern could be a marble statue of himself. What pigeon would dare to roost there? There is no sign that somewhere he is dervishing, that somewhere his daughter will not forgive him, that somewhere his novel is unwritten—no, his will, or perhaps his arrogance alone, supports him. How easily the man is replaced by Robert Brownburn, stepping out to the podium—handsome, middle-aged, famous Robert Brownburn, the man whom Less met at the beach, who invited him here to City Lights, who will live with him for fifteen years—rearranging his papers, as poets do, then looking up at the crowd to speak and the only things in existence are Arthur Less and Robert Brownburn and the poem.

Our hero looks on, stupefied, as Mandern brings the audience to a boil. Perhaps this is what will become of Less. Grown to this age, this stature on a stage, holding an audience rapt with storytelling alone. Able through his talents to swindle love and perhaps even death...

For are we not that fraction of old magic that remains?

SOUTHEAST

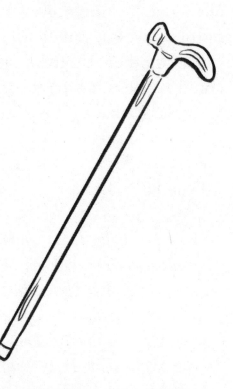

ARTHUR Less is now halfway across America and halfway (he imagines) to fixing all his woes.

Burdened with a pug and a poncho, he trembles his way down from the mountains; he will not see snow again on this journey. And what is it he feels on this leg of the trip with no Freddy to support him, no famous author to direct him? Oddly, he feels free. Alone and free and a fraction of whatever that old man said. No ghost can keep pace with a conversion van on these twisting roads, and no *uncertain* feelings can arise when there are more immediate crises: Arthur Less might perish by coyote, or from thirst, or from exposure to the elements; he might even face the blunt barrel of a pistol and escape with the joy of knowing he has stolen another day from Death and sleep well. You could say he is having the time of his life. You could say, at least, that Less is lost. At last.

Dear Mr. Less,

We are delighted that you will be joining the Last Word Theater Troupe for our little tour of the South! As you are probably aware, we present literary works in their entirety through dialogue, dance, and song (our Marjorie has a famous voice). I am sure you have heard of our six-hour performance of To the Lighthouse *(I myself played the Lighthouse) and our eight-hour performance of* Gravity's Rainbow *(I myself played the Rainbow), which had the unique honor of being shut down by the health department. I hope you will enjoy our presentation of your short story!*

   As you know, we will perform first in Natchez, Mississippi, followed by Muscle Shoals, Alabama, and Augusta and Savannah in Georgia. So looking forward to meeting you tomorrow at Bramblebriar, my family home, outside of Breaux Bridge, Louisiana. Give a call if you have any problems getting here. I myself will play the part of the Southern hostess!

Your devoted reader,
Dorothy Howe-Gorbaty

It's four days' travel from New Mexico to Louisiana, and the only way is through Texas: a long, dry section of America that, for cross-country travelers, is equivalent to the long, dry section on the "Whiteness of the Whale" in *Moby-Dick,* the tedium of which drives most readers to madness. Less and Dolly pass through Amarillo (hello, Reilly O'Shaunessy and your beloved dentist!) and into a land of sagebrush, dead armadillos, more churches than doughnut shops and more doughnut shops than gas stations. The rest is sun and hard earth. I know this because Less called me daily ("Ladder down!"), babbling about RVs.

All sorts of wonderful things lie outside Arthur Less's field of expertise—higher-level physics, disassembly and cleaning of rifle barrels, the clean and pure love of a woman—but over the past few days, he has had to educate himself in a field for which he is woefully unprepared: recreational encampment or, in the vernacular, camping.

The first hurdle is the campsite itself. Having been a mere child in his earliest camping encounters, when his father (public anemone number one) chose a series of Civil War massacre sites as appropriate locations for father-son bonding, Less is unaware of where a middle-aged man with a conversion van and a pug might be accommodated. His first forays are a series of false starts: tent-only state parks, human-only county parks, wino-only city parks—until he discovers he belongs to that rarefied set: RVers. He begins to notice signs (WELCOME, RVERS!) that provide a solution: private parks. And here he enters worlds previously unknown. The first, south of Muleshoe, Texas, proves an excellent education: rows of concrete slabs beside a pond, abandoned except for two elephantine vehicles whose Christmas lights presume a semipermanence, each slab provided with its own concrete wigwam. Too small to sleep in, too enclosed to cook in, the wigwams remain a mystery unsolved. Arthur finds the "host" in one of the Christmas vehicles (a man resembling his uncle Chuck, only wearing a bolo tie), signs some forms, and is given an orange cone. This item is equally inexplicable. He places the cone inside the wigwam and is pleased by life's symmetry. Then he goes through the task of transforming Rosina into a cozy lodge: popping the top, storing the table, unfolding the sofa, making the bed, drawing the curtains, and, in a rather advanced puzzle for this hour, attaching various opaque oblongs to their corresponding windows. Dolly settles in, a crescent on indigo wool. A mesh opening in the fabric above allows a breeze and, in the darkness, an unexpected half-moon of stars. Soon, Less floats upon a river of sleep. The next morning holds its own witty metaphor: the shower that works on purchased tokens, each producing a minute of lively animation, in which one has to perform one's heart's desire before existence ticks away. Death is everywhere.

It goes pretty much like this, with variations: white people, mostly resembling Uncle Chuck, giving him forms, waving to him from RVs (whose makes—Airstream, Southwind, Bounder, Hurricane, Horizon, Phaeton, Zephyr—sound to Less like 1980s rock bands), concrete slabs, barbecue grills as sturdy as oil derricks, token-operated laundries, showers, and so on. People's accents remain unchanged as well, and, more important, Less's goes unchallenged. Until he crosses the border into Louisiana.

"Hello, you got space for my van tonight?"

"We sure do!" says the smiling host. "Now, you're not from around here, are you, honey?"

"Nope. Is this a place that allows dogs?"

"It sure is!" She is an elderly lady with curled silver hair, tinted glasses, and a HOOT 'N' HOLLER T-shirt resembling that worn by his uncle Chuck. "Just watch out for the gators. You from the Netherlands?"

"No. No, I'm from Delaware. Gators?"

"See, I thought from how you sounded, you was from the Netherlands."

He knows what this means. The query takes many forms—"Are you an actor?"; "You remind me of my cousin, do you know him?"; "Anyone ever tell you you look like..."—and he has never known what to say. Because the question she is really asking, without at all knowing she is asking it, without meaning anything in the world except that she detects a linguistic flourish, is *Are you a homosexual?*

He sure is!

Once he parks Rosina on the concrete slab (beside an artificial lake from which the "gators" will presumably emerge) and transforms her into a sleeping coach, he heads immediately to the communal bathroom and looks at the beard he has grown crossing Texas. Who was it who said they killed queers down south? (It was me.) He trims everything but a handlebar mustache. The next day, he stops by an aircraft-hangar-size store and purchases a red bandanna, wraparound sunglasses, a HOOT 'N' HOLLER T-shirt, flip-flops, a baseball cap, a cowboy hat, a bolo tie, and six miniature American flags. Arthur Less changes out of the muddied suit and poncho and puts on some of his new purchases. He disposes of the dream catchers, attaches a flag to each corner of the van, and sticks the other two in the rear window, just to be safe. He waves at the parking-lot attendant on his way out. Arthur Less feels relief rain down inside him as he turns on the wipers to wipe away an accumulation of what the attendant called "lovebugs." He caught the danger just in time; now (he believes) nobody will ever suspect he is Dutch.

And what of Dolly? Less, bereft of Tomboy, has turned to her for solace. He realizes she has been parted from her one true love (like so many of us), and so he makes her comfortable each night in bed, imagining how she must be suffering. But let me tell you something (and don't tell a soul): She is not suffering. Not at all. Her grunts and sighs, her haughty mien, seem unchanged after Mandern's absence. Is she a songbird who sings for any crowd? Is she truly heartless? Or are her passions more like Less's than he imagines?

Each night, when the big-top tent has been lifted, the curtains all drawn, and one sole reading light shines upon the bedclothes, her performance begins. Standing on her little bed, taking the corner of her filthy bath towel, Dolly enacts a danse Apache. One imagines a score by Offenbach as she first coaxes the towel into the figure of her beloved and then tosses it across the stage, only to retrieve and abuse it some more, sometimes lovingly, sometimes viciously, until at last she has created the shape she desires and lies down, satisfied, upon her conquered beau. Less watches this display with interest; he recognizes it. The seemingly pointless struggle with the inanimate, the cries of anger and frustration, the sobs of love, to create something held only in the mind of its creator, who looks upon it with a sigh, delighting in what she has built, and falls asleep in a world where one thing is just as she would make it. Our protagonist looks down on her with envy, this creature so like himself, recognizing in her (though more successful in her chosen field) a fellow artist.

As for his own work, Less has written nothing. It is, he tells himself, the fallow year after finishing a book. A year to read, to choose the winner of a literary Prize. And yet, every evening as Dolly performs her danse Apache before settling in, he has picked up one book after another and failed to vanish into the pages. Grown too old for Neverland, our Peter Pan? Too stout for a rabbit hole? Could be (and what will he tell the Prize Committee?), but I propose the opposite: Less has come alive to his senses, his curiosity, his fears, his memory, and entered that separate realm of being in which the outer world does not vanish, not at all, but pricks with painful detail, the province not of the reader or the critic but of that suffering creature trapped behind the looking glass: the writer.

For now Less is paying attention.

Less arrives at last at Bramblebriar, the "family home" of the Howe-Gorbatys. Parking his conversion van below this brick Palladian manse, he feels less an author than an air-conditioning repairman. A breeze arrives and sets his American flags aflutter.

An elegant woman in a green sweater set walks toward him, hand outstretched, her carefully coiffed hair the exact rosewood shade of his parents' bedroom suite. She is Dorothy Howe-Gorbaty, the leader of the troupe. Her wide exophthalmic eyes (perhaps caused by a childhood condition; we all carry great burdens) give her an incredible range of expression, so one imagines that even when she is cast in nonspeaking parts, her mute reactions can command an audience. It is certainly true outside the theater, such as in her pantomiming approach today, where her frozen gesture and steady gaze call to mind a character about to deliver a vial of poison.

"Arthur! I can't tell you how thrilled we are you could fly in!"

"Well, actually, I drove here."

"You came all the way from California in a van?"

Less has sized Dorothy up as a suborder of Nancy Reagan: white, slim, chic, attractive, with the frantic myomorphic expression of a squirrel in search of a nut. He explains: "No, well...in fact, yes."

"*Through Texas?*" she asks in a low, dramatic register.

"It's a long story."

"Well, bless you, that is going to solve a *big problem* of ours!"

What problem the van might solve is a mystery. Then he thinks. "Oh, the hotel!"

"Actually, I wasn't thinking of the hotel. *You've solved the problem of the set!*"

"The set."

"You're not in the theater, I know, but we made this wonderful set! For your wonderful story! Rocks and trees and so forth. But we just weren't thinking! How were we going to carry it around, in our little cars? But you've got your wonderful van! Aren't I the enfant gâtée?"

"Pardon?"

"This is my husband, Vladimir Gorbaty, but we all call him Vlad."

Vlad seems at first glance to be a typical world-weary Russian businessman with silver hair and irises the sea-ice blue of a polynya. Yet Less can detect, inside this somber shell, a man alert to and amused by his position as foreigner. And (to further matryoshka the poor man) Less vaguely senses yet another man within: the man in love with Dorothy and, through her thoroughly American charms, America itself. Surely deep within this nested set of Vlads, completely concealed, is Vlad himself, carved from a single piece of wood, Vlad the Lad: the nut Dorothy is searching for.

Vlad holds out a bear's paw to shake. "Hello, Mr. Less."

"Hello, Vlad, call me Arthur."

Dorothy laughs. "And now come meet every-body!"

Everybody turns out to be a constellation of six women and one man arranged in the garden like the Pleiades, twinkling in various shades of pastel, and indeed Less approaches as if they were alien visitors from that very star cluster. What is he to make of so many smiles? So many false lashes? So many manicured hands reaching out to take his arm in fellowship? They are not all white—Marjorie, the famous singer, her Ghana braids in a bun, and her brother, a handsome man in glasses named Thomas, are Black—but they are all of a type: Theater People.

Less asks, "You're doing my story 'Nutrition Play,' is that right?"

Dorothy lays a hand on his arm. "I tell you, you were a challenge to find! The foundation just asked us to perform a story by Arthur Less. Did you know there's an Arthur Less in Christian rock? And real estate? There's a million of you out there! But Leila here hunted you down on the computer, and when I saw your photo, I just knew we'd found the right one. So we picked a story from your collection!"

"Thank you." As Less's mother taught him to say.

Thomas approaches with a shy diastematic smile. Shorter than Less in a pastel-blue turtleneck and jeans and the gray suggestion of a beard, Thomas must be somewhere around forty and holds himself like a dancer, shoulders back, chin high. "Hello, sir, I like your van," he says to Arthur Less. Less cannot tell if he is teasing. Thomas lowers his chin and says: "I'm portraying you in the play."

"Oh my gosh!" Less says, mostly in reaction to hearing himself called "sir." "Me? Of course, it's not me. It's a composite. Anything I can help with?"

Thomas adjusts his plum-colored glasses, revealing a freckle beside his nose. "I guess I had a few questions."

"Anything you want," says Less.

Less is expecting him to ask about his youth, his father, his mother, all of it. But instead, Thomas bends his head to his shoulder, looking off into the distance, then says to Less, "I'm working on a backstory and I want to feel what it was like."

"Being gay?"

Thomas smiles. "Being in Delaware."

"Delaware!" Less says, utterly perplexed. He can think of nothing to say about Delaware. It is like trying to describe an airplane meal you had half a century ago.

Thomas nods. "Or being gay in Delaware," he says, quite serious now, moving closer to Less and looking up at him. Chestnut eyes. "I'm just trying to build a story."

"A story?"

Thomas says, "About a boy who does not know if he deserves to be loved."

Less stands there with this man for a moment and simply says nothing. What does one say before beauty? What does one say before truth? Thomas waits patiently.

Our hero takes a deep breath and says, "Well, there was a bar in Dover called SecretS . . ."

The set is not small; it consists of three fiberglass stones, two actual trees mounted in concrete, a set of timbers (presumably meant to be the school?), and a life-size papier-mâché statue of a male saint. All these to delineate the small town of his story, copied from his own small town of Camden, Delaware? Less feels the burden of a creator who has not thought for a moment about the effort necessary to turn his ideas into reality. And the burden is real; he is the one who will have to carry it.

"What do you think, Arthur?" Dorothy asks.

"Very artistic."

"I mean about the van?"

"I'm sure I can fit it in," he says. "I'll have to put them outside at night."

In a deep whisper, Dorothy says: *"They'll make a seductive tableau."*

He asks Thomas to help him with the set ("Two strong men!" Thomas jokes), and they load it into the van despite strenuous objections from little

Dolly, who barks at the statue continuously like those dogs in movies who recognize an impostor.

"We'll see you in Natchez!" Dorothy sings, and the other actors wave along with her. He sees Thomas hold out a falconer's arm for his sister. "For our first performance!"

To be honest, Less is excited to see the performance. He has never seen his work anywhere except on the page. He has never had rights "optioned," as they say in publishing (a kind of polyamory where only the writer must remain exclusive), in the theatrical, cinematic, or televised realms. He has never even been translated into another language, unless you count the British version of *Dark Matter* in which the word *color* was de-*Webster*ized to *colour*. He has never known his words fed into the reel-to-reel projector of another's mind and cast upon the psyche's silver screen, never heard the orchestrations each new spirit writes beneath his simple melodies, never opened a reader's skull and seen the flashing, colored mechanism there. In brief—he's hoping it will be a musical.

I am ashamed to say that Arthur Less is not comfortable with Southern hail-fellow-well-met friendliness. Perhaps because he grew up on the Eastern Seaboard, where affection was kept in the cupboard with the hurricane lamps, or perhaps it was merely because his parents, including a loving mother who, like a famous actor omitting from a script lines she cannot pronounce, simply could not say "I love you." Less used to tease her about this; he knew she loved him, knew this beyond any doubt, but he would end each phone call with "I love you, Mom," which was like trying to get a Buckingham Palace guard to smile because she was temperamentally incapable of answering anything but "Goodbye, son." Perhaps it was homosexual teenage anxiety around friends: *Play it cool, don't let on; above all, don't say you love him!* Perhaps it was his life with the poet Robert Brownburn, fifteen years beside a man whose entire career was based on steering clear of sentiment. It might be nice to be married to Byron or Shelley or Keats, with a love note nailed to a tree now and then, but living with a twentieth-century poet meant making do with "today / my scar / is pinker / than yester-day" (a literal quote from a valentine). Perhaps he was simply born too late for LBJ love-ins, too early for Clintonesque raves. A buttoned-up, goody-goody, suburban gay white boy of the eighties. What plant could flower under the cold sun of Reagan?

"—up the Mississippi into Arkansas and across to Natchez, then to Muscle Shoals, that's Alabama, and onto Georgia—"

I ask, "And your dad's going to be at one of these?"

"More important, we'll be two-thirds repaid. But yeah. That's what he said."

"What does Rebecca say about all this?"

Less sighs. "She says he's dying. But he could be up to his old tricks."

"He's died before?"

"Basically. Tell me about Maine."

"I might leave before the course is over," I say. "There's some writing I want to get done."

"Writing?"

"Just something I'm working on. I found an island. Valonica. The easternmost inhabited island in America."

Less: "You never said you were writing something. You're leaving?"

"Let's say you've inspired me."

"Will you be there when I get to Maine?"

"I will," I tell him. "And if you don't make it, I might take that train back across the country—"

"I'll make it, Freddy! I miss you."

"You know where to find me."

Less takes the scenic route to Natchez, driving past mangrove swamps, alligator farms, and various ship-repair docks that seem always accompanied by gentlemen's clubs, like Confederate troops and their camp followers. Spanish moss festoons the road just like the weathered small-town banners Less passes beneath, advertising events—RICE FESTIVAL!

FROG FESTIVAL! POSSUM FESTIVAL!—many months in the past. Within the van, the set jostles itself noisily until reaching a gentler equilibrium, with only Saint Joseph wobbling to and fro in the rearview mirror.

The troupe is staying with friends of Dorothy Howe-Gorbaty (on air mattresses, like true troupers), but Less has Rosina. He finds a sort of gravel pit across the river from Natchez proper where gargantuan RVs nuzzle beside each other like oxen at a trough and box-turtle tents dot the riverside. "Your first time in the South?" the dried-apple-faced camp host asks, smiling, and adds: "What's your favorite Bible verse?"

He understands, from her welcoming expression, that the question is not a test. For her, it is as bland as a New Yorker asking about his favorite bagel.

"'Arise and shine, for thy light has come,'" Less says without a pause. "Isaiah, sixty, one."

"Now, ain't that sweet?"

"What's yours?"

The woman shows her dentures in a smile. "'As a dog returns to its vomit, so a fool repeats his folly,'" she tells him. "Proverbs, twenty-six, eleven."

The performance is in a former riverboat launch, reached from town via a narrow incline that Less cannot imagine was any less treacherous one hundred years ago when folks were waiting on the

Robert E. Lee, and it feels like a small miracle that Rosina arrives safely. The moment they park, little Dolly begins barking at Saint Joseph all over again and keeps barking while Less unloads him from the van and carries him to the door of the strange little building. I say *strange* because the theater is not in Natchez proper but "under the hill": a townlet set beneath the river bluff whose charming antique buildings belie its past as a refuge for scallywags, rapscallions, whoresons, and knaves. That is to say: The theater district.

Thomas approaches with a wave and together the two strong men begin unloading the rest of the set.

"Arthur, you made it!" says Dorothy when Less and Thomas enter the theater hoisting Saint Joseph between them. They set him down and Thomas wipes sweat from his brow. Dorothy: "We're *so* excited for you to see the performance, and I'm not going to say a *word* because we want it to be a *surprise*! Now, let's get you a drink from the bar! I'm going to spoil you with Southern hospitality!"

"Where's Vlad?"

"Oh, he's at home, but he'll find us in Savannah! Now, get yourself a seat."

"I have to get in costume," Thomas says to Less, departing, and Less wonders what costume could possibly transform Thomas into the cringing boy Less used to be.

Less searches the auditorium carefully for his father's presence. There are five seats marked RE-SERVED in the second row, and, holding his bourbon, Less takes one. The others are never filled. The audience seems to be elderly and perplexed, as if they had expected something different. Perhaps the elderly always wear this expression? It is half full, which is good enough for Less (only now noticing he is in a room of all white people), and as the lights go down, Less nods with recognition that his father will not be here in Natchez. Maybe in Alabama. Less sips his bourbon and takes some pleasure in not knowing what is to come. Music starts, and then singing, and then Less's heart begins to sing as well because at least one person's dream has come true tonight: it is a musical after all.

If only Less had known, he would have invited his sister! Marjorie has transformed herself, with ribboned Afro-puffs and a fuchsia jumpsuit, into the confident and oblivious little Rebecca, readying herself for the school nutrition play in the song "Half a Whole-Wheat Sandwich." And here is little Archie Less—played by Thomas as both contemporary narrator and, donning the ruffled shirt little Less insisted on wearing, the boy still in the thrall of his father's charm. In fact, he has a song entitled "My Father's Charm." Thomas sings it in a low and trembling voice with a blinking awkwardness that is a startling imitation of Less. An actress named Georgia plays his quiet, doting mother. And— surprise, surprise!—Dorothy Howe-Gorbaty herself portrays his father, Lawrence Less, in his entirety. Charismatic, joyous, full of outrageous promises; all of her affectations previously noted have vanished, and here onstage is Lawrence Less! Fringed denim jacket and all! When, at the climax of the piece, the other half of the whole-wheat sandwich fails to appear ("Half a Whole-Wheat Sandwich, Reprise"), when Lawrence Less as well fails to appear and Thomas-Archie realizes his father is gone for good, gasping in understanding, Arthur Less breaks down in racking sobs that are equal parts relived sorrow and musical-theater joy, and show me the homosexual who could sift out which is which.

"That was wonderful!" he tells Thomas when it is all over.

"Really?" The actor is still in makeup and contact lenses that make him blink repeatedly—or is he still imitating Less? "Was it what you imagined?"

"No," Less says, then watches the poor actor's composure drop. "It was better! It was so much better!"

Mrs. Dorothy Howe-Gorbaty, beside them, sighs in delight. "Was it? Oh, good! We were *terrified,* simply *terrified,* you wouldn't like it."

"Arthur, are you crying?" Thomas asks. "What happened?"

"Nothing, nothing. And the talkback was nice," he says, though it was mostly audience questions about what kind of pen he uses (his mother's antique one), whether he writes with whiskey (wine), and why on earth a theater troupe would perform literary works in their entirety (though not in so many words).

She claps her hands. "We're so glad you're here for that! It makes such a difference for *our sponsor.*"

"About your sponsor—"

"Oh, come along with me and have a drink!"

Less turns to Thomas. "You coming?"

Thomas turns away, smiling shyly. "Oh no," he says. "I better rest, you all have fun." He looks up at Less before he walks into the Natchez night. He vanishes behind the van. Less finds himself being led down the road to a wooden building whose front porch is taken up by men in rocking chairs, smoking cigarettes and nursing beers. Motorcycles are parked out front in a kind of dogpile. Across the way is the old steamboat launch—now a mere parking lot—and beyond that, of course, is the Mississippi moving by, as turbid and as quiet as the evening sky above.

"Mrs. Howe-Gorbaty, I wonder if you could tell me something about my benefactor."

She laughs. "Well, isn't that funny? I was gonna ask *you!*"

"You mean you don't know?"

"Not a thing!" Could it be complete coincidence that his father wrote not just *see you in the South* but that he was happy to *support your literary efforts*? And that he runs an arts foundation? But reader, there are no coincidences on this journey; there are only the signs we refuse to recognize...

Miss Dorothy has put her hand on his arm. "By the way, Arthur, down here, everybody calls me Miss Dorothy." Again she uses the deep voice he heard when they met. Less is discovering that, just as early movies had portions tinted blue to imply night, the actress has an artificially altered register. This is her voice for intimacy. "You'll find many married ladies are called that. And you're already so charming, you'll want to know that down here, you'll be hearing 'ma'am' and 'sir' all the time. People will love it if you do that too. You just 'sir' them to death!"

My notes show that Arthur Less—outside of a college registrar's mistake that had him briefly training with the ROTC (he thought it was an improv class)—has never called anyone "sir."

They pass through the saloon doors into a large room whose stamped-tin ceiling is covered in dollar bills (memories of Bombay Beach). Mostly white people are moving tables toward the corners and a band seems to be setting up; the lead singer, though a worn and wiry man, has the long blond hair of a Miss Possum Festival contestant. Less follows Miss Dorothy to a seat at the bar and asks: "Am I Mr. Less?"

"Not to me, Arthur. You're just Arthur. What are you having?"

Now Miss Dorothy does something it has never occurred to Arthur Less to do: After she orders from the cauliflower-eared barman (a whiskey sour for Less, a white wine for herself), she asks to buy a round of beers for the boys in the kitchen. He nods his head and takes her credit card.

"Arthur," she asks above the music, "you said your family was from the South?"

"My mother was from Augusta. My father's family was from Delaware."

"Did you come down much?"

Less lets the cocktail soften inside him. "Christmas, to Georgia. To see my grandparents. My sister and I slept on the sewing-room floor—my grandma was a seamstress. Ladies would come with a page torn out of *Vogue* and she would just make it for them."

"And your grandpa?"

"A butcher," he says. "For Piggly Wiggly."

She bats her heavily mascaraed eyes. "Arthur, I'd never have thought your family was working class. In fact, I reckoned you were foreign. You speak so . . . crisply. Like somebody in a novel."

There is nothing he can say but "Thank you."

A cheer comes from the kitchen and Miss Dorothy

smiles and waves through the little window; the cooks wave back. None of them are white.

"Mine was working class," she is saying. "I know it doesn't seem it, from my house and everything. That's all my husband, and it's false. He bought that house when it was falling down. Don't be fooled by anything 'round here, Arthur. There's a way of seeming that maybe you're not used to. My mother grew up in a shack in the hills. You know, with a rickety front porch and a Chock Full o'Nuts can nailed to the post to spit tobacco into. They used to say about her family"—and Miss Dorothy smiles— "they 'couldn't set a table.' Meaning they had no matching plates or forks or anything. Ain't that funny? To judge people like that."

"You don't sound like you're from the hills."

"You can't hear it. But when I've had a few drinks, like tonight, I'll slip up. Maybe you will too." Less thinks to himself that it's not poverty his voice reveals.

A thought occurs to him. "Miss Dorothy, where are your ancestors from?"

"Lachlan Doyle, came to Charleston in 1717! He was a rascal!" She laughs. "Ó Dubhghaill in Gaelic, meaning 'dark foreigner.' Don't I seem like a dark foreigner to you?"

"Not really."

"Hear tell he was kicked out of Ulster for *too many wives*. And you, Arthur?"

"Well, in 1638 . . ." Less begins, then pauses. How are all these stories the same? Luckily, he has no time to spread more tales of Walloonery.

"Oh, it's the Tams!" Miss Dorothy exclaims; she means the song the band has started. The man with the beautiful hair is plunking at his guitar and nodding as he approaches the microphone. "Shall we dance?"

She hops off her stool and onto the little space left clear for dancing, and other women also sashay from their tables to snap their fingers and sway their hips. A few men join as well, but not many.

The man with the beautiful hair begins to sing:

Don't let love slip away, slip away

Less watches in amazement—not Miss Dorothy or any woman in particular, but collectively, because they all seem to know the same dance style. They are swaying, slightly bent, elbows drawn in close to their ribs as in imitation of shorebirds with their wings half raised; they close their eyes and smile, clapping now and then, rocking not from their hips but from their knees; it is the Carolina shag. What hoodoo is this? Because, to Less's surprise, from the thick Mississippi air, his mother has been summoned. She is dancing in a Delaware kitchen, crab cakes in the pan. She is dancing just like this. He can see her brave smile, her skin soft from Oil of Olay, pale girlish lipstick, and two clip-on amethyst pendant earrings that Less covets dearly. She grew up poorer than he can imagine. She takes his hand, little Archie Less's, and swings him around, then steps away as if tapped by an invisible partner. Bopping and shuffling and smiling some private smile. Then she turns to Less again and grins. She spins him, and spins him, and spins him and they both laugh, though he does not know why. But here: It is the Carolina shag she must have danced as a girl. Shy in her slender frame and flipped brown hair, a green ballerina dress, silver shoes. Waiting for someone to choose her.

So be young, be foolish, but be happy

Miss Dorothy looks at Less, wiping away her tears of laughter. Robert Brownburn comes to him—the tears are black.

"Bee, looks like you've got a new decorator!"

We are in the RV park outside of Natchez, Mississippi, talking to Rebecca. His sister is again on a screen, but this time behind her is a large fishing net and buoy. Less mentions this and she says, "Oh yes. Robinson Crusoe."

"I love his work."

"It's castaway chic. How's the South?"

"Dad hasn't shown up yet," he tells her. "But I'm going through Augusta."

"Oh, Augusta! Christmas!" she says with a smile. "You know, I've inherited something from Grandma. Maybe you inherited it too."

"Her silver?" Less says. Outside the open door of the van, what seem to be a dozen teenagers are attempting to assemble an army tent, that old-fashioned Tinkertoy puzzle, in a cloud of marijuana haze.

"Sort of. Remember how we'd visit her at Christmas and she'd run around the house cleaning and cooking things and then, right after she set everything on the table, she'd begin to sort of... quake? I've inherited that. Her nervous system."

Less pauses a moment and examines her image. She seems calm enough. "So you sort of quake?"

"No, it's even better!" she says, smiling madly as she lifts her hands into his view. "Remember Grandma, she'd kind of, both of her hands would tremble, right? With me, it's just the right hand. I'll see if I can do it for you in a minute. I'm used to suppressing it. But my right hand closes up, like this, and starts to tremble." She takes her left hand out of view, lifts her right hand, presses the fingertips together, and begins to shake it back and forth. "I call it 'Ring for the Maid.'" And, indeed, she looks exactly like an antique matron holding a tiny bell.

"Oh my God, Rebecca."

"Jeanette!" she calls out to an invisible maid as she rings her invisible bell. "Oh, Jeanette!" Then she breaks down in laughter.

"Rebecca! What's causing it?"

"Terror," she says, shrugging. "Some kind of terror—that's not new, is it? But this terror is whenever I've made a mistake. Like forgotten to call someone. Or whenever I even *think* about a mistake I made, long ago. Then all of a sudden, I Ring for the Maid."

He's aghast. His little sister! "Does it hurt?"

She puts her hand down. "No. Sort of. Yes, I guess. It's exhausting. My therapist calls it a tic disorder, which sounds like an infestation, but it means it's *in*voluntary but not *un*voluntary. Meaning I don't start it, but I can stop it."

"When did this start happening?"

"After the divorce. It was the day I left. And I went to a hotel, a really nice hotel in SoHo. I took a long bath and I ordered room service and had a chocolate sundae and lay around in the big bed and watched the worst movies, and it was wonderful! And then, out of nowhere." She rings her invisible bell. "Ring for the Maid. I felt terror. Not like, *Oh, I'm worried about how things will go.* Like ... horror-movie-level terror. Like, tiger-attack level. It went on all night. And it goes on, I don't know, half a dozen times a day. Oh, here it is!" This time, her arm rises by itself and begins to shake violently. "I know. It's dramatic."

"You're going to break that bell."

"Doesn't anything like that happen to you?"

"No, but..." Not this. Not exactly this. Not this absurd religious quavering. But when she said "tiger-attack level," he knew exactly what she meant. Why had they never talked about this before? He thought he was the only one for whom ordering a deli sandwich and wrestling an alligator held equal levels of terror. It is one of the reasons I always think of him as the bravest man I know—for who can guess what feats of valor he has overcome simply to arrive at your door? To get here, for instance, he has lost his first love, caused the early landing of an airplane, flooded an architectural treasure, and crossed the Mississippi with a pug.

Dolly sits at the window, avidly watching a mustard-yellow cat make its way across the gravel saying, *Ciao...ciao...ciao.* Some memory tugs at him.

Rebecca says she has to go. "Say hi to Augusta, Georgia, Archie."

"I will."

"And say hi to Dad for me."

He tells her neither of them should count on Lawrence Less.

Less takes Dolly outside one last time before bed. He can feel the cold, that persistent lover, trying to get at him through his thin suit; he embraces himself against the chill. But here the world is quiet, and dark. A few voices emerge from the other side of the RV park, and Less can now make out a candle guttering in a mason jar and, gathered around a bottle of wine, a group of four or five young people. Shift the scent from marijuana to clove cigarettes, the pattering sound from gravel to eucalyptus pods, and he is on a porch near San Francisco ten years ago talking to a young man in the dark. The same candle in a mason jar casting the same magic-lantern light. Above the rumble of a streetcar, beside a potted lavender, the young man is talking about American literature, and Less turns to see him, and the young man, removing his red glasses to clean them with the hem of his shirt, looks up at Less and stops talking. A night bird says, *Ki-ki-koo!* The young man is me. I take one step closer; Less does not move, and this is when, ten years ago, I kiss him.

For one moment, the past is before him, not memory, but the past...

The young people erupt in laughter. Less lets it fade and be replaced by the gravel, the candle, the South. Too bright, my Walloon? A time-darkened work of art restored to its original hues? Too unfamiliar, those gaudy feelings now?

Less goes back inside Rosina and transforms the

van into its sleeping form, and Dolly curls up beside him.

You would think nothing would be as well oiled as the derricks pumping along the Mississippi River. And yet they squeak all night.

Less, Dolly, and Rosina travel northeast along the Natchez Trace, a long sinuous path from one corner of Mississippi to the other, decorated on either side with green lawns and, beyond them, carefully maintained forests, in imitation, perhaps, of those old wild days when European wagons would roll by carrying flatboats back up to Nashville, or the times when the Creek and Choctaw blazed trails along the ridges, or even long before humankind, when bison broke the first paths in search of salt formations (there are no moose in the South). There is something American, too, about the rolling lawns and peaceful shade. And yet: the unshakable sensation that something awful happened here. Less finds himself looking around in fear; there is nothing to see but green glades. No ghosts are known to walk; a surprise, considering the deadly highwaymen for which this route was once notorious and the Africans forced to walk, shackled together at the wrists and ankles, in coffles the long road down to Natchez. Just this long green road like a river.

No shoulder for stopping in times of trouble—
for what trouble could there be?

Less takes two detours. The first is to Oxford,
where he shyly peeks into the bookstore and com-
mits a writerly crime: he asks for his own book.
The clerk, a young Black woman in an orange
headscarf and matching glasses, her literary glee as
bright as her attire, quickly produces it; it is the
work of the other Arthur Less. "It's a masterpiece,"
the clerk says in awe. "Just a masterpiece!" He buys
it, of course. He places it next to Dolly in the van.
The title? *Sunday.* And he visits Rowan Oak, where
William Faulkner's body lies a-moldering in the
grave, and elderly tourists come to his home and
inquire politely about his furniture but rarely, these
days, about his fiction.

Then he heads to Grinder's Stand. Signs lead him
to a log cabin; a reconstruction, it turns out, but
faithfully made with an enormous chimney just inside the entrance to block the wind. It is the log
cabin where Meriwether Lewis spent his final night.
Standing before the chimney, Less can imagine the
thirty-five-year-old explorer wiping the mud from
his shoes as he is greeted by Mrs. Grinder and
shown to his lodgings. By sunrise he would be dead,
having taken his own life, they say. Clark wrote,
upon hearing of the tragedy: "I fear the weight
of his mind has overcome him." Thomas Jefferson
spoke of Lewis's "sensible depressions of the mind."

Alcoholism, failure, loneliness. And there is also a popular theory that he was gay. Based on nothing more than his failed marriage, his fur stoles, and his complaint of an army coat: "The lace is deficient." He wrote ardently to Clark: "I should be extremely happy in your company." Poor gay Meriwether! Less looks upon the cabin and thinks of lonesome Lewis out here in Tennessee. And lonesome Lewis far away in Texas. And Arthur Less, my Prudent, are you lonesome too?

Less now arrives in Alabama's northwest quadrant, passing abruptly from the green fantasy of the Natchez Trace into the stark reality of back-road wilderness, where tiny towns of weathered wooden shacks alternate with larger ones of black cast-iron arcades. He stops in one of the latter for a cup of coffee and a sandwich for the road, a spacious room decorated with antique signs that must have hung all over town—optician, shoe repair, dressmaker— with a chromed bar set like an island in the middle where two young women tend a hissing espresso machine; the white woman has purple hair and the other has none. No hair, that is; her head is shaved. When Less takes a seat, she immediately serves him coffee and asks where he is from; he politely returns the question, and she says she is from here. "Went to Nashville, but my mama got sick so we came back," she says, placing a sandwich in a panino press and gesturing to her partner. "I had to get out—you know what I mean." And she gives a wink; with a shock, Less understands she has identified him, for she, too, is from the Netherlands. (So they don't kill them here in Alabama?)

On his travels, Less has begun to talk to Dolly—not just the typical "Good girl," "Come here," and "Get away from my gumbo!" but now in more elaborate monologues, rants, and confessions. Dolly listens attentively and without judgment. They have arguments over the use of a particular couch pillow; they make up tenderly. Less begins to revert to some old habits. One morning, for instance, he slams open the little bathroom door and shouts, "Champagne!"

He passes from sugarcane into the land of cotton, on roads where the stuff blows everywhere and sticks to his windshield, past snowscapes as far as the eye can see and behind trucks heavy with their burdens, which he fears will upend upon him at the next pothole. He meets new insects, passing an unhappy hour ridding himself of a stinkbug that has made its home on his steering column and later screaming to find the husk of a cicada attached to his own sleeve. Down a long back road that winds through pine forests smoky from a nearby fire, he finds himself passing a wrought-iron sign for a hound-dog cemetery; there he stops and eats his lunch (a lesbian panino), and he and Dolly read the headstones of perhaps two dozen dogs, some with sculptures of their likenesses baying up a tree, some in shining granite inscribed with their names and prizes, but most of them simple wooden markers carved with love. One in particular stands out, for a hound named Mason Jar who died in 1996:

HE WAS NOT THE BEST
BUT HE WAS THE BEST I EVER HAD

Less stares at this for a long time before getting back on the road.

All the while, the radio plays one song after another full of longing for a lady or a long lost home or a chord outside the obvious four; none are found. And still the phrase keeps haunting him: "I should be extremely happy in your company."

He comes to Muscle Shoals, where the performance is to be held (and where Less trembles at the question: Will his father be here?). The RV park sits on a point between two rivers (presumably so gators can fill their buffet plates from either side) where willows droop like spurned suitors, raccoons act as garbage inspectors, pulling up the past, and Less can make out, in that magical spot where the rivers meet, a tessellated surface not unlike a back-gammon board where the clear and muddy waters coexist but refuse to mix. Such is love. In the spot sits a bench and beside it two enormous ceramic roosters.

Less enters a trailer with a sign reading HOST and is greeted by a mournful basset hound. Less goes for a brief meander with Dolly, then reenters the trailer to find the basset hound has transfigured, as in a folktale, into a heavyset elderly white man with a beard. Less is given a spot beside the roosters, which are especially prized by the host: "My grandma brought them over from France." Less is warned about the gators and handed an orange cone.

"Son, where in Europe are you from?" And so on.

His father is not here. The rest of Muscle Shoals must be at a barbecue; barely half the seats are taken, and no Lawrence Less on any of them. Our hero turns his face to the stage. One strand of tinsel remains from last week's COLLARD FESTIVAL along with the sole banner fragment: LARD. The lights go down. *Archie?* comes a voice in the darkness—oh, must be forty years ago now. *Archie, what are you doing up?* The front door of his mother's house opens to the nighttime streetlamp brilliance of his neighborhood and, silhouetted against it, his father's bulky form. *I just needed a few things, I didn't want to disturb your mother or you kids. How are you doing, son?* The frozen childhood feeling of not knowing what is right anymore. *Archie, warum bist du nicht im Bett?* The music begins and Arthur Less is not in Delaware anymore and not in Alabama either; he has achieved liftoff into the unbothered empyrean of theater.

Does it matter that the tunes are derivative, the music prerecorded? That his story's plot of betrayal during a school play comes across onstage as creaky and suspect? We can say definitively no. The audience, previously all too present with their coughing and whispers and warbling electronics, vanish and all that is left is Arthur Less and the stage. He is transported to his childhood when, taken to a show by a neighbor, he watched in awe and thought (as he thought when he first saw the Rocky Mountains): *Why did no one tell me life could be this?* As if they had been hiding from him that, instead of Puritan hard work and failed get-rich schemes, promises broken and pointless battles waged, life could be sequins and song. He felt he had been lied to from the Pilgrims on down. The secret had been kept from him like a mad aunt locked in the basement, and now a neighbor had innocently set her loose—and she was wonderful! He understood everyone was wrong about life, and if they were wrong about that, then they could be wrong about him. It seemed possible—only for those two hours—that he as well, somewhere inside, could be sequins and song.

"Bravo!" he shouts, standing at the end of the performance as the rest of the audience applauds in befuddlement, and we can forgive his error in gender and countable nouns as we have so often forgiven Arthur Less in these rare, well-earned moments of delight.

"Come along, you'll love it," Thomas says outside the theater. He is trying to persuade Less to come to a party given by a fellow acting troupe. He wears his plum glasses, and his heavy sweater is yellow as the moon. "It's an Alabama troupe that also does works in their entirety. They don't sing, though," Thomas adds with a wink.

"Um," Less says, picking up a prop tree.

"There'll be improv!" Thomas's eyebrows raise with this tempting offer.

"Um," Less says, taking in Thomas's eyebrows, his freckle, the scent of oranges somehow in the air. Less feels terrified of something. "I think I'm gonna pass. Listen, Miss Dorothy said in Georgia I should visit Gillespie?"

"Oh yeah," Thomas says, dropping the load of Saint Joseph into the van. "You could do that. Hey, do you really live in this van?"

"Just on this trip. It's comfortable. You never been in one?"

"Oh," says Thomas. "Not me. I've not seen much besides the theater stage since college. Buses, yes, and hotel rooms, I can draw you a picture of every one. All the same. All across the South now. Grew up in Pickens, South Carolina, and got out of there fast. My teacher said I had something. Went up to New York City—turned out something wasn't enough. So I came back and me and my sister took up with Miss Dorothy. You could say I'm a wanderer, but I've never been in a van like that. Guess you're a wanderer too?"

Less feels without words for once. "It's got a cockloft," he says.

Eyebrows again. "What, now?"

"A...you know, the top pops up," Less says. "More space."

"For what?"

"For...sleeping?"

A laugh. "What's it like to sleep in there?"

"It's peaceful! You should try it sometime," Less says, then frowns. "I mean..."

Thomas looks shyly away, his head bending to his shoulder. "You'll have to give me a tour when it's not filled with our set."

"I'd like that."

Thomas smiles sadly. "So, no theater party?"

"Not tonight, thank you." Less pauses, then asks, "Thomas, why are you wearing a sweater when it's so warm out?"

Thomas shrugs slightly and says, "As my grandma Cookie says, we're all having different experiences."

We certainly are.

Less watches Thomas depart. A loneliness has overtaken him, perhaps from what he has just turned away. He drives until he finds a roadside bar whose backlit sign reads STAGGER LEE, ALL WELCOME. He takes it at its word—as he takes all strangers and lovers and politicians—and walks Dolly through a drizzle to the entrance. It is a low brick building with a flat roof, sitting alone in a desert of gravel; in a previous life, it could easily have been a fried-chicken joint, or a dry cleaner's, or a muffler shop. The windows are all blacked out, and Less is brought back to another bar, also blacked out, that terrified him as a young man: a bar called SecretS. It was in Dover, Delaware (for all I know might still be there), and young Less, only eighteen years old, had circled the block for an hour before gaining the nerve to enter SecretS, in reality, nothing more than a pool table, a jukebox, and a garishly lit bar with a mistrusting and lonely clientele—much like STAGGER LEE.

"What'll you have?" snaps the bartender, a short woman in a yellow lace-up top whose impressive ponytail hangs to her belt. At first glance she is young, with vitality, bold eroticism, and a mien of mischief, but on closer analysis, she is not young at all; in this way, she is like Less. She points her finger at our hero to make one thing clear: "Now, I'm a beertender, not a bartender, but pick your bottle and I'll make sure it's cold."

It is a large black room empty of everything except some tables, chairs, a jukebox, and the J-shaped bar set up in the corner; it is almost uninhabited except for a few elderly men, a blond fellow around Less's age, and a diminutive young woman with bright pink hair and thick glasses. They are all at the bar and they are all white. Less seats himself on a red-vinyl bar stool beside the blond man, who wears a trucker's hat and an unchanging expression. He is smoking with his only hand; the other is missing, along with his arm. And yet the pistol on his hip shows he is fully armed. He does not look at Less. No music plays from the jukebox. It would be pointless to count the tattoos.

"Nice ass, Teresa," says one of the elderly men.

The beertender turns around and shouts: "Nice ass? You must be blind, old man. I ain't got no ass! I got titties."

"Nice ass," he quietly repeats.

She addresses the room: "He ain't seen a real ass in years. What'll you have, good-looking?"

Less surveys his fellow patrons' drinks: Bud Light, Bud Light, Bud Light, Bud Light.

Our Minor American Novelist, oddly, feels safe here. Not in spite of but *because* he is so out of place—as out of place as he felt more than thirty years ago sitting at the bar of SecretS. The same looks of suspicion and appraisal, the same dark room and jukebox, the same limited variety of beers, even a similar blond man in a trucker's cap smoking beside him. "What'll you have, good-looking?"

This is so familiar, so terrifying, and yet not nearly as terrifying as when he'd sat in that gay bar, ordered a beer with someone else's ID (the ID, in fact, of his friend Ben, whom Less considered so much better-looking that he felt he was pulling a double con), and sat there wondering, *Is this where I'm meant to belong?* He does not wonder that here; he does not belong at all, and they know it and have let him know they know. After all his global travels, and his regional ones as well, after years of tae kwon do lessons and debate team and college singing groups and West Fourth Street and Baker Beach and the Russian River and the Shack on the Vulcan Steps with Robert Brownburn and with me, Freddy Pelu, not to mention his old home in Delaware, it feels ordinary to Arthur Less not to belong. What could be more normal than to be out of place everywhere you go? What could be more American?

"Bud Light, please," Less says, then hastily adds, "ma'am."

"You call me T." Less tells her his name and she leans forward against the bar. He smells her floral perfume as she stares him down. "You just get out of jail, Arthur?"

Has the mustache worked at last? "I . . . I'm . . . we're just passing through—"

"She's just joshing you, sir," says a disembodied voice. Less realizes it must have come from the man beside him, but the man is currently drinking his beer (old ventriloquist's trick).

T. chatters on, vanishing into a cooler below the bar so it's just her voice: "We get a lot of boys just out of Lauderdale fixing to get back in trouble. My ex-husband, for one." She reemerges with a Bud Light and opens it for him. "Just the other day a boy came in, a stranger like you, asked first thing, 'Where can I get some pot?' Now, you don't do that! Show up at some strange bar and ask for pot! That'll be two dollars, hon. Lief, you were here, that boy was just—*what is that?*"

Less is frozen. T. stares at him as if he'd tried to pay for his beer with raw uranium.

Now the entire bar is staring.

"Is that the cutest fucking dog in the world?"

Less looks down; Dolly has emerged from her slumber on his lap, lifting her head above the bar with one paw; the pose is that of a celebrity rolling down the window of her limousine, ostensibly to look at the crowds but in actuality to be adored by them.

"What the fuck is your name, baby?"

"This is Dolly."

"Well, hello fucking Dolly!" Less cannot tell if she is referencing the 1964 Jerry Herman musical or the 1969 Gene Kelly film version or simply speaking English.

Dolly is allowed to crawl onto the bar and is groped by an ecstatic T., in all probability neither the first

health-code violation nor the first groping to occur
at STAGGER LEE. Less wears a smile of resignation
until he realizes the room has warmed considerably
toward him, the greatest sign of which is that the one-
armed man beside him meets his eye and speaks:

"That is some crazy-ass dog."

T. hands Less two quarters. "Here, Arthur, go
put something on the jukebox. I warn you, it's all
songs recorded off the radio. Owner's one cheap-ass
bastard. They all start halfway through and have all
the good parts bleeped out."

Arthur Less, whose taste in music does not extend
much past original cast albums, is faced with an
utterly foreign selection of songs and merely picks
at random. It is a song called "Rednecker."

T. bursts into guffaws. "Oh, this song is so ridiculous, have you heard it?" Lief shakes his head no. T.
turns to the others at the bar, and they start laughing as well. "Turn it up!" Has he found a place in
America where people are kidding? Do they laugh
when they pass under the courthouse banner OUR
CITIZENS ARE THE GREATEST PEOPLE IN THE WORLD?

You might think that you're a redneck
But I'm rednecker than you

"Did you go to that funeral today, Slot Machine?"
T. asks. "I call Lief 'Slot Machine.' He's my one-
armed bandit."

Lief shakes his head. "I been to eight funerals this year. I just couldn't go to another. This goddamn town."

T. takes a sip from her own Bud Light. "Lief's been stuck here for years, taking care of his mama. I think maybe she's in her last days, don't you?"

Lief nods solemnly.

"And then what will you do?"

Arthur Less has said this, and T. looks at him with interest.

"I got a van. Like yours. I got it all fixed up with a fridge and heating and a bed and everything. The first minute I can, I'm gonna take it out on the road. I want to see all the places I had to drive by in my truck."

"What's the first place?" Less asks.

T. breaks in, laughing: "Not to Mississippi, I know that! Now, Arthur, you stay out of Mississippi. They're mean and country there. They won't cotton to you like us here."

Perhaps she is trying to save Lief, to change the topic to one well loved around here. But Lief takes a drag of his cigarette.

"I hear there's a spot in Maine that is the first place the sun strikes America. I want to go see that. That's what I want to go see. The first place the sun strikes America."

Less swallows his beer quickly. Here, in this bar in Alabama, Freddy Pelu has appeared. In curly dark

hair and red glasses, but surely not drinking Bud
Light. Less is silent; he knows he cannot say his
lover is in Maine. In any case, Less does not know
where he is. And then Lief taps out his cigarette and
surprises him. "I got a question for you, friend."

"Shoot," says Less, drinking from his Bud Light.

"I never met a gay guy before," he says thoughtfully. "What's it like to be gay?"

Less spit-takes his beer to his left, where it does
no harm. And he gets no chance to answer—a hoot
'n' holler sounds from the entrance. It is another
pink-haired woman apparently named Lil' Bit and
a short man with an eyepatch named Rooster. The
room feels sharper, more threatening, as if some
truce has elapsed, and Rooster starts shouting, "Get
ready!" Lil' Bit has to calm him down. When Less
turns back to Lief, his companion has gotten caught
up in a conversation with a young welder down the
bar, a skinny man with an amateur's mustache (Less
is the professional) who says it's too hot in summer
and too cold in winter. Lief advises him to become
an electrician; you always work indoors. The young
man takes this advice hard, and Lief tells him, "You
got time to change what you want out of life."

Rooster starts shouting again—"Get ready! Get
ready!"—and stands up with something dark and
heavy in his hand. Lil' Bit runs back to stop him,
but it's too late; Rooster raises it to chin level. Less
feels some frozen agent filling his blood; he ducks

down slightly behind Lief. The jukebox music stops; the room freezes like a cold snap. Then he sees: Rooster is holding a microphone. He is about to sing karaoke. The song is cued up: "Hey Jude." Time to go.

To Less's surprise, as he exits, T. runs from behind the bar and gives him a big hug. "Now, you come back if you're headed through here! This bar's for everybody, you hear?" He stares at her and his face is a question mark.

As for what it is like—don't ask a bad gay.

Tonight in Alabama, inside his conversion van, Less manages to attend the next meeting of the Prize Committee. This time, the jury convenes in new chambers. Finley Dwyer has arranged a video meeting in which their faces are displayed in adjoining cells, calling to mind that ninth circle of hell in which Mordred, Cain, and others of the damned are frozen with just their heads above the ice. It is pleasant but curious to see his fellow jurors displayed in this fashion: Freebie with his unexpected Shirley Chisholm head of curls, Vivian looking stern and sharp-chinned, apparently seated in a Gothic manor, and Finley Dwyer with a black velvet beard in a brown velvet suit on a green velvet couch, smoking. He looks like he might purr. Only Edgar's face is missing, replaced by a gray square (for reasons that Less suspects are more obstinate than technical) from which emerge mutterings and the sounds of things crashing. And of course Less can see himself, that mottled, pink-white, rabbity old ghost in the mirror. With a handlebar mustache.

Finley: "Arthur, have you done something with your hair?"

Less realizes he is in his Southern disguise: "No, I've grown a—"

"And we really missed you these past few meetings. Perhaps you're more comfortable as a nominee. Would you like me to remove you from the jury?"

"No, I just—"

"Let's let some others get a word in, Arthur," Finley says. "Edgar?"

From the square comes a coughing fit and then: "I like Overman."

Less sighs a little. Reading an Overman novel is like being put in the care of a neglectful uncle; any character might die, any violent memory might appear, any drug might be shot into any vein. Also: Overman is gay.

"*Overman?*" Finley asks. "Has anyone else gotten to it?"

Less begins: "Not yet, but I—"

"In a minute, Arthur. Freebie?"

Freebie frowns and says, "I don't know if it was the Overman or the Underberg, but I didn't like it."

"Neither did I," says Finley. "Edgar, what did you admire?"

"The language, the experimental structure. The gay love story. I cried at the end."

"I cried too," Vivian says.

Finley waves his hand. "Yes, yes, of course we all cried at the end. Yes, yes, the experimental structure. But I take a strong stand against the gay love story."

Less says, "Really?"

"Arthur, you're quite the chatterbox today. Yes, really. I'm sure you'll agree with me. We both have lived through a time when *no* queer stories were up for prizes like these, when our agents begged us not to write queer stories, not to say we were queer, not to participate in the queer literary world in any way. I know you took that advice. And I am overjoyed to see the world changing. When they asked me to serve as head of this jury, I accepted it swearing I would work to promote queer literature and writing about queers. I have read the Overman novel with an unbiased mind. The question is not whether it is any good. And I am firm in my opinion."

The heads all wait expectantly.

"That's not..." he begins. "How you write..." he says. "About queers."

There is nothing more to say; the jury is silenced by this judgment. The set of little heads nod solemnly. But Arthur Less is visibly squirming within his little square on the screen, like a grammar-school student who knows the answer—knows the answer!—but is not allowed to speak.

"Are you, are you—" Less begins.

"Yes, Arthur?"

"Are you—"

"Yes?"

"Are you saying he's a *bad gay*?" he blurts out when a sort of digital gavel comes down upon the proceedings: a blinking light.

"I'm sorry," Finley says, "but we have to end here. I have a free account and they limit us to forty-five minutes. No more missed meetings, Arthur. Until later!" One by one, the faces vanish from his view, just as Less is revving up speed. Perhaps next time.

The next morning, Less is awakened by a crash outside his window. The camper is completely dark, so Less trips over something (his shoes) before managing to open the door. It is early; a pinkish mist rests on the troubled waters. He sees that one of the roosters has fallen from its plinth and lies in shards upon the ground. Two terrified teenagers holding towels stand beside it; instantly, the bearded old host comes out of his trailer carrying a baseball bat. He strides up to the teenagers, swings the bat—and smashes the other rooster. Disbelief ripples through the air. He walks back to the trailer, then catches sight of Less and stops. "It would have been too sad to see it alone," he says, then he enters his trailer and closes the door.

Less looks back at the two shattered roosters. Dolly wails poignantly for breakfast. His phone begins to ring.

"I-have-Peter-Hunt-on-the-line-please-hold."

Arthur Less sits on Rosina's pullout bed, blinking at the morning sun, while Céline Dion performs the entirety of Metallica's "Enter Sandman," followed by an interlude of silence, followed by the voice of Peter Hunt: "Arthur, let me get right to it—"

"Peter!"

"How's show business?"

"Like no business I—"

"Good news! You've got a lecture tour of the East Coast. Sounds like you've already been in touch with them?"

"No, what? No, I—"

"Balanquin Agency, but let me handle it. You start in Dover, Delaware—"

"I grew up there!"

"Did you? Dover to Baltimore and so on with a total fee of—"

"—enough to cover the whole rent, Freddy! I've almost done it."

"Wait, how long will it be?"

"Another week or so, I have to get the details. Maybe three. But just in time."

"You know, you don't need to do this. You can still come to Maine. I can borrow from Carlos—"

"I'm never borrowing from Carlos! Anyway, I get to see my sister, and maybe it will be kinda fun!"

"Sounds like you've got the theater bug."

"I admit it's nice to be celebrated."

"Less, I went to a party last night."

"Really? That sounds fun."

"I might be out of phone range for a while."

"Because of a party?"

I say, "I found a bed-and-breakfast on the island."

"Island? Party? What's going on?"

"The island I told you about. The easternmost inhabited island in America. I have a new project."

Less asks, "Will I be able to call you?"

"The woman who owns the inn said the only phone that works is her old Bell telephone. She's quite a character. She told me she's the Oldest Living Whaler's Widow, whatever that means."

"When do you leave?"

"Tomorrow," I say. "It's called the Oldest Living Whaler's Widow's Inn. They're so literal up here."

Less: "I'm understanding we won't talk after tomorrow."

"You have your adventure. We'll talk when I'm back from the island. Maybe we can take that train I always wanted to take."

He asks, "Are you leaving me?"

I laugh. "No, Less, of course not."

"Then what is happening?"

"Less," I say, "something needs to change between us."

A pause; his confidence shatters like a ceramic rooster. "Freddy. I'm so sorry I haven't been there for you. I'm sorry. It's been money, and my dad, and—"

"You sound scared."

"I am scared, Freddy! I can't do this alone," he says, then adds: "I can't do this without you. Don't leave me!"

"I love you, Less," I say, and realize it must sound like I love him *less*.

"Don't leave me, Freddy."

The shock of this statement makes me pause.

"What are you talking about?" I say to my lover. "I'm not going to leave you!"

As for distant lovers...well, as a great philosopher once said about a boomerang:

I guess it half works.

Crossing into Georgia reveals more of the same cotton-blown landscape, but all Less can think of is our phone conversation. "I'm just doing what I have to!" he finds himself telling Dolly. "I have to see my father. I have to see my sister. We need the money. I have to say yes!" Dolly cocks her head as if she cannot place his accent. As they approach Atlanta, he begins to come across towns that have more than just fry-up shacks and a dollar store, towns with wine bars and candy shops and those "art galleries" that sell cutouts of ladies' posteriors to plant in your yard. In one exhilarating moment, he drives through a townlet advertising a "Lavender Pride" event, with kissing booths and musical performances and an actual closet door for anyone wanting to "come out." It is sponsored by a local closet-door manufacturer. Alas—it takes place the following weekend. He checks into a state park above an enchanted lake and is just preparing to depart for the theater when—for the first time—he fears for his safety. A man's voice behind him:

"Nice van." Smiling there, a short white man with a white goatee, perhaps six or eight years older than Less (hard to say at these fifty-something altitudes). He wears a floral shirt, suspenders, and the curious redundancy of tinted glasses and a blackjack dealer's green eyeshade. Our hero is forced to explain the workings of his curious vehicle (how its cockloft extends and retracts) and the man nods and replies, "I got a good setup over there. My wife and I got satellite TV, microwave, everything. Come and take a gander." Less crosses a mulchy divide where sits an RV no ophthalmologist has ever owned: dusty, tear-stained headlights, oak-leaf shadows on its awning.

"Come in," the man says. Inside, it's worse: a sepia-tinted sanctum whose couch is a depository of old magazines and whose dinette table is a display for the vast and marvelous variety of hamburger condiments. An open cabinet reveals an impressive DVD collection. Somewhere beyond, in a dusty sunbeam, lies an unmade bed. The small man (his improbable name is Stubbs) gestures to this paradise. Blocking the sunlight slightly, and the exit, Stubbs takes hold of Less's gentle hand. "You know," he says, "my wife ain't back for two or three hours. We could have a good time here, you and me..."

How Less escapes this solecism, we do not know. But we find our hero again in a thoroughly locked Rosina, where Dolly pants a cloud onto a cold window. Safe and sound—from what particular horror, Arthur Less? The explosion of your Walmart incognito? The desperations of middle age? The extinction of the DVD? A poor man looking for something so common, it is scrawled in every rest stop? Or is it a glimpse of life without your Freddy, delivered in the plain brown wrapper of Stubbs?

Less drives to the venue and helps unpack the set. He looks at the audience; no Lawrence Less here either. Our hero begins to understand. As a dog returns to its vomit, so a fool repeats his folly—his father is not coming. He was never coming. It is all the same lie stretching back over fifty years. A vision of Stubbs knocking on his van door. The lights go down in Georgia. And Thomas begins to sing.

Less has somewhere to be tomorrow but, possibly to avoid another Stubbs encounter, he delays his return to the campground by stopping at a bar—GIBSON's in pink neon cursive, his mother's maiden name, he's feeling lucky—the outside very much like STAGGER LEE, the inside as well, except he finds he is the only white person here. Less is quite accustomed to being the only queer person somewhere; it is like being the only person in costume at a party. But look at Arthur Less in a setting whose awkwardness is *not* familiar to him, watch as he struggles his way, tensely smiling, through the jukebox light to find his place at the bar.

The bartender, a petite woman wearing cat ears with the shy, perceptive demeanor of a librarian who knows just the book for you, goes up to Less and says, "Welcome, sir, you want a setup." It is not a question. Less glances at the elderly man in bifocals beside him, who nods. When it comes to drinking, should we know no *no*? Less nods. She tells him, "Jack and Coke." He nods again. When she brings the setup (bottled RC, bottled whiskey, ice in a bowl), she leans forward and says: "Sir, I hope you feel safe here." Less is startled into dropping an ice cube. The man in bifocals nods in agreement and turns away. "Yes, ma'am," Less says.

"Yes, thank you, ma'am." She smiles and adjusts her cat ears. He recalls saying these words himself the times he brought a straight male friend into a gay bar, the same words you say to someone carrying an unconcealed weapon—that you hope they feel safe, because of course they themselves are the danger...

A song comes over the sound system, a blues song in a smoky voice. It takes Less some whiskey to realize it is the man in bifocals singing; his head is bowed over a microphone. Afterward, the microphone is passed to the next one at the bar. When it is Less's turn and he is almost through his setup, dizzily content, the bartender asks him to name his song. "'Anything Goes,'" he says, and without judgment she picks it from a laptop computer, and the bar quietly listens to Arthur Less sing "Anything Goes." *Since the Puritans got a shock,* in his clear and slightly flat tenor, *when they landed on Plymouth Rock*...When he is done and has been politely applauded, the bartender takes the microphone and begins her rendition of "Hey Jude."

In the bathroom of the RV camp, in the steel of the safety mirror bolted above the sink, Less catches sight of a menacing visage and jumps in terror—not Stubbs. It is Arthur Less. On that scratched surface, Less sees only a lean and sunburned country face, a handlebar mustache, his Georgia grandfather's

Adam's apple and receded chin; a "yokel," as his mother scornfully called her relatives. A frightening camouflage, like the moths that avoid predators by imitating their poisonous cousins. "Sir, I hope you feel safe here." Poisonous cousin, indeed.

So Less shaves off the handlebar ends of the mustache, shaves the rest of his face clean. He tosses the T-shirt in the wastebasket along with the baseball cap. From now on, his only clothes are clean white shirts and his gray suit, which he always hangs outside so it will not wrinkle. His disguise has fooled nobody but himself.

So he wears, once again, his unremarkable mustache to the next morning's destination.

"Good morning, I'm Lynn, and welcome to the Gillespie Plantation. Built in 1830 as just a log cabin, by the twenty-first century it has expanded to two thousand acres. The invention of the steam-powered cotton gin in 1879 by Robert Sylvester Munger and his wife, Mary Collett Munger, will be of no interest to you, Arthur Less, nor will the botanical life of the cotton plant as its 'squares' become creamy flowers that brighten to pink before they wither. No, you are looking at me, Lynn, a white woman in her sixties whose mouth is covered in white powder from a doughnut I ate just before this tour and at your fellow visitors today, also covered in whiteness: the French couple in sunglasses and unisex indigo jumpsuits, the three elderly ladies whose sweatshirted breasts are freckled with rhinestones, and the young heterosexual couple in vintage 1950s attire from some vogueish town like Asheville or Nashville. You are judging them all, as you are judging me, a widowed retired high-school teacher from Athens just trying not to vanish soundlessly into this uncaring world. But have you judged Arthur Less? You think you're not part of this, you Californian? You told us you were from Delaware, a slave state even after the end of the Civil War, and I happen to know your people have been there a very long time. Long enough. You are in this, too, my friend. Now come and try the cotton gin, which as you know is short for 'engine,' replacing a gin developed in India around five hundred years after the death of Our Lord Jesus Christ. Have you ever touched a cotton boll? Have you ever touched a rice panicle? A sugarcane stalk? Any of the actual world? Well, come and try, but watch your fingers, Arthur Less. Cotton is sharp."

Arthur Less's daydreaming mind is yanked back to attention by the movement of his group out of the cotton mill and into a dithering Georgia rain. Miss Dorothy had suggested he visit Gillespie Plantation, and Thomas had given his approval, so Less awoke early and searched among the fields until he spotted a sign: GILLESPIE PLANTATION, CONTINUOUS TOURS. Police tape cordoned off the western edge of the property, but Less parked, entered, and found *continuous* meant he was to catch a tour already in progress, as one used to do in movie houses when one could watch proleptic romances in which lovers married before they met.

And now Lynn is leading them across a lawn to a squat log cabin, roofed in birch, inside of which they take their seats. "This is the original log cabin; you're to watch a little film. Afterward, you're going to take a tour of the outbuildings. Bye, now."

The film is written and narrated by one of the new owners ("Hello, I'm Ethel Doss, and welcome to ... Gillespie Plantation"), a beautiful blond white woman in a green satin dress whose fullness suggests supportive petticoats. The quality of the film is lacking, especially the music—"Greensleeves" plays whenever England is mentioned, and for Egypt, the "Hoochie Coochie" song—but despite this incompetence, her history is accurate and unsanitized: "The ban on importation of enslaved people did nothing but heighten brutality on forced-labor plantations such as this one." The film ends, somewhat prematurely, just before the Civil War; Miss Ethel appears again, dressed as Mrs. Claus: "Come back in December for a Christmas at Gillespie!"

They are once more treated to "Greensleeves" before the lights come up.

"How'd you like the film?" comes a voice from the back.

"C'était bizarre," murmurs the Frenchwoman.

One of the elderly ladies turns around and says, "You're not Lynn!"

"No, ma'am. I'm not." Behind the pews now stands an exceptionally tall Black woman with a plain, bare beauty and her hair tied up in a bun. She walks down the center aisle with her head bent sideways to get past the low rafters; she wears a loose indigo dress and silver beads, which she grips in one hand. "I'm Gwen. I grew up in an old sharecropper's cabin at the edge of this property. And I'm going to take you to see where the people used to live."

She opens a side door of the cabin and they walk out again into rain; the grounds have begun to muddy. As they pass around the cabin to an open yard, to their left, police tape cautions them. "What's all this?" Less asks.

"Oh, that's the old house for the planter and his family," Gwen says, smiling. "Burned down last year. Never found out how."

One of the ladies asks, in a panicked voice: "What about a Christmas at Gillespie?"

"Now, this here is the smokehouse," Gwen announces to the group, raising her hands to get attention. Less notices the young 1950s couple have broken away and are headed for the gift shop; perhaps the smokehouse is where they came in. Gwen puts her hands on her hips, pulls herself up to her full height, and addresses the six of them: "You gave us four pounds of pork per week per family, that's what we lived on. You gave us cornmeal and we made hoecakes. We each had a little plot to plant vegetables, and we worked that at night. Because all day long, we worked in your cotton fields."

The only sound is the whispering of the Frenchwoman translating for her husband. Has she translated the shift to the second person? Is her English good enough to notice? Our novelist, of course, has noticed. The light rain has gathered at the tips of his umbrella's spokes in drops that hang there and do not fall. Gwen has no umbrella; her hair is covered by a lace bonnet of raindrops.

One of the rhinestoned ladies asks, "Is a hoecake the same as a johnnycake?"

"It is, ma'am. Some say it was cooked on the blade of a field hoe hot from the fire."

Less asks, "You said you grew up here?"

"Just down the road. Started working after I got my master's in June. History," Gwen says, pulling back her shoulders in pride. And now a memory makes her smile: "You should have heard my sister, she was in a rage of jealousy! Never liked when I did something she couldn't. Same thing at Christmas when my pies are better." She clutches her beads and laughs.

"What kind of pies?" Less asks.

She looks at him; she seems to have caught herself.

"Sweet potato and pecan," she says, releasing the beads. "Now, follow me into this cabin here."

"This cabin here" is a cramped house of age-bleached wood divided into two parts by a fireplace. The supportive timber of the tin roof suggests it must be a modern addition. An iron bedstead, painted white, sits in one corner, strung with ropes to support a mattress. Its plainness speaks in the same monotone as Miss Ethel from the video.

"A bedstead like this would have been rare, but let's say this was a favored family." Gwen touches the iron of the bed. She gazes upon it as if her jealous sister were sleeping there, with all their complex love for each other. The room, for a moment, is silent except for the buzzing of flies. When she speaks again, her voice is quieter, deeper: "Now, I recall this bed was coated in lime— that was to keep away the bugs. And us kids, we slept on straw mats," Gwen says, gesturing to the concrete, now a world away from them. "Here on this floor."

Less notices that the Frenchwoman has stopped translating. The Frenchwoman's husband whispers to her and she shakes her head.

The rhinestoned lady is unperturbed: "Can you tell us about the folks that owned the plantation?"

Gwen exits her reverie and smiles. "Not much to tell; there were only ever five or so. There were two hundred of us. See the newspaper glued to the walls for insulation? That is not period, of course; it's from sharecropper days. We weren't allowed reading material. You'll find useless old Confederate money pasted up there too. And you all probably know about the Underground Railroad." The group nods hastily. "They say us on the plantations would sing at night to warn those making their way to freedom. Harriet Tubman herself said so. If we knew you all were out with hounds on the roads, we'd warn people to get in the creek to drown the scent."

And then, astoundingly, she begins to sing:

Wade in the water
Wade in the water, children

Arthur Less watches himself from above, here in this antique cabin that has survived far longer than thought possible by the ones who built it; he can see his bald spot and his sunburned nose as he listens to the tour guide singing in her slow, powerful voice this slow, powerful song. His hands folded with the umbrella that drips onto the floorboards. His back pressed against the wall. He can see the expression on his face, and what is one to do with pity? Is it all just useless Confederate money?

Wade in the water
God's gonna trouble the water

When Gwen is finished, the only sound is some mechanical device whirring in a far-off field. The French couple look as if they do not want to be here. But who would want to be here?

The rhinestoned lady, perhaps, because she asks a question of Gwen: "How much did a bale of cotton weigh?"

Gwen turns to her; it seems she is twice the height of the old woman. She puts her hand on her chest over the silver beads. "Ma'am, the Lord has so blessed me," she replies, "that I do not know."

A call takes place outside Savannah:

"I'm trying to reach Peter Hunt. This is Arthur Less."

"Please hold."

Céline Dion performs the entirety of Iron Maiden's "Hallowed Be Thy Name." Then Silence. Then a voice:

"I'm sorry, Arthur, Peter's not available, this is his assistant, Laura. Can I help?"

"I want to get hold of the lecture agency," Less tells her. "I'm supposed to start a tour on Sunday and—"

"It's all handled, Arthur. You're in Dover Sunday morning at a church."

"A church?"

"Your contact is Deaconess Perkins," she tells him. "After that, your driver takes you to Baltimore for an event the next evening. We'll send the whole itinerary."

"Okay. Great. I was just worried because I hadn't heard anything—"

"The lecture agency got confused with your name."

He laughs. "Oh, that happens. A lot."

"You're at the State Street Inn in Dover, which looks lovely!"

"That's also why I called," Less says. "You can tell them to cancel the hotel. I'm staying with my sister..."

"Thank you, Savannah, for coming tonight and for staying for our little talkback! I know a lot of you have things to do, so we're so grateful that you're giving us this time. I am Miss Dorothy, and tonight we have the author himself, Mr. Arthur Less, joining us onstage after this, our final performance."

A smattering of applause; Less can see none of the audience with the bright lights on him, none at all, but he bows slightly and takes his seat beside Miss Dorothy. How he will miss these nights, these tributes to his prose! How he will miss the Last Word troupe and Dorothy. And Thomas. Tonight Thomas sang "My Father's Charm" with tears in his eyes. Then directed the last line to Arthur Less.

Dorothy asks for the first question, which is about his writing habits. Less answers automatically that he awakens at six each morning and writes three pages before noon with his mother's antique pen—his usual lie. Then Miss Dorothy asks for another question, and a man's deep voice comes out of the blind spot where the audience must be:

"Mr. Less, what is your philosophy of life?"

Less starts from his chair. Dorothy turns to our onstage author expectantly. Who would not want to hear Mr. Less's philosophy of life? But Mr. Less is not thinking of his philosophy of life, not exactly. He is thinking of another stage, another spotlight. An anemone. A satellite dish.

Dorothy touches his arm gently. "Mr. Less," she says, "the gentleman wants to know your philosophy of life!"

Have his eyes adjusted enough to the stage lights that he is able to make out one particular shape in the crowd? An elderly man in a safari suit, smiling from the third row? Could that shadow be the same one holding a birthday cake, smiling down on his son?

Dorothy: "Your philosophy, Arthur."

He becomes aware, again, of the room, the stage, the hand on his arm. And because it is the last thing he wants to think about, he reaches for the closest philosophy at hand:

"Know no *no*."

My uncle used to carry around, in his wallet, a delicate photograph of his mother at the beach, which on request he would produce and unfold with the minutest care (for it was folded in eighths), spreading it flat on the table, where one could enjoy the image of my grandmother, trapped behind the whitened creases that this folding and unfolding had worn upon her: A cage. I have such an image to place before you now: the last photograph of Arthur Less and his father.

Easter, late 1970s. There is a cherry tree in blossom, and Lawrence Less and his children embrace its glossy, carbuncled trunk as, perhaps, a surrogate for the missing mother (photographer). All are in matching jumpsuits—little Rebecca in pig pink, Archie in cadet blue, and Lawrence in burnt umber—an incomplete set of crayons of varying heights, but Lawrence is, of course, the tallest. His left hand rests on Rebecca's head. The smiles are slightly out of sync, and Lawrence's is caught in decline, as if he doubted the photographer's abilities or had waited too long posed with one arm around the tree or perhaps saw something in the distance either pursuing him or drawing him onward. The long bronze hair, swept across his forehead. The pointed nose and full lower lip, the worry lines around his eyes. Arthur Less has not looked at this photograph in years, but if he had, he would realize that, at fiftyish, he is the spitting image of his father.

"Hi, Dad."

A few pounds heavier, a few shades pinker. White

hair grown slightly wild above the ears, waves foaming on either shore, but otherwise unequivocally
bald. Dressed in a belted safari suit and leaning on
a Lucite cane. His smile might glow in ultraviolet.
Somehow rich? It goes without saying Lawrence
Less is old. Not old in the way Less is growing old,
where you can so easily see his younger self, or as
Mandern has grown old, affecting a hat and sunglasses to resemble his author photo. No, old as in
you'd never guess he'd been young. You wouldn't
recognize him from his youth, as Less does not.
How simple; the man hobbling toward him down
the aisle, leaning simultaneously on his cane and
on a thin blond white woman, is not his father,
Lawrence Less. Rather, he long ago ceased to be.

"Archie!" Lawrence Less says and stumbles forward for a manatee embrace; scent of sandalwood.
Instantly familiar—the pursed smile, the closed eyes
as he shakes his head in disbelief, as he so often did
at Less's baseball games—without a doubt his father,
with waves of pride and disappointment reverber-
ating from the past. He gestures to the woman
beside him, who carries a garment bag. "I want
you to meet Wanda. Wanda Young, but we call her
Wanda Y."

"Wonder why?" Less says gamely.

They all laugh. The woman, turning to him in a
manner not unlike a satellite dish, says, "I've heard
so much about you."

Lawrence Less leans in. "Now, this play of yours. I recognized somebody in that awful father!" Why is his face so pink? Is Less doomed to a flushed old age?

"It's so beautiful," Wanda says, and she is coming into focus now: confectionary hair, plucked and tidied features, like a Renaissance garden, and a confident daffiness. She says, "You're such a talented writer, Archie. Your father is so proud of you."

Less searches inside himself for one last bit of antipathy, one speck in the heart's pantry, but he does not even search very hard. How strange. The moment holds neither disappointment nor delight. Realizing we are no longer in love is not the heartbreaking sensation we imagine when we *are* in love—because it is no sensation at all. It is a realization made by a bystander. And so it is today for Arthur Less, feeling no heartbreak at the sight of his long-lost father.

Less shakes the woman's hand. "Nice to meet you, Wanda."

Lawrence Less touches his son's shoulder. "Hello, son. It's good to see you doing so well."

"So you live here now?"

Lawrence looks proudly at Wanda. "We live on Hilton Head. It's an island just off the coast of Savannah. What a beautiful spot!" He holds out his free hand as a partial frame of an imagined paradise. "Beautiful houses, Spanish moss, harbors and restaurants and shopping! Isn't it, darling?"

Wanda embeds a smile in her face, plumping her cheeks. "Well, I've lived there for thirty years, I can't really say!" She turns the smile to Less, and the smile is sincere. "We're so glad to support you. We brought you something of your father's."

"It was Wanda's idea."

She blinks with pride as she holds out the garment bag for Less. "It's been hanging around forever and your father will never fit in it again!"

Lawrence, in false rage: "Wanda Y.!"

Less takes the bag and she tells him she thinks it will fit perfectly; he's just like his father was at fifty.

Raised eyebrows from Lawrence. "Archie, how long are you in town?"

"I leave tomorrow for a lecture tour," Less says distantly. "Actually, it's for a reading in Dover."

A laugh. "Delaware! I haven't been there in years."

"I haven't been there since Mom died."

The redness of his skin deepens, coarsens. "Of course." *I think he's afraid of you.* Then Lawrence swiftly lifts his hand, as if tossing up a thumbtacked dollar. "Here's an idea! Why don't you stay with us tonight? Have dinner, a drink—what do you say, Wanda?"

"Oh, that's a wonderful idea!" She claps her hands together, and the clap is sincere. "We've got a guest cottage and everything."

Lawrence rests his hand on Less's shoulder. "You could make it a little writer's retreat! Stay for a couple days!"

Less speaks firmly and evenly. "My event in Dover is Sunday morning."

"Stay overnight," Lawrence says.

Wanda is charmed by the idea, charmed by Lawrence, perhaps even charmed by Less. "Do, Archie! I'd love to get to know you."

Less speaks firmly and evenly. "I'll let you know."

"Sag ja, mein Sohn," his father says with a glint in his eye.

[*The following is translated from the German.*]

"Say yes, my son."

"Let you know I will."

"Archie, I'm dying."

"Told me Rebecca did."

"I have stage four prostate cancer." He lifts the cane. "It's gone everywhere. I asked my doctor why they still call it prostate cancer if it's all over the place, and he told me its heritage is the prostate. That's the word he used, *heritage*. Isn't that ridiculous?"

"Ridiculous I do not find, Father."

"I told your sister it should be Walloon cancer. Because that's its actual heritage."

The old man has managed to get a laugh out of his son. "Wallonischer Krebs," that is the phrase his father used. Arthur watches Thomas and Marjorie bringing Saint Joseph out to the parking lot, and

Thomas looks thoughtfully at Less's father and then at Less.

"Stay, Archie. It's taken a lot to get here." He must mean the sponsorship.

"Perhaps."

[*End German translation.*]

Lawrence Less turns to Wanda, grins as wide as a gator as he switches back to English: "He's coming."

Wanda bats at him playfully. "Oh, Larry!"

Less is breathing rapidly, terrified of this old feeling. But he manages his voice. "They're throwing a little party for me at the Chatham Club, so I'll let you know."

"Oh, that's the good one," Lawrence says. "They let in gays and Jews. The other one's for assholes."

"Oh, Larry!" Wanda says in faux shock. "I'll have you know the other one's my father's club!"

"As I said..."

Another playful bat. "Oh, Larry!"

Oh, Larry. Where is the man who stroked little Archie's head one sunburned summer, the man with the thick bronze hair that fell over his left eye, the deep brown beard, the smile, the lines drawn in the golden parchment skin? That man disappeared forever. This man is not him. The man in the safari suit waves farewell as his new wife (wife?) helps him out of the theater. You could almost have it both ways—you could forgive this Larry, struggling with his cane and Wanda and harbors and restaurants and shopping, his cancer and gays and Jews and assholes, forgive him and let him die forgiven. And still never forgive the one who left.

Less arrives at the "wrap party," already well in progress at the Chatham Club, tucked on the top of a hotel, providing a rain-soaked view of the city from its orange-slice windows and furnished with chandeliers, mossy velvet furniture, and a bar. He wears, of course, his gray suit as well as a tie as bright blue as a poison dart frog, a tie kindly offered by the desk clerk; the Chatham Club has a strict dress code. He finds the bar packed (not as entirely white as he'd expected) and the guests warm and welcoming; he is told with a grin, "Oh, this is the club for Jews and gays. The other one's for assholes." Often, a hand is put on his arm to reassure him he's in the right place. They serve Netherlanders here.

"Hello, Arthur Less," comes a voice beside him. It is Vlad, the Gorbaty to Dorothy's Howe, sullenly waiting for a refill of his martini. "I hope performance has been success."

"Thank you for coming. I hope you enjoyed it."

Vlad grunts. "You are married?"

"No," Less says, somewhat taken aback. "No, I'm not married."

"Do you not love her?"

Less is stunned silent by the question, mostly

because Vlad is the first person who cannot hear his "accent."

"Ah, is serious decision. Very serious," Vlad says. "Example: Must attend wife's performances. Must clap-clap-clap. Not to support is crime of love. Punishment death!" He lifts one hand, and the bartender arrives and produces another martini. "But you should be married."

Crime of love. Less touches the left breast of his jacket, as if the phrase were embroidered there in scarlet thread. *Crime of love.* But isn't Freddy on some island off the coast of Maine where his lover cannot reach him? Isn't it Less who kept his word, who is about to fix their problems? In the court of love, who is the criminal?

"Also serious decision," Vlad tells Less, "when to eat olive." He winks; Arthur has already eaten his.

And now the Last Word troupers surround him. Marjorie and the other women seem transformed, as if by this magical rain, from ragged troubadours to sequined selkies, and Thomas, in his green suit, to Poseidon. The gap in his smile has lost none of its charm.

"Thomas!" Less says, taking his hand. "Thank you for impersonating me night after night."

Thomas lowers his eyes. "Oh, Archie is a great character. He's so . . . vulnerable."

A laugh. "Yeah, that's true."

The smile again. "Thank you for your advice in Breaux Bridge. It really helped."

"Oh?"

"Well, Archie is this boy who's always been left," Thomas says, laying it out with his broad hands. "So as a man, he doesn't know any other kind of love. And he has to, sort of, find a new way."

Less is speechless. Once again, he wishes Rebecca could be here to see this.

"After meeting you, I tried to play him like you. You know, a really handsome man who can't see it. I mean," Thomas says, laughing, "not that I'm so handsome!"

"Oh yes, you are!" Less can feel himself blushing.

"And I can tell you now," Thomas says shyly, moving closer and speaking quietly. "I . . . I kind of fell in love with Archie." His eyes meet Less's and hold his gaze.

Less laughs nervously. *AH-ah-ah!*

He feels Thomas take gentle hold of his arm, feels the warmth of his breath as he leans close to his ear and whispers: "You know, you never showed me that van of yours."

Less turns in amazement. "Well—"

"Arthur, look at you!"

Less swivels around; Thomas lets go of his arm. Miss Dorothy is smiling at him, almost in tears. In the looking glass of her eyes, Less sees a young man in a cloud-gray suit stepping into a private club and asking her to dance the Carolina shag. Perhaps she was Dotty then, in a hand-me-down dress, a girl whose recent success in a local production of *Bell, Book and Candle* has given her a giddy feeling of possibility. In her eyes, Less must be Jimmy Stewart.

"Where are you off to next?" she asks.

Marjorie's jewelry winks, and Thomas winks too.

"I'm off tomorrow early!" he says, glancing at Thomas. "I have a lecture tour up north. Dover, Baltimore, Philadelphia, and so on." He adds, "So I can't stay."

"Yes, go north. You know there's a hurricane coming our way. Best to outrun it."

"A hurricane?"

"He's named Herman and they say he's a hellhound. Une vraie crapule. I'm sure it will peter out before Virginia. And thank you for taking the set to the dump outside town! Merci, merci! I have something for you. From your benefactor."

Dorothy hands him a sea-green envelope. The check (his stipend as an artist) is for even more than I-Have-Peter-Hunt-on-the-Line-Please-Hold said. His heart fills with the helium of relief. His relationship is saved. He is saved. He must call Freddy. But how?

Thomas touches his arm again and asks, "Happy, Archie?"

Less turns to him, then to the check, then to Miss Dorothy, who asks, "Would you like to meet them? A few are here at the reception."

"Them?" Less asks.

"People from the foundation, the Gantt Center. They came all the way from Beaufort."

He looks at Thomas. "Happy to," he says. He is confused; if Lawrence Less is his benefactor, then who has he roped in from this foundation? But just as Less glimpses the sequins and bow ties of the foundation members, there is a tap on his shoulder. It is the desk clerk, who whispers an urgent message. Less's eyes, turned to the disco ball on the ceiling and spangled by reflected light, widen in surprise.

He says to Miss Dorothy, "I'm sorry; I have to go immediately, I'll be right back." He turns to Thomas, who adjusts his glasses and seems about to speak. "I'm sorry," Less says. "I'm sorry."

Less dashes out of the bar of the Chatham Club, and the others are left in stunned silence. A moment later, of course, he is back and rapidly returns the tie to the desk clerk. Then our author is off again into the damp Savannah night. Thomas stands there in his suit, blinking, hand still grasping the air where Less's arm used to be.

The representatives from the Gantt Center watch this flurry with looks of concern and bewilderment. One lady, touching her brooch (a diamond boomerang), turns to Miss Dorothy and asks, "You're sure that was the author?"

Waiting for him in the lobby, dressed in a black patent leather coat lined in faux fur, holding a quilted purse

and a gray umbrella, stands a middle-aged woman
with two dramatic gray streaks in her hair. She
has the look of a Spanish condesa examining him
through a lorgnette. "Mr. Less," she says, her smile
as firm as her handshake. "My name is Xiomara. I
have an urgent message from Mr. Mandern." She
opens her purse and produces a picture postcard.

Dearest Prudent,

*Alas, it is time to be reunited with my Dolly. Xiomara
will escort her to Palm Springs, where my daughter
has agreed to visit me. My final adventure? As for
Rosina, let her take you as far as she can. If she dies
and you must abandon her, have no regrets! After all,
we are that fraction of the old magic that remains.*

Best,
Parley

Rosina is parked beside a streetlight with a gas
flame. Less notices the sidewalk is set with oyster
shells. He slides open Rosina's door to reveal—
the second-most-ridiculous creature. Dolly, sleeping, comes to life in parts, as if by ancient magic,
opening her uncomprehending eyes, uncurling her
tail, stretching out a paw, before trembling all over
with joy at Less's return. She cleans Less's face
completely as he lifts her into his arms, but he well

knows her true passions lie elsewhere. He gives her a kiss, and then she is handed to Xiomara, who wraps her in fur lining. With a jolt, and too late, Less realizes Dolly has been his companion across the country, that he has gotten as used to her snore as he has to my own, as used to her nightly danse Apache and absurdities and rituals as he has to my sleeping bonnet, and that they will not, in all likelihood, see each other again. Less reaches out, but Xiomara is already departing, and her umbrella hides any attempt by Dolly to look back. Anyway, dogs never say goodbye.

Less is about to return to the party when a pounding on the roof announces a sudden downpour. He jumps into the driver's seat and slams the door, but it is too late; he is drenched to the bone. Beyond the streaked windshield, a view of Orleans Square, presided over by a parliament of live oaks, bearded in Spanish moss, their long arms frozen in the uncanny gestures of inverted octopuses. In their midst lies a toadlike fountain dedicated to German immigrants. The view is black and slick with rain.

He looks up at the orange-slice windows of the Chatham Club and smiles. Then he puts his key in the ignition and brings Rosina, once again, to life. Maybe dogs know best; no goodbyes. He will write Miss Dorothy a charming letter: *Thank you, ma'am, for the dancing lessons and the bourbon.* He will let Thomas be; surely the footlights have dazzled his heart. Who would fall in love with a middle-aged gay white novelist nobody's ever heard of? Behind him, Saint Joseph goes into his old wobble. Arthur Less is off to see his father. Then to the dump.

There is not much to see from Savannah across to the island at night; unlike the back roads he has been taking, the highway is so featureless that Less imagines he has entered some alien simulation until he feels himself rising over a bridge and sees the signs for Sea Pines. Without realizing, Less has passed from the land of cotton to rice. When the rain stops, he pulls over and changes out of his soaked suit jacket and shirt into the only clothing he can find: his mud-spattered poncho. It will have to do. He takes the exit and approaches an entrance gate guarded, at this hour, by a woman in a white shirt with the nameplate STARLET. With her platinum-blond hair, marcel-waved, and the beauty spot above her left eye, the Black woman indeed looks like a starlet.

"I'm sorry, sir, no RVs or campers allowed on the island."

"What's that?" he asks.

Starlet leans out of her shed. "No RVs or campers allowed."

"But I'm going to see my dad. He lives here. This is just my car."

"I understand, sir, but your vehicle can't go any farther than this gate."

"I can't drive to his house?"

"No, sir."

"Can I park it here and have him drive me to his house?"

"Absolutely not, no, sir."

"Why?"

"That is the island policy."

"But why? Do you live here, ma'am?"

Starlet laughs. "No, sir, I do not."

The moss from the trees shimmers around them like tinsel hanging in an auditorium. He looks up at the guard and asks, "If you were me, ma'am, what would you do?"

The beauty mark above her left eye lifts with her brow. Starlet looks at him intently, then slowly closes her eyes and opens them.

"I'd call my dad," she says quietly.

Less is game. "Okay, let's call him."

She laughs. "I mean *your* dad."

"I know this sounds weird, ma'am, but I don't have his number."

"I'll look it up. You could also call the two RV parks on the island," Starlet adds, gesturing to where he exited the highway. "Maybe they have space? And he could pick you up?"

"Thank you, that's a great idea!"

But at the first park, he is informed that, while

they do indeed have space, they only accept RVs with "black water"—meaning RVs with a toilet. "Why? Don't you have toilets?" Less asks, mystified; it is as if Noah's ark allowed Tyrannosaurs but not chickens. He is told that it is the island policy. The second park, happily, not only has space but accepts chickens. However, it is "age-qualified." Less asks what that means. "Well, sir, are you older than fifty-five?" Less says that he is not. "Oh, I'm sorry, sir, but you'll have to find another place to stay. The resort is only for mature adults." That is also the island policy. In one place, he has the wrong plumbing; in the other, the wrong birthday. He wonders how he got lost in this maze of exclusions and how he might find a secret passage. Then he glimpses himself in the rearview mirror: muddy poncho, neat blond mustache. He catches sight of Starlet behind him. There is no secret passage; he and she are precisely who are meant to be excluded.

"Sir?" Starlet calls to him. "I don't find an owner named Lawrence Less."

"He doesn't live here?"

"Now, could be he's a guest of somebody?"

"Wanda," Less says. "Wanda something."

She laughs again—cool, clear water. "Oh, my friend. Everybody in this damn place is named Wanda!"

He senses some beast waiting for him in the

darkness, some private Herman, its breath already stirring the strands of Spanish moss.

A vision of confectionary hair and he shouts: "Y.! Wanda Y.!"

Within a minute she is telling him his dad is on his way.

From the moss-swaying darkness, headlights of a car approach; Lawrence Less gets out, slowly disengages himself from the vehicle, and cane-walks over to Less. With the headlights, the guardhouse, the palm trees, the safari suit, the cane, it all feels like a spy novel. There should be a briefcase of diamonds, a microchip, a forged masterpiece. Has Mr. Yes become a villain?

His father is lit from all sides; his nose casts three Picasso shadows onto his face. "I'm so sorry, Archie, they're just very particular here."

"Well, I probably don't meet the dress code either."

A smile from the Picasso. "Actually, you don't."

"I'll find a Walmart parking lot somewhere. I better get going, in fact. If you're late, you have to park under the floodlights. Good to see you again, Dad."

Less approaches with his arms out for a final embrace.

His father makes no move from his station in the streetlight. "Old lady here a month ago, a gator came out of the water, went after her Chihuahua.

She went to fight him off, and he took her arm. Terrible tragedy." He shakes his head. "Though the paper did add that her diamond ring was returned to the family." His father looks out into the dark bayou night. "If the cancer gets worse, I might sacrifice myself to the gators."

Less drops his arms; he will not escape this conversation after all. "All the options sound awful."

"I want you to know that I left you and your mother and sister to protect you. It got complex. I went to jail."

"I heard about a satellite dish," Less says.

"Oh, that!" The old smile is back. "Archie, I was working for the government. My point is that I didn't want to leave you. I did it to protect you. You understand?"

Less repeats the phrase he has memorized for just this occasion: "I have understood the words you have said."

Lawrence tilts his face into the light. "Archie, we're not going to see each other again."

Whether it is the cancer or the alligators that will part them, Less does not know, just as he does not know the truth of anything here—the only witness, his mother, is dead, and these are possibly more of the same lies that Less has heard for years. But Arthur Less knows this one statement is true: They will not see each other again.

He says, "Thank you for going to all this trouble."

Lawrence shakes his head. "It's no trouble."

"I mean the tour," Less explains. "The Gantt Center. All of that. It must have been a lot of trouble just to get me here to say goodbye. Thank you."

His eye catches that of Starlet, eavesdropping in the booth. She gives him a quick wink.

But Lawrence cocks his head like Dolly. "Archie, I don't know what you're talking about."

"The performance," Less says. "The Last Word."

"Ah, that!" Wide grin. "You can thank Wanda. It was Wanda who saw the ad in the paper. She searches your name a lot since you got so famous. Seems you've got a doppelgänger! Wanda urged me to come see you. So I did."

Less stands in the wet night, his arms at his sides. Of course Lawrence Less didn't arrange this tour, this play, this stipend. Didn't Less just walk away from the real sponsors at the Chatham Club? Why would Lawrence Less have anything to do with the Gantt Center? Wrong again, Arthur Less.

"I don't understand anything anymore," he says.

Wind arrives, and around them, the Spanish moss swings like chimes. The Picasso (our forged masterpiece) leans forward slightly, and the shadows vanish. He is all in white light now. "About the awful father in your play," says Lawrence Less. "Son, I think it's time for forgiveness, don't you?"

Less sighs; perhaps he hoped it would not come to this. Perhaps he hoped this whole muddle with

the van and the gate would allow him to elude
unnecessary entanglement with the past, as we all
hope that we will be spared the pain and shame and
humiliation we work so hard to avoid. But things
go wrong. And perhaps what stands before him is
a man who can do no harm anymore. A magician
with no more tricks up his sleeve. "Dad, I'm in my
fifties. I've had a whole life without you. I don't
even know why I came here."

"Are you ready for forgiveness?"

"Sure, Dad," Less says in a gesture of submission.
"I'm ready for forgiveness."

"All right, Archie," his father says, embracing his
son with his bulky arms and scent of pipe tobacco
and wood stain. Less cannot stop a tear from
welling in his right eye as he hugs his father. Then
Lawrence Less, leaning heavily on his cane, nods his
head ecclesiastically and says:

[*The following is translated from the German.*]

"I forgive you, son."

[*End German translation.*]

What do we want from the past, anyway? For it to
trifle with us no longer? For it to cease its surprises,
its stirrings, its stings, for it to be fixed forever—
for it to die? But the past is like those jellyfish that,
when harmed, coil into themselves and revert to
immature blobs from which they begin new lives
and become, in simple terms, immortal. What can
we do but look away from such painful miracles?

"Bye, Dad," says Mr. Yes. He helps his father back to his car and embraces him one final time. *You are seeing suffering,* Less tells himself. *You are seeing someone in pain.* Less watches as the headlights disappear into the dark tunnel of trees, then goes to Rosina and brings her back to life. In the rearview mirror, Starlet is staring off at some memory this has awakened in her. May the gators never get her.

As for what Less came all this way to say, there is really no reason to say it out loud.

Wind shakes rain loose from the Spanish moss and it falls on the road like a briefcase of diamonds.

Magically, even at this late hour, Less finds a free spot north of Savannah on Hunting Island and performs what is now a ritual: Removing the set and Saint Joseph and placing this nativity scene beside Rosina (the dump must wait). He hangs his gray suit on the side mirror for the moment. He pops Rosina's top, blacks out her windows with curtains and oblongs, transforms her into a bedroom, and, sitting there, he looks east. What luck! The spot even has an ocean view—black palm trees tossing their shaggy hair before a dimly glowing sky and an even blacker ocean—but, as in a folktale, at midnight the enchantment ends.

A loud knock on the window. A Lessian hand claps back a Lessian scream (silent). He removes the oblong from the glass; nothing but the park manager (a Black version of his uncle Chuck, bearded) warning him: "Hurricane Herman coming, thought you knew, that's why everyone else left. You wanna repark yourself facing southeast. Take the winds head-on that way. Good luck, son." Then the wind starts. First as a wolf whistle, then as a howl; he feels Rosina faltering slightly northwest and realizes he is about to be swept away to some unfriendly Oz. So he does as suggested; he starts her up, looks to which direction the palm trees are moving, aims at the storm, and cowers in his coffin. Less peers out into the darkness but there is almost nothing to see, not even a henhouse floating by, just the dim headlights of the manager's camper weathering the same hurricane. Arthur Less stares out at the nothingness and hears the rain, drumming like a heavy metal band with eternal encores, louder and louder, and realizes that he is not going to die from heartbreak or a bad father or bad reviews, as he has always imagined; not from AIDS or cardiac arrest or cancer or an auto accident (as the actuaries would have it); not from shame or humiliation or arrogance; not from cocaine or meth or mushrooms; not from Twinkies or Spam or cigarettes or any of the hubristic excesses of homosexual American living—he is going to die from this. From Hurricane Herman. As simple as this.

"Freddy?" he calls into his phone, but there is no connection to the outside world. And yet he keeps calling into the void: "Ladder down! Freddy? Freddy?"

Before him, great creamy waves fold in the water, enormous pages of a novel being turned by some bored titanic reader skipping to the end to learn the murderer—but Arthur Less knows all too well who the murderer is: it is Herman. What did Arthur Less do, exactly, to awaken this ancient curse? Laugh at a lover's funeral? Flood a commune? Look upon the home of the Spider Grandmother? Step within a sacred hound-dog cemetery? Leave a dying father to the gators? Or is this the price for taking love for granted? A Shakespearean price indeed. The wind is gusting, beating like a heart all around, and there is little to do but be terrified.

Crime of love. Punishment death!

He looks out the window and realizes what he has forgotten...

First goes his suit, plucked from the side mirror and taken to a heavenly dry cleaner who can remove mud and humiliation.

Next, his childhood. Outside his eastern window, a flash of lightning illuminates the tableau: the set and Saint Joseph. This rude sudden light confers on these mute objects everything the labors of theater have not; namely, the magic light of reality. For it is only in this instant (and not, as he had hoped, during beloved performances) that they come to life— the trees, the shrubs, and the very saint that stood

near his childhood home, Saint Joseph, whom his
neighbors, the Reeds, implanted in their front yard
and decorated with pastel eggs one sunny Easter—
and of course it is only in this moment of rebirth, at
which he gasps, that Less is treated to its twin: destruction. For he is witness as, one by one, Herman
plucks the pieces of his childhood from the earth
and hurls them into his own maw, devouring them,
and Arthur Less is merely a witness as the dogwood
tree decorating his curb is taken skyward, then the
shrubs lining the drive, and then, at last, after a
pause during which Herman considers whether to
have an entrée after all, Saint Joseph swivels sideways
in the mud and, with a final glance at our hero, is
raptured heavenward at last.

The air stills; the eye of the hurricane has arrived,
portending that we are only at intermission and
worse is still to come. In what is perhaps his final
motion on this earth, Less leans forward to peer
through the windshield, and there he sees, within
the eye, as through a porthole, a constellation...

And here, for the moment, we must leave him.

★   ★   ★   ★   ★   ★

★   ★   ★   ★   ★

★   ★   ★   ★   ★   ★

SUNRISE

A dear departed poet once noted that, in book 4 of *The Odyssey,* there appears one of the most restrained cameos in all of literature when "out of her scented room" comes Helen of Troy. There is no description of her, the most beautiful woman in history. Perhaps her beauty is beside the point and always was; we will never know.

But I would never do that to you. Readers, may I present:

Me, Freddy Pelu.

★   ★   ★

Around the time Arthur Less sat in STAGGER LEE being asked what it was like to be gay, I was attending a faculty party at the local Down East college. My host was a giantess of the German department— quite literally a giantess, a white woman towering above the party in coiffed wig and thick glasses. She asked me a question in German when I arrived; Arthur Less came vividly to mind. I was speechless. Disappointed, she indicated the bedroom where I could leave my coat, then drifted off to other guests. I walked into the room, saw two young people kissing, and walked back out. I made my way through the academics looking for wine.

I found it and, glass in hand, stepped out onto a cold porch where graduate students were flirting and drinking around a lantern. They burst into laughter and I warmed myself on that fire; for a moment, a memory of lavender and streetcar sounds intruded, of me rubbing my red glasses on my shirt. *Ki-ki-koo.* As I turned to leave, I saw another fire glowing beside me: a cigarette. Attached to it was a person, a man in a bow tie; his long black hair framed his amusement. Some people have the luck that an awkward feature marks them, like the potter's thumbprint, with a charmed beauty; in this Asian man, it was his ears, which jutted boyishly from his strong face. "Didn't see me here, didja?" the man asked. I recognized, in his hamburger-hamburger speech, a fellow Californian.

"No, no, sorry," I said. "Hello. You're faculty?"

"Sociology. Jason Fidelino." He was my height; I thought he might also be my age.

"High-school English. Freddy Pelu from San Francisco." I put out my hand but the man did not shake it; he shook his own head in the negative.

"Sorry, I can't."

"Oh." I wondered what higher academic etiquette I hadn't learned.

"It's not you," Jason explained, setting down his drink, putting out his cigarette in a little tin box, then placing the box in his blazer pocket. "I'm part of an experiment. It's why I had to come outside. I've had too much to drink and it's risky to be around others."

A relief. "Well, that's the most intriguing thing I've heard all week."

"It's really more of a contest with my grad students." Dr. Jason Fidelino took out another little tin box and offered it to me: mints. I took one, as did the sociologist, who then placed the box in another pocket. I wondered how he avoided mixing up the little tin boxes. "My group has a theory about human contact, physical contact. So to test it, we all agreed we would go without any human touch. No hugs, no kisses, no child on your lap. And no handshakes. I apologize." He gave a formal bow of his head. I again noticed his ears, like the handles of a fine amphora.

"For how long?" My tongue stumbled nervously over the mint.

"As long as possible. Most of them broke down within a week. They're young, after all. You see a few here, drinking and flirting." As if he had pressed a button, all the young students laughed together. Jason went on: "They can't live without touch. So now it's just down to my student Hari and me." He looked at me. "Six months."

"Six months," I repeated as automatically as I had taken the mint. "Oh, you haven't touched another person in six months! What have you learned?"

Jason studied me for a moment with a little grin. "I'll tell you something. Five years ago, I had a heart attack."

"My God!"

"I know. I was only twenty-five." With a shock, I realized he was much younger than I. He went on: "My doctor said my heart couldn't take any strain, so I had to make a choice. I could choose love. Or I could choose cheese."

"That was the choice? Love or cheese?"

"That was the choice. And Freddy," Jason said, smiling ruefully, "I chose cheese." There was the sound of horse chestnuts falling on the roof. "I think I'm one of those people who can live without. Maybe Hari is as well."

I said, "There must be all kinds of temptations."

"I'm a cold-water swimmer," Jason said. "That

helps with temptation. And being Asian and gay in New England—well, it keeps you single."

"And Hari?"

"Deaf and Bengali. We're untouchables." He stroked his long hair and looked out at the students.

But I found myself, like some armchair detective, going back over an earlier scene and spotting a vital clue I'd failed to notice before. "Is Hari here at the party?"

"Somewhere, if he hasn't left. As I said, it's a risky room. And the drinks!" He picked up his drink, pulled out the olive, and popped it in his mouth.

"I think I saw him kiss a girl."

"Hari?" Jason said, shocked.

"Tall, curly hair, clear-framed glasses? He was kissing a young woman in the coatroom. I didn't think anything of it."

"That's him!" Jason said, then stared at the floor. "Oh God."

"What's wrong?" I asked. "You've won."

He looked back out at the students. The lantern cast light on every movement of his sharp features: the curve of his cheek, the hollow beneath his lip. There seemed to be any number of handsome young men standing beside me. I thought of how long it had been since I was touched.

"To be honest, it's a little confusing," he said. "I've gained a certain . . . resolve. Cold-water swimming."

I asked him what the prize was.

"A wheel of cheese." Jason smiled a little. The students laughed again and I took a sip of wine. Jason seemed to glow with private thoughts and pleasures, perhaps considering his trophy.

I asked, "Would you like to try it?"

"Try what?"

I merely smiled and put out my hand. Jason examined it carefully, as if it were a great sum of money, but did not take it. Instead, he reached out his palm and placed it on my chest, just inside my jacket. The man looked only at his hand and seemed to be taking a deep breath. We heard the chattering of the students and the sound of glassware clinking. Then I reached up and undid the first few buttons of my shirt, and Jason, still gazing only at his own hand, pulled the fabric aside and rested his palm on my naked skin. I felt his cold fingers growing warmer from my body, saw his expression of shy amazement, sensed my own heartbeat moving into the other man. Perhaps it was the wind blowing the horse chestnuts, rattling like the passing of a tinker's cart, that tipped the moment over and made your narrator burst into inexplicable tears.

Jason removed his hand and at last looked up. His eyes were also wet. I buttoned my shirt with embarrassment and tried to subtly wipe my eyes. Jason gazed out at the darkness and took a deep breath.

"Thank you, Freddy," he said in his quiet, formal voice. "I can go back to the party now."

"And collect your cheese."

"And collect my cheese," he said. Jason's face was all shadows and lantern light as he stood there, not moving. Then my name came from his lips: "Freddy!" The expression on his face was one of panic. Slowly, he stepped toward me and opened his mouth as if about to speak. He closed it and swallowed. I asked what it was, but he shook his head and said, "Nothing."

I believe he almost said something else. But after those words, he vanished into the giantess's house and I stood there feeling an untried terror. What had he meant to say? And if he had said it, what would I have done? What to call how I felt?

Uncertain.

The next morning, as Arthur Less was listening to Gwen at the Gillespie Plantation, I was no longer at the American Teachers' Colloquium and Conference for a breakout session on narrative structure; instead, I broke out of my own narrative structure. I left the story entirely. I found myself on a bus bound Down East (as they say in the Pine Tree State). I had spent almost a month in the conference center and never saw more than a beauty-marked seagull headed to an unseen harbor, but as the bus took off, I began to see my northeastern surroundings at last: The cannonball pyramids like sweets in a candy shop, the Greek-temple mansions that alternated with burned-out abandoned factories, the faux lighthouses (landlocked) selling art made from sand dollars and starfish, and the yard sales by the thousands presenting wares that weather would ruin—pianos, settees, cast-iron pans, paintings, posters, stuffed animals—as if they were not items for sale at all but offerings to the gods. Then the bus turned windward and I managed to glimpse— the Atlantic Ocean! At last. Was I mistaken, or was that the naked torso of a man in the chill waters of the bay? Cold-water swimmer or some mythical monster, an ichthyocentaur half hidden by the tide? But the bus moved on and he was gone, replaced by a wishing well. And then a cemetery. And then a fish market with the sun on it all in sequins, bringing to mind a boy in Arizona Less had told me about.

Leaving my conference, I felt perhaps the same wildness that Less felt driving out into the Mojave Desert with an old man and a pug, a quixotism, jousting with wind farms and donning a trash-bin helmet. I was led from my bus to yet another bus—like a hostage being purposely confounded as to his whereabouts—and, finally, I stepped out at my waterfront destination: the Rockland Ferry Terminal. The nation is so wondrous and varied that the idea that there might not be ferry service in late autumn would never occur to a Californian like myself. I smiled at the sign on the nearby lobster shack (boarded up), amused by words I almost willfully refused to connect to my own fate:

CLOSED FOR THE SEASON

REASON?

FREEZIN'!

"No fairies today."

The voice came from behind me.

I said, "What's that?"

A middle-aged woman in bright yellow foul-weather gear glared at me from the end of the dock. Reading glasses nested in her dandelion-white hair. She acted as if she had been expecting me for days. "No fairies today," she said. "But I'll take ya." She wore a beaded necklace from which depended a carved blue whale.

"No *ferries*," I repeated as my mind corrected the first sentence and then I responded to the second: "But you don't even know where I'm going."

The woman looked me up and down. "You're going to Valonica, yeah?"

"Yeah."

"I'll take ya." Asked the cost, the woman mentioned a sum most high-school teachers are not accustomed to. She said her name was Captain Eliot Morison from Gay Head (Wampanoag tribe). Not, she pointed out, Elliott Morrison or Elliot

Morisson or any other variation: "One *l*, one *t*, one *r*, one *s*. I do take cash or check."

"Oh."

The sea and sky were deepest gray. The wind tugged at the flags atop the shed before me: The Maine state flag argent, charged with a pine tree and a moose couchant, supported by two homosexuals flirtant. Above it, the American flag seemed far less fanciful: four dozen eggs and bacon. I turned back to the woman in overalls.

"Cash or check," she said. "One *l*, one *t*, one *r*, one *s*."

After I paid her, Captain Morison smiled for the last time that day, and we blindly plunged like fate into the lone Penobscot, heading toward Valonica Island, where (according to the ferryboat pamphlet) "the sun first strikes America."

On tiny Valonica, I found my way to a saltbox house labeled OLDEST LIVING WHALER'S WIDOW'S INN and knocked on the door. It opened upon an elderly white woman with eyes deeply encamped in the pink forbidding canyon of her visage.

"Mrs. Nicholson?" I asked.

"Lad, you are speaking to the Oldest Living Whaler's Widow!" she shouted, shaking with indignity as one hand held a plaid shawl around her shoulders.

"I beg your pardon," I said with a little bow.

Of course I had no idea what this meant except that I might have to change my sleeping quarters. Unfortunately, there was not much to the island except a floating lobster pound, some rocky beaches guarded by Chaplinesque puffins, and the OLDEST LIVING WHALER'S WIDOW'S INN. It seemed the choice was puffins or widows. What was a Pelu to do?

"My late husband, Captain Nicholson," she informed me with her severe expression, her eyes the gray of pewter tankards melted down for bullets, "was on the crew of the *John R. Manta*. Sailed into New Bedford in 1927, the last of the old New England whaling ships." She shook her head, silver hair neatly parted and combed back to a bun. "The last! There were no more."

Seagulls sat on the roof, listening to her tale. Off somewhere, the harbor bell was ringing. I smiled, set down my bag, and gently pursued a line of questioning: "I called about a room—"

"Don't tell me about the *Wanderer!*" Mrs. Nicholson broke in, one finger emerging from her shawl to point heavenward. "The *Wanderer* never returned! We did." The finger dropped. "I was with her."

The seagulls and I were lost in gender. "With whom?"

"The *John R. Manta*," she said with a nod. "They retrieved me in the Azores, and years later, we married." Mrs. Nicholson smiled bashfully. "I was a bride of tender age."

What was it like for whalers' wives and widows? Years away at sea, husbands coming back—if they came back—having seen things you cannot imagine, having wrestled with the unknown and, somehow, won? All this with barely enough money made to cover the debt accrued? I imagine it was like being married to a novelist. I liked her immediately.

She smiled. "You know, young man, you remind me of my great love."

"Captain Nicholson?"

She did not seem to hear me at first, staring out at the gaudiness of autumn leaves (how the Puritans must have blushed at nature!). Then she turned to me. "No, oh no," she said hastily. "Come on in, come on in, you're letting in the cold..."

Every morning, I awakened with the dawn and the harbor bells. When was the morning ever my friend? In my youth, it used to be so hard to take— the unmade bed, the unmade day—but here on Valonica, it felt like something had been repaired at night, as if by elves. Something was changing— I was changing. It had happened before, when I awakened one morning to a sky all Lessian blue, when I flew across the world so every day would be that blue, when I waited on the steps for Arthur Less, having cast off the world's plans for me. And that next morning: Sunlight filtering through the trumpet vine onto the white bed and the body sleeping in it. A tangle of thin blond hair, his cheeks in high color. And me, looking at Less's sleeping form. Filled with the freshness of love. Where had that gone? Where was the beautiful middle time together, the time he and Robert had shared? Had I missed it? Or was it still to come?

On Valonica, there was no blue. The landscape was reversed; the ocean was now in the sky, in ripples and foaming waves, and the surface below seemed merely to reflect the turbulent thoughts of the weather. How long had this been going on? For all time? Was everything changing along with me?

During my stay with Mrs. Nicholson, I found myself taking walks around the tiny island; it could be done in forty minutes. And my favorite spot was a small marker set into the stone giving the name of the deceased lobsterman, his buoy number, the longitude and latitude of his death at sea, and BROTHER, SAILOR, HUSBAND, FRIEND. It was that of Captain Nicholson. I reported this to his widow, who harrumphed, as she also harrumphed at my desire to learn her first name and at my desire to see a whale. "Not 'round here this time of year," she informed me as she stirred her cod soup and the fire ticked like a clock. Even less likely: a moose. But I went back time and again to her husband's marker, looking out at the variations in the water that to me seemed like rivers and ponds in a gray land-scape below scudding gray clouds. An anecdote: My favorite movie as a child was *The Wizard of Oz,* and I knew that it began with gray clouds just like these. Every time any black-and-white scene with gray clouds appeared on television, I would clap my hands with glee. No number of disappointments could dissuade me; I always thought it was *The Wizard of Oz*. And life is actually so threaded with hidden enchantment that, one time, it was.

Similarly: One Valonican afternoon as I stood beside his marker, a grayness different from the water rose in a creamy froth, churning its wrinkled skin until it blew, like a fountain, into the air.

"Thar she blows!" I shouted to nobody at all. "Thar she blows!" And then the whale sounded, heading back into the deep.

Don't tell me about folktales. Don't tell me about hope.

So there I stayed, with Mrs. Nicholson and her stories and porridge and lobster stew, learning at last that her first name was Adele. One night on Valonica, wandering the island, taken by the spirit of freedom (and perhaps by the spirits in Adele's larder), I threw my phone far out to sea to join Adele's husband in his grave. It made not a sound in the surf. Now I was lost. There I stayed, communing with the puffins, working on a book I had been thinking about a long time but never found the confidence to write, a book about a trip around the world made from his tales and my imagination: a love story.

★ ★ ★

Let us return to Arthur Less.

We have now reached the part of his story that might be called "Dolly Disparue." Having survived a hurricane, Rosina, empty now of all cargo except Less and his meager belongings (including the T-shirt and shorts he is wearing), makes her way northward from Savannah, and a languid sadness overtakes the journey. The miles go by, as does a relay race of local radio stations. Without Dolly, there is an emptiness. Less fills it with food—from the bar of the crystal-chandeliered Childress House, where a white male bartender with plucked eyebrows eyes Less meaningfully as he serves the tarted-up shrimp and grits, to the run-down Rhoda's Famous, a house built on a shack, where Less sits with the elderly Rhoda (black turban and beads) as the Black woman fills sweet potato pies and tells him of when this used to be a juke joint while her granddaughter (red braids, two gold teeth) wearily prepares Low Country boil and warns, "Now, Mama!" when Rhoda tries to get her attention with a flyswatter. "Now, Mama!" There is no wriggling dog to greet Arthur Less when he returns to the van or bark ceaselessly at the RV parks, which are no longer manned by hosts with traffic cones but by efficient office workers behind Plexiglas screens. These workers hazard no guesses as to where Less might be from. No wild fool cuddles him to sleep each evening. Nobody steps on his face to wake him. For now, Arthur Less is truly alone.

Tonight is the Super Beaver Moon. That is what the radio states, loudly, in the bookstore/doughnut shop in Rocky Mount, North Carolina, where Arthur Less sits at a table decorated with H. H. H. Mandern's face. Is he already reunited with his Dolly and his daughter? Less has four doughnuts before him: bacon, bacon, bacon, and candy corn; he is considering these limited options when he hears the words *Super Beaver Moon* announced, loudly, into the room. He turns to the doughnut clerk behind the counter. "Excuse me, what did he just say?"

The clerk is a young woman whose false eyelashes flutter on her face like lovebirds in a bower. "He said a Super Beaver Moon."

"I just...I thought I heard wrong." He begins to giggle like an idiot.

"A supermoon is when the moon is full at its closest point to the Earth," the young woman explains, quite seriously. "I'm taking astronomy."

"Which is the Beaver part?"

"The full moon in November. The full moon in January is the Wolf Moon. My favorite is August," she says, then leans forward on the counter. "The Sturgeon Moon." She shrugs with a *Beats me* expression. "Sturgeon Moon! Anyhow, it's going to be the biggest moon any of us ever saw. At around nine tonight, you sit out on your porch. It's warmish for November."

"Could I exchange this candy-corn doughnut? I didn't realize—"

"No exchanges or returns, sir."

"Oh."

"You enjoy your Super Beaver Moon, now."

He is just crossing the parking lot to Rosina when an elderly Navajo woman comes to mind. There, on the stony hillside: water coming out of the rocks.

He checks his messages to find he has (inattentive juror) missed the final Prize vote by one day. He learns this not from Finley Dwyer, who apparently cannot be reached, but from Freebie.

"Well, but could I add in my vote?" Less says, panicking as he tries to manage phone conversation, navigation, and manual transmission. "You see, yesterday I was detained. I sent a message."

"We did talk about that! I stood up for you! But Finley said if we started bending the rules now, where would we end up?"

"But yesterday *was* the end. You bend the rules at the *end.*"

"Sorry, but yesterday we voted to kick you off the jury."

"What?"

"If it helps, I abstained."

"Thank you, Freebie." Less wipes his eyes with one hand. There goes more money. Well, the recent check will help cover any deficiency in funds.

The council has voted to expel you permanently from Ambrogio.

"Actually, it solved a lot for us," Freebie says. "Finley wanted Natasha Ashatan, but of course, she's a poet. Vivian wanted Michael Saint John but she forgot he won last year. Edgar voted for Overman, which took some sorting out."

"I thought that wasn't how you wrote about queers?"

"It took some sorting out."

A truck honks at him and he realizes he is between lanes. "Freebie, to be honest, I have to go—"

"We threw out everything and started over. Finley got who he'd wanted from the beginning. Anyway, it was the only compromise we could reach. I can't tell you the winner, though, Arthur."

"Honestly, Freebie—"

"We announce it Monday!"

"Great, gotta go—"

"See you in New York!" says Freebie as he ends the call, apparently forgetting Less is no longer on the jury.

Less breathes deeply and shakes off this new shame. After all, tomorrow is the start of his lecture tour of the East! He will make his little pile of money to add to the other piles of money, and some new miracle will make up the rest. For don't men like Arthur Less always end up safe?

As he passes from the Carolinas to Virginia—strange, how keenly he feels the sensation—the landscape metamorphoses, as if by the removal of a kingdom's curse, into old familiar shapes: the jagged tree line individuates into dogwood, tulip, red maple; insects (rest-stop terrors since Palm Springs) transform from urinal-crawling aliens into good old daddy longlegs; the highway grass turns an ordinary green, the sky a prosaic gray; even the air loses its perfume, as the exotic particles of these long weeks fade, revealing mere asphalt and burning leaves, and now, as he passes over a bridge, arrives the scent of mud and wet stone: the Potomac. A spell has been broken and the world around Arthur Less loses some of its sting and glory, becoming safe and commonplace— the sensation of arriving home.

He passes the gaslit colonial village of Alexandria, where, on one side of the highway, white diners are served replicas of George Washington's meals (mutton and yams), and, on the other side, Black families sit and chat on row-house stoops, sharing pink-tinted sheet cake. Off to the north, in plain-visaged Rockville, are the graves of F. Scott and Zelda Fitzgerald, consigned for eternity to lie beside a shopping mall. Less crosses the Potomac, and here it is: Washington, DC, stern gray city of law! How well he knows this route, and, after a few scratches, how easily the stylus falls into the vinyl groove of memory.

Out your right-side windows, passengers, you can see the very spot where teenage Arthur Less waited tables for three miserable summers: Thee Wayside Inn, allegedly founded in 1784 and allegedly visited by President George Washington. Less was forced to wear breeches and a tricorne in candlelit rooms, greet guests with "What cheer?," and refer to them as "Goodman" and "Goodwife." His buckle shoes wore thin as he bustled among the tables, and his vocabulary retrograded to eighteenth-century patois. "What cheer, Goody Less?" he would say to his sister, Rebecca, to which she would respond: "Fuck you." Our hero's suffering was brought to an end when he arrived at work one day to find a crew of firemen examining a pile of wet and blackened timber where Thee Wayside Inn had stood. These modern men turned to Less, in his breeches and tricorne, and perhaps saw there a teenage Rip van Winkle.

By then, however, his humiliation had already reached its apotheosis. Let us picture a particularly wince-inducing evening when the quarterback of DelMarVa High had celebrated his birthday there. The quarterback who, with his friends each morning in homeroom, smirked at gangly Less while reciting: "I pledge allegiance to the *fag* of the

United States of America..." And who, that night, took cruel and easy pleasure in watching Less, in hose and breeches and tricorne, serving them a flaming pudding while chanting, "Huzzah! Huzzah! Huzzah!"

The heat of the flaming pudding, of the burning inn, and of adolescent shame begins to cool as Less mounts the great Bay Bridge over the Chesapeake. The sunlight sparkles on its dark waters as it seems to exhale into the Atlantic. Sailboats are in movement today, and somewhere down there is a place his mother had taken them to, a waterside joint where butcher paper was thrown over the table, buckets of blue crab were brought in, and adolescent Arthur Less was handed a hammer and told to follow his heart's desire. He crosses over to the marshes of eastern Maryland and miles of scrubby winter farmland and, at one point, road construction, featuring a pregnant woman with long yellow hair, an orange construction hat, and a STOP sign who holds Arthur Less in place for ten full minutes, her eyes never leaving his, before reversing the sign to SLOW—for this, he gives a grateful wave. Briefly he imagines her life. The thought is diluted by still more miles of stubbled farmland before he crosses the Mason-Dixon Line.

And now he is in Delaware.

Cross the lower part of the state and you will arrive, of course, at the Atlantic, and the town you will arrive at is called Rehoboth. It looks similar to many beach towns in the mid-Atlantic, with its saltwater taffy and fudge, its rinky-dink midway of bumper cars and cotton candy, its beaches cleaned and then dirtied by the tide, garlanded twice a day with seaweed. There are a hundred of these towns. The difference is that this one is queer. It didn't start off queer; it started off as a Christian retreat by the ocean. But things went another way. Who knows why? Who knows why anything happens in America?

The house is one of those beach houses on stilts, and Less walks up the steps and knocks on the door. It opens on a woman with a low cloud of silver hair, thin lips, sharpened nose, and elongated chin recalling Viking invaders from the Bayeux Tapestry.

"What cheer, Goodman Less?" asks his sister. "You've grown a mustache!"

"What was he like?"

They are in the kitchen of her little house, clapboard arrayed with crab nets and starfish, rustic and simple except for the oceanside wall, which, like the one indulgence of a hermit saint, is made magnificently of glass. Less is sitting on a stool in a borrowed college sweatshirt; Rebecca is chopping onions. The Atlantic of their childhood shimmers in the autumn air.

"Harmless," Less answers.

She smiles over her Dewey beer. "You see?" Rebecca wears a jumpsuit, but hardly like the one from their Easter memory; it is black with a white stripe down the side. She told Less she wears it almost every day; life has become easier.

"Almost harmless," Less cautions her. "Pink, bald, old."

"Aren't you glad you went?"

"He told me he forgives me. *He* forgives *me*!" He trembles at the final effrontery: "In *German*!"

Rebecca tosses the onions into a pan. "That's what dying people say, Archie. They say they love you and they forgive you. I think it's a script the hospital hands out."

"I didn't hear the *love* part. And he was mad about something I wrote. It was the strangest thing. Then he invited me to his house... well, not *his* house—"

"*Nutrition Play.*"

"What?"

"He's mad because you put him in *Nutrition Play*."

"The father is fictional; it's a composite character, nobody understands that..." Less sighs.

Rebecca says nothing. Less looks out at the ocean and the mess of seaweed and trash tide-washed onto the shore.

"He came and he was charming and... it's not even his house. He's sponging off some rich woman named Wanda. Like always. And I...," he starts and closes his eyes against the shame. "And I had this stupid idea he'd sponsored my tour."

"Oh, Archie."

"It's not his fault," Less tells her, setting down his Dewey lager (flicker of a rafting memory). "I got it into my head that he'd brought me out there. That he was rich and throwing money at me and...of course he wasn't. He just saw it in the paper. No, Wanda saw it in the paper. He just attaches himself to some woman for stability and tells lies to get by and..." He trails off, staring out at something over the water.

"Archie?"

Less says, "What I came all that way to say to Dad, I realized I didn't need to say to him."

Rebecca is silent.

"It's simple. It's just 'I don't want to be like you.'"

"Oh, Archie."

"And I am."

"No, you're not."

"The arrogance. The Robertness. Maybe it's the only thing I know. That's what Freddy thinks."

"That's nonsense, Archie. It's nonsense."

A night bird says, *Ki-ki-koo. Ki-ki-koo.*

Less wipes his eyes, chuckles, and asks, "What about you? Still Ring for the Maid?"

A grin. "Oh! I'm so glad you asked. I fired her."

"It's hard to get good help."

"Now, instead, I kind of...shudder. It's still very

ladylike. Like I'm a dowager and you've suggested I take the public bus, and I sort of…" Here Rebecca closes her eyes, lifts her hands, and trembles in disgust. "I'm keeping it very Maggie Smith."

"Does that mean your anxiety's better?"

She says, "My doctor doesn't know. Nobody knows. I'm a curiosity. I think my anxiety has reached middle age. I think it's going to age right along with me."

"Just keep it ladylike."

A gesture of impatience. "Oh yes! I think this is just who I am now. Your friend Zohra says this is the price I'm paying for being divorced and happy in a Puritan country. I think in a 1980s comedy version, Steve Martin would be a Pilgrim who's, like, cursed by a witch and time-travels and ends up very, very tiny living inside my skull. And the witch is Lily Tomlin and she's immortal and now she's running an oil company I work for or something."

Less raises his eyebrows. "You've got a hit on your hands."

"So to speak!" She lifts her hands again and trembles and they both laugh at the ghastly thing that has happened to her. "Oh! I have your mail." He remembers he had forwarded his mail from the Shack and finds, among the pile of bills, a card with the simple message *Dear Arthur, I visited Robert today and can report that no ghosts walk. Today I finish my last rug. I hope your travels are well. Love, Marian.*

"What is that?" Rebecca asks.

He begins to explain about a debt and a weaver and a poet—

"No, in your hand, Archie." She is pointing to Less's right hand, in which sits a pen that he has removed from his breast pocket, perhaps an automatic motion in the presence of bills. "Is that Mom's?"

"Yes."

She frowns. "Wait, did you steal it after the funeral?"

"You probably don't remember we talked about this," he explains calmly. "It was stuck. The cap was stuck on, maybe the ink leaked and dried, I don't know; you said just take it."

"That doesn't sound like me."

"Well," he says, "I took it. And the cap was stuck for good, nobody could get it off. None of my friends, nobody, it was a joke in my house. Robert said whoever could take it apart 'is rightwise king born of all England'! If I have that right." Less laughs.

Rebecca asks him who took the pen apart.

He describes how one morning he was making a phone call and asked for a pen and was handed his mother's with the cap miraculously removed. Just like that, his mother's pen. Like it was nothing at all. "Of all people," he says. "It was Freddy."

That's right; it was me.

"Sword in the stone," she says very simply.

A pause. "Yes, I suppose," he says. "Sword in the stone. What are we making for dinner?"

Crab cakes, of course. Delaware crab cakes and mango salad with a curry dressing, something their mother used to make when she allowed herself the luxury of crabmeat—for her birthday or a visit from her children—and as always, it is accompanied by a celebratory awe. For though they grew up by the sea, they hardly ever ate from it; their mother had grown up inland in Georgia, and poor. To cook a whole fish or clams or mussels seemed as bizarre to her as sushi seemed to her parents. As Thomas's grandma Cookie would say, we are all having different experiences. After dinner, they do something else their mother would never have done: take a walk on the beach on an autumn night.

Less wears his poncho. Rebecca is wrapped in a blanket and has brought all her minibar bottles. She apologizes that she can't come to his event tomorrow. "I did see one of the posters and..." She laughs.

"Oh no."

"It's not your photo, Archie!"

"They keep doing that!"

They laugh and walk until they reach the rocks, then turn back. The view now is of the beach houses, mostly empty and shuttered against winter storms, but a few lit up out of season. From one comes the sound of a party; Rebecca says it is her lesbian friends. They could join them, if he wants a party, but Less demurs. He says he needs to have a clear head in the morning for his Lecture Tour—one more stage and the debt's repaid! His Lecture Tour. One can almost hear the capital letters in his voice. But Rebecca does not ask about the lecture tour.

"How are things with Freddy?"

Less takes a deep breath and closes his eyes. "Bee, he ran away to an island off the coast of Maine. For some project I don't know about. He said something needs to change among us."

"Among us?"

"Between us." *Romeo and Juliet and Robert*. "But he didn't say what!"

"This is the guy who flew across the world—"

"Yes. And he's not answering his phone."

"Do you still love him?"

"Of course I do, Bee! But he's changed."

"Have you changed, Archie?" she asks.

"I don't want to change, Bee! I'm in my fifties," he says decisively. "I've changed enough."

The moon is not out yet, but there are stars, and the world that these Delawareans probably take as ordinary or even ugly—the mounds of kelp and sea litter, the hard stonelike sand, the rocks spattered with the candle wax of bird droppings, the smell of rot and life, the waves breaking into applause, and everywhere, everywhere, unstoppable life hidden or crawling or swimming—is, to anybody else (to me), extraordinary, beautiful, exotic, strange. Somewhere in the water, the fish lie listening, arranged like magic daggers in the dark.

"Zohra and I got close after the divorce," his sister says, bringing out her phone. "She went through something similar, you know. And I'll read you what she wrote me. I've got it right here. I said something like what you said, I said I didn't want everything to change, I just wanted this *one thing* to change. My marriage. Zohra said"—and Rebecca clears her throat before channeling Zohra's British accent—"'Fuck that.'" Less sees his sister transform into his old straight-talking friend as she reads from her phone. "'Fuck that. You don't get that, Rebecca. This isn't redecorating, this is house-on-fire shit. This is grabbing what to save. This is leaving shit behind. This is once-in-a-lifetime suffering and pain and heartache and yet it may be your only chance to decide what you really want. None of this *I don't want to change* bullshit. Hell no—you've changed. That's happened. Now what? Everything changes and this one fucking time, you're in charge of it, my God, so choose! Make the wrong choice, that's fine! That's fine! But choose.'"

Rebecca looks up with a smile. The waves give an ovation as she laughs.

There is a lesbian noise and Rebecca turns to

look. People are gathered on back porches and balconies along the shore. His sister makes a hooting sound, then pulls out of her pocket her miniature bottles. Arthur asks her what is going on; perhaps the police are on their way, as they might have been in decades past when the Lesses were underage here at the shore. But his sister just pauses to look at him and laugh.

"Archie!" she says with delight. "It's the Super Beaver Moon!"

Here, tonight, up and down the beach, he sees the Americans. Out on their porches or on the beach in plastic chairs, wrapped in blankets or afghans, gazing up at the moon. With their beers and snacks on their laps, eating them by streetlight or, in one instance, by the light of a floor lamp that has been dragged out into the yard. From more than a few porches, on more than a few lawns, American flags ripple in the breeze. The moon rises, large and bright, among the stars that cover the sky like dollar bills. We have seen, already, the constellation called the Question Mark. And what is the question? Could it be the one that Vit asked him back in San Francisco: *What if the whole idea of America is wrong?* It occurs to Arthur Less that here, looking upward from their porches on this Universe Appreciation Platform that is their home, his fellow countrymen await the Answer.

As, perhaps, do I.

America, how's your marriage? Your two-hundred-fifty-year-old promise to stay together in sickness and in health? First thirteen states, then more and more, until fifty of you had taken the vow. Like so many marriages, I know, it was not for love; I know it was for tax reasons, but soon you all found yourselves financially entwined, with shared debts and land purchases and grandiose visions of the future, yet somehow, from the beginning, essentially at odds. Ancient grudges. That split you had—that still stings, doesn't it? Who betrayed whom, in the end? I hear you tried getting sober. That didn't last, did it? So how's it going, America? Do you ever dream of each being on your own again? Never having to be part of someone else's family squabble? Never having to share a penny? Never having to bear with someone else's gun hobby, or car obsession, or nutrition craze? Tell me honestly, because I have contemplated marriage and wonder: If it can't work for you, can it work for any of us?

"Huzzah!" Bee shouts beside Archie, raising her bottle of rum. "Huzzah!"

"Arise and shine, for thy light has come" (Isaiah 60:1).

Less awakens while his sister is still asleep, showers, and pulls his father's suit out of the garment bag; through the haze of naphthalene, he can imagine his grandmother's house, some holiday, and this suit shimmering beside a Christmas tree or perhaps shimmering the evening of the school play when his father leans down to say he will join them later. Thomas played little Archie Less, and now Less has been cast in the role of the father. But he has no choice—he dons his one good shirt, slips into the suit, and finds it is nearly a perfect fit; the waist is a little tight, the sleeves a little short (perhaps the lace is deficient?). Less stands before his sister's bathroom mirror and sees a stereoscopic view: himself today and his father fifty years ago.

The suit is of the brightest possible blue.

He packs his few items, leaves a note for his sister (*Good morn, Goody Less!*), and goes outside to start up Rosina. The early beach light recalls summers spent at a rental house here, the piles of orgied horseshoe crabs, the sunburns, the backshore littered with seaweed and treasure, the piles of orgied flip-flops, his own particular hermit crab, and stories of an island close by where the wild ponies roam. He is back on Delaware farm roads that look best in the snow (it has not snowed), heading to his event in Dover, when Rosina breaks down at last.

It happens like this: Less finds himself trapped behind a small red car upon whose roof sits a sign, like a pageant queen, proclaiming STUDENT DRIVER. Moving so, so, so slowly along this small ordinary road of steel mailboxes arranged on their posts like feathered caps. So, so, so slowly and almost imperceptibly serpentining within its lane. Less knows he is not trapped behind; it is the STUDENT DRIVER who is trapped *before,* glancing terrified at the hulking ancient van trembling in the mirrors, trapped *within* the teenage Delawarean body Arthur Less remembers well. Is this why he ignores his own blinking dashboard light?

To relieve the STUDENT DRIVER's anxiety, Less detours; he knows the area, after all. His detour takes him, not without some pleasure, to his old hunting grounds. No building rises above a single level, no church or post office or hair salon. And then, rounding the corner, he catches sight of them: a dormant dogwood on a curb, a line of bushes on a drive, and, standing where the Reeds affixed him forty years ago, Saint Joseph raising his hands to the Delaware sky.

They have been here all along; it was Arthur Less who abandoned them. This childhood kingdom deserted for college and cities and after his mother's death renounced for good, everything given away or sold, so that Less was later forced to reconstruct it, painstakingly, with words. What is the term, I wonder, for a stateless citizen born in a country that vanished long ago and now living without passport or portfolio?

Walloon?

The most popular street name in America is Second Street (*First* replaced mainly by *Main*), and it is on Second and Elm (no elm) that Rosina takes her final turn. The cockpit lights up, the engine gives a telltale death rattle, a shudder passes through her system from nose to tail, and she voids, through her exhaust, a puff of white smoke such as the Vatican emits when it has chosen a pope. From this moment, she is never to speak again. Yet on she moves, as Less presses pedals in a panic and turns the key and tries to find an ally (no Dolly either), until Rosina rolls at last to a stop. Her final breath hangs in the air abaft, spreading wide like an archangel. Before them, a sign:

DELMARVA HIGH SCHOOL
GO HORSESHOE CRABS!

I pledge allegiance to the fag . . . Of all the places in the world to stop . . . *of the United States of America . . .*

But the archangel has called down a savior:

"Hey, is that old Archie Less?"

A small red car has pulled up beside Rosina, and a white man's white face is grinning from the passenger's side, waving at our hero. Beside him sits a frankly pregnant red-haired teenage girl. The man's bushy gray hair and mustache are unknown to Arthur Less, yet there is something familiar in his smile . . .

The sign atop the savior's car?
STUDENT DRIVER.

Let us enjoy Less's luck, for it is soon to run out:
The teacher for the STUDENT DRIVER turns out to be
none other than Andrew Pollack, the quarterback
who ridiculed Less so many years ago and who
seems to have no memory of this. "You back home
for long, Archie?" he asks and it takes some effort
for Less to find the lithe footballer and fetch him
through the wormhole of memory to this moment,
to this shaggy-haired man leaning out the window
of a STUDENT DRIVER car. Apparently, he teaches at
DelMarVa High: history and driver's education. In
an impressive act of abridgment, Less explains his
life leading up to the nearby literary event that he
now has no way to attend. A pause; the autumn
wind bats kittenishly at the high-school flag. "Well,
hop on in!" Andrew says, and Less takes the back
seat and is driven, by the terrified teenage STUDENT
DRIVER, all the way to Dover, hearing Andrew's
unabridged (but mostly uneventful) life until now.
Less comes to understand that life for some goes
smoothly, as free from incident as it is perhaps from
poetry; a fainter kind of happiness than Less has ever
perceived. We are all having different experiences.
With a wave goodbye, Andrew leaves Less at the
door ("Give me a call sometime, Archie! It's great
to see you!") of the United Baptist church.

★   ★   ★

"Hello, dear," says the woman holding a sheaf of pamphlets between the entrance columns, a freckled woman in a scarlet skirt-suit and glasses whose shoulder-length hair and wide-brimmed hat give her the pastoral aspect of a Quaker. The Black woman's smile for Arthur Less is somewhat rueful. "I'm Deaconess Perkins, can I help you?"

"I'm sorry I'm so late!" Less says, quite breathless and not insignificantly beginning to perspire through his one clean shirt. He takes a deep breath and explains: "My van broke down, I had to get a ride!"

Deaconess Perkins's face fills with genuine concern. "Oh, what a shame!"

She has found the perfect word: *shame* (though today's particular shame lies elsewhere). Less buttons the second button of his shirt, pulls his face into the smile he learned in the South, and says to Deaconess Perkins: "Well, ma'am, do I look okay? I hope I'm not too late."

With one beringed hand, she adjusts her hat and says, "I'm afraid you are. The event is just ending. But you look lovely, dear."

"What do you mean?"

"You can get your book signed if you like." Deaconess Perkins hands him a pamphlet, which he takes but does not read. "Are you a fan of Mr. Less?"

"Who?"

"Arthur Less, dear," she explains with a sympathetic smile. "He just finished."

As two rivers at an RV park might trouble each other's waters before joining, two realities now ripple in the air.

He stretches his head forward, tortoise-like; the skin between his eyebrows puckers.

"But I'm Arthur Less."

Each looks at the other as if they were insane.

Deaconess Perkins stands temporarily stunned into inaction, so our hero looks elsewhere for answers and, seeing the open door, simply walks through it into the church, whose tall nave windows, divided horizontally into clear and amber panes, butter the room with topaz light as one butters a cake pan, revealing in their autumnal glow a line of people waiting patiently before a table, behind which Arthur Less perceives both a familiar-looking man signing books and, more important (as Less finally reads his pamphlet), his own part in this folly. The title on the pamphlet:

SUNDAY WITH ARTHUR LESS

Frozen at the transept, bathed in golden light, our Arthur Less lets out a series of plangent sighs.

Ohhh!

He was confused; I cleared things up.

Not what I expected.

Ohhh!

When I saw your photo, I just knew we'd found the right one.

You're sure that was the author?

It's not your photo, Archie!

Ohhh!

The great floodgates of the wonder world swing open. The various strange events of this voyage—the various adventures he had no right to be on, these unlikely things, these honors and horrors that mystified our poor man until he simply shrugged his shoulders at the absurdity of life and his good fortune—come down to a simple explanation: It was all meant for the man who shares his name.

The other author; the alter Arthur.

Ohhh!

I am reminded of a magpie, screeching at his reflection in the mirror before realizing, with a cry, that the intruder is himself.

★   ★   ★   ★   ★   ★

    ★   ★   ★   ★   ★

★   ★   ★   ★   ★   ★

"Arthur fucking Less!"

Our protagonist sits in the back of a black town car on its way from Dover to Wilmington, Delaware. Sunlight floods the compartment. Beside him on the gray leather seat sits his temporary travel mate: a man in the vicinity of his own age, in the neighborhood of his own gravitational mass (shorter but broader), in the district of his own hair loss, sporting a mustache in snow leopard and not Lessian fox and a velvet suit of deep, almost Marianas blue. Something flashes in the sunlight—wire-rim glasses, wedding ring, steel diver's watch—but *he* does not dazzle; he absorbs, quietly, like the velvet that he wears. The impression he gives is of a bashful schoolboy who knows the answer but does not care to raise his hand. He is Black and his name is Arthur Less.

"Thanks again for the ride," says our protagonist.

But now the other Arthur is laughing, almost in tears, waving his hands. "No, I'm sorry, I'm sorry I find this so funny! It's funny, come on." He is clearly amused by the situation and has offered to drive (or, rather, let the Balanquin Agency's escort drive) our hero to broken-down Rosina to retrieve Less's things and then deliver Less to the train station in Wilmington, Delaware. He looks, smiling, at our hero. "So Arthur Less, we meet at last."

"At last."

"Wait!" The Black man's face knots itself into

mock fury. "You canceled my hotel last night, didn't you?"

"Oh my God, I did," says the white man, putting his hands over his face. "I'm so sorry."

"Shame on you!" Goofy laughter: *ha-ha-HA*. "Canceled my hotel!"

"It just never occurred to me that Balanquin—"

"Well, apparently your agent has been emailing them the whole time *I've* been emailing them—"

"So I took all those offers from you? I'm so sorry about this." Our Less lowers his hands. "I have to ask you. This is so embarrassing..."

"Out with it."

"Did a Southern theater troupe contact you about performing your work?"

"In its entirety?"

"Oh, shit."

"They called back and canceled. Said they'd made a mistake. Don't tell me...oh, well, shit!" *ha-ha-HA*.

Our Less laughs as well: *AH-ah-ah*.

A clunk and jostle signals they have passed onto a high bridge overlooking a straight shining waterway. The other Arthur's eyeglasses go flying off into the seat well; his composure vanishes as he pats blindly around his feet. *Of course*, our Less thinks to himself. The velvet and voice are as much a disguise as a cloud-gray suit; down deep, he's an awkward novelist like any other. Is he also from the Netherlands?

The other Arthur Less says in a confidential tone: "Hey, it's a little early. But this is a momentous occasion, right? I took some bottles from the minibar and—"

Less produces Rebecca's rum from his breast pocket.

"Arthur Less! Look at you! Okay, give it here, we're going to do a mystery shot." He tosses all the bottles into a suit pocket and invites our Less to pick. After rummaging in the velvet pocket, our Less emerges with spiced rum. The other gets Southern Comfort. Less notices now the pierced left ear from the author photo.

"Damn it," he says. "I hate Southern Comfort! Well, we take what comes. Here's to Arthur Less."

"And Arthur Less."

They toast and share a laugh—*AH-ah-ah; ha-ha-HA*—as they might share in great good fortune.

The bridge tower's shadow rolls across the chauffeur and Arthur Less and Arthur Less. Our Less tries to sit very still in his seat, but during this part of the conversation, each expansion joint the car passes over causes our hero to bounce slightly as if on a trampoline.

"Hey, we almost met once!" says the other Arthur Less. "I was passing through San Francisco, and Silvia Tsai had a dinner party and said she was inviting you; she thought we should finally meet! But you didn't come."

"I don't remember that."

"I do—you were on a trip around the world!"

The poignancy of this remark surprises our Less; he has to blink back tears. He could not even tell you why this is happening.

Our Less asks, "Did you ever interview H. H. H. Mandern?"

"I was asked to, but honestly, it's not my thing."

"Well, I did."

"You did? Bet he was a piece of work."

The theater of the Southeast. The tour of the East. The mad Sancho Panza–ing across the Southwest. Lucky breaks—all stolen from this man?

We are crossing the Chesapeake and Delaware Canal, suggested by Benjamin Franklin in 1788. Since it spanned two states—Maryland and Delaware—a typical fraternal struggle ensued, with a properly absurd solution that stands to this day. On the Chesapeake side of the canal, a Maryland pilot boards the ship and takes it as far as the state line; there, a Delaware pilot boards the ship, still in motion, ousts the other, and guides the boat to the Delaware River. A reverse buccaneering happens east to west. And yet the halves of the canal are as identical as twins.

With a jolt, they reach the other side.

Our Less says, "I think I have something that belongs to you." Out of the inner breast pocket of his father's suit, he pulls a worn wallet and, from it, a worn envelope. Our protagonist stares at it for a moment, then hands it ceremoniously to his mystified fellow writer. "It's a long story," he says as the other opens it. "But in Savannah, a foundation gave me the wrong check." Our Arthur Less barely suppresses a sigh, thinking, *I'm sorry, Freddy. I just gave everything away.*

The other Arthur Less holds out the sea-green piece of paper and reads aloud: "The Gantt Center." And then he reads the amount. "Holy shit!"

Our Less lowers his head meekly. "I have no doubt they gave it to the wrong Arthur Less."

The other points at our hero: "You mean the white guy!"

Less is silent, head bowed.

"Because it's a Black foundation!" this Arthur Less explains, laughing. "For Black authors!"

"It is?"

"It is, Arthur," he says, then laughs again, pocketing the check with a shrug. "What are you gonna do?"

"Well," says our Less, "I know what we don't do, Arthur. We don't cash checks meant for someone else."

"Arthur Less," the other says in sudden animation, "I'm cashing any check I get!"

Signs appear for the airport, and the landscape takes on the blandness of functionaries around a king—rental cars, parking lots, flimsy motels, auto-repair shops—and one neon-lit sex shop, the jester. We could be absolutely anywhere in America.

The other Arthur Less's expression becomes quizzical. "What do we do about our names? They're going to get us mixed up forever." And now one of alarm: "What if the *Nobel Committee* announces that Arthur Less has won the prize for literature?" He laughs, but our Arthur Less freezes.

"Arthur," our hero says, very seriously. "I have a question."

"Should I take another mystery shot?"

"You weren't asked to be a juror for"—and he mentions the name of the Prize.

"You're on your own there," says the other Arthur. "I'm not eligible for any of that. I'm not even American. I'm Canadian!"

Our hero suggests they do another shot anyway, and they do. He brings out his mother's pen. "I wonder if you could sign my book?"

"You know," our hero says with a bright expression, "you might have given me an idea for my next novel—"

"We should both write the same book," says the other Arthur. "Blow their minds!"

Ha-ha-HA; AH-ah-ah.

(Does the world really need two of these creatures?)

At the Wilmington train station, they part and a formality returns. After all, they are likely to run into each other for the next twenty years or so and must keep the cordial distance of neighbors whose shared tree keeps dropping apples on both sides of a fence. Less retrieves his duffel and waves; only his reflection responds before the limousine heads off toward Baltimore.

The inscription in the book: *From Arthur Less to Arthur Less: May every day be Sunday.*

If this trip had a mantra, it would be "Wrong again."

Wrong about the weather. Wrong about the route. Wrong about manual transmission, boomerangs, and blueberries, inland seas and desert roads and canyons; wrong about wigwams, dive bars, and ferry schedules. Wrong about lovers. Wrong about fathers. Wrong about Famous Authors and theater troupes and Prizes. Wrong about Walloons.

But above all else, wrong about people. No surprise, in fact; novelists, with their love of structure and language and symmetry in novels, are frequently mistaken about the people who inhabit the actual world, much as architects are about churches. What is acceptable as true in a novel—that the waitress, existing merely to drop soup on the protagonist, need only have a hairdo and a hand—is, in the real world, an unforgivable moral error. For while our middle-aged author would probably consider himself a Rosencrantz or Guildenstern, certainly never a protagonist, the truth of existence has not quite pierced his soul: That in real life, there are no protagonists. Or, rather, the reverse: It's nothing but protagonists. It's protagonists all the way down.

And here is Arthur Less at the Wilmington, Delaware, station where the other's limousine has dropped him off. Look at him: Reading the train schedule, dressed in his blue suit, facing the gusty emotions of the autumn sky here on the site of the failed New Sweden, the very spot where Prudent Deless stepped onto American soil. Where can his supposed descendant go from here? Is there, on the schedule, some train to long-lost Wallonia? Or wherever he is from—surely Less is as much a pasticcio as any of us. Wiping away a sniffle with a Kleenex (his favorite handkerchief given away what seems like a year ago now), he very calmly takes out his phone.

"Freddy," he says to a deep-sea voice mail only Captain Nicholson will answer now. "Freddy. I don't even know where you are."

HaaaaaAAAAAAAAR! cries out an approaching train, the sound shifting from distant whine to imminent thunder (his sister, using only her hands, used to imitate a train in exactly this way, innocently portraying the theory of relativity; perhaps we are born knowing all).

Less stands very still and calm, eyes closed, preparing himself for the somewhat pleasant blast of air accompanying a train rushing by. He takes a deep breath and smells the lavender bush, the coolness of the muddy Delaware. His right hand creeps up to rest on his heart, the breast pocket of his jacket, where the solidity of his mother's antique pen so often offers a calming satisfaction, like the sensation of her floury hand on his in a long-ago kitchen. But there is no solidity today. He grabbles at the outside of the pocket, then, contorting his arm, searches inside. The limousine comes to mind, the other author signing a book, perhaps pocketing the pen like a handkerchief at a funeral. Less touches something and with great relief says "ah!"—but the autumn light reveals it to be a roll of mints. His fingers search, then search again. And again. But there is nothing there.

HAAAAAAAAAAR!

Less hurls the mints toward the train's passage, then collapses against the wall. He stares into the chaos as the train stampedes by. His father's jacket is swept open, and his hair, so carefully arranged this morning, is blown back, revealing the pink innocence of his scalp. He looks so much older. Bald, scared. And he is breathing in heaving sobs now. His body begins to tremble uncontrollably in the torrent of sound. His back to the wall, his eyes filled with tears.

"Freddy, I made..." He gasps. "I made a fool of myself!"

I traveled the world to win Less back, and the day he found me, I was at the top of his stairs, sitting on my luggage, smiling through tears of joy. And joy is how those days were in the Shack, filled with the freshness of love. Days of reading and sleeping and working and making love in the shadow of the trumpet vine. It was so easy to live that way, but for Less, did it somehow feel too easy? Unsurvivable if it ended? One morning, I found him in the bathroom crying. Are you all right? I asked. What's happening? He shook his head, eyes closed, and said that people always left him. He wiped away his tears, but he could not look me in the face. "So if you're going to leave me, Freddy," he whispered shakily, "please do it soon."

HAAAAAaaaaaaaar!

I saw on his face the years of despair and I said to my lover, "What are you talking about? I'm not going to leave you!"

As the train fades into the distance, the wind calms around him, and Arthur Less steps away from the wall. He looks to where the train has vanished. His face wet with tears, he searches for a Kleenex and feels, in his pants pocket, the cool cylinder hidden there. *Sword in the stone.* With a shudder, he lifts out his mother's antique pen.

Beside the Wilmington train schedule is an antique phone booth (devoid of a phone) and Less enters its prism to avoid the rising wind. He does some searching and calling around before reaching a hotel in Maine:

"Lad, you are speaking to the Oldest Living Whaler's Widow!"

We return to our narrator already in motion—

Did I not tell you, readers? The story has been writing itself while you were away...

Alas, my Walloon, you will not find me at the Oldest Living Whaler's Widow's Inn. I bade farewell to Adele, to Captain Nicholson, and to all the puffins of Valonica and took a bus down to Boston, where I had booked myself onto the train I always begged you to take with me. What is a man in love to do? As you stand there windblown in Wilmington, I have made it as far as Chicago, the tips of whose corporate temples rise above clouds of frankfurter steam, and I am waiting for my connection to the next train in my own crosscountry trip.

My first was called the Lake Shore Limited; I treated myself to a sleeping compartment called a "roomette" that I assumed would be shared with a stranger in the European manner. Not so; Americans have no interest in bunkmate comedy. Strange; I was relieved. I felt in myself some spore of Americanism coming to life. I tried to drown it in the lounge with whiskey (against penthos and kholon), then fell into a dreamless sleep as the train bumped noisily out of New England. At some point the conductor's voice came over the speaker, announcing: "Eerie... Eerie..."

I am afraid to say I napped through the entirety of Ohio and Indiana, which leaves them as pure as youthful crushes, as exotic and enticing as when I first read their names on the map: Elkhart and Waterloo, Sandusky and Elyria. When I awoke, outside the window: the Super Beaver Moon.

My next train is here—the Empire Builder!—and I board and find my new roomette (no roommate), its fold-down bed in daylight incarnation as a couch. It is probable that, as I put away my bag and settle in, as the Empire Builder builds steam (so to speak) and moves westward, Less is already talking with Adele, who informs him that I left two days before. He asks why did I go there? She cannot say. He asks why did I leave? She cannot say.

But I can say:

I have never seen America. But I need to, perhaps to understand my partner—his love of colonial-era ketchup and Prohibition-era "root beer," the Mont Blanc of ice in every sip of water, his terror of talking about race, his fascination with the island of Great Britain and indifference to the continent of Africa, his defense of the Democratic Party, his defense of the Fahrenheit scale, his belief, despite centuries of evidence to the contrary, that we are free to become our true selves, that we are free to love as we choose, that happiness is within our grasp if we reach for it.

Perhaps. But also—to understand myself. What if you had to wake up every day with someone promising a miracle, and every day you believed it, and every day it didn't happen? Don't we all look at our beloveds sometimes and think, *Why do I stay?* Why do we stay? There is something vital in staying.

(Are you looking at train schedules now, my love? Rental-car companies? Are you checking flights to Eerie, St. Cloud, Wishram, Redding?)

From Chicago, I cross the great Midwest. Night falls upon the icy lakes of Minnesota. I awaken once to visit the train car's shared commode, and while waiting for the occupant (all I see is the back of a dragon kimono), I chance to look out the window. There, in the dim light, lies a narrow shining strip of water that vibrates like a guitar string with the movements of invisible birds, replaced suddenly by the faint outline of a house with one lit window, a diamond, through which I can plainly see a man in overalls, exhausted in a chair, with a hammer in his hand—precisely the cover illustration on a book of American folktales my great-uncle gave me as a child. The ones that have fed my dreams. The conductor murmurs through the speaker, "Cloud...Cloud."

I awake in North Dakota to find a child staring at me through my window; I neglected to shut my curtains. We are in Minot and apparently it has snowed. The child gives me a dubious appraisal and moves on, revealing a train station astir with baggage and people; I could believe we have traveled to Budapest, and a long coiling serpent of steam intimates we have also traveled in time. The attendant who knocks on my door, offering coffee, even speaks with an accent. In this moment, I feel complete delight (the steam reveals its source: a hot-dog cart).

As we cross vanilla-frosted North Dakota, I think of Arthur Less.

(Have you gotten a call from I-Have-Peter-Hunt-on-the-Line-Please-Hold? Have you seen the morning papers? Have you heard the news?)

I do not need a ring. I tried marriage before, as many know. Let me state here that Tom Dennis was a good, decent man who treated me gently and, when I asked, he let me go. I do believe he loved me. But my fiancé was no easy roommate, leaving glasses on wood tables (wood tables, dear reader!) and dropping socks and candy wrappers whenever they ceased being of immediate use; he became like those beachgoers who assume their litter will go out with the tide. I should have known from this that my relationship was in some trouble. But I knew all couples had these fights, and I assumed they were not a detour from love but its bumpy path. So imagine my surprise when (Tom Dennis far in the rearview mirror) I moved into the Shack with Less and this new roommate began to exhibit the same tendencies—socks on the floor, underwear behind the bathroom door, unwashed plates—and, reader, I didn't care at all! I remember making the bed and finding underneath his pillow a mushroom-like profusion of tissues (for his morning nose-blow) and being filled with...not rage, but tenderness! With Tom Dennis, it was a chore I was willing to bear. With Less—I did not care at all. I stared at those tissues, stupefied. I did not care at all. The difference, you see, dear reader, is that I love him. How do I put it? He is not the best, God knows.

He is not the best.

But he is the best I ever had.

Because to love someone ridiculous is to understand something deep and true about the world. That up close it makes no sense. Those of you who choose sensible people may feel secure, but I think you water your wine; the wonder of life is in its small absurdities, so easily overlooked. And if you have not shared somebody's tilted view of the horizon (which is the actual world), tell me: what have you really seen?

From North Dakota, we glide across Montana. After days of Great Plains (America thoughtfully flattened into two dimensions), the approach of mountains feels as alarming as Frankenstein's creature lumbering toward a hermit's hut. Snow-topped, colored in sunset's bloodbath, the peaks rise from the plains with the glamour of movie stars and it feels incredible to realize we have moved past the velvet rope of foothills and are being ushered into their presence; I am starstruck. Rose-and-turquoise-tinted crags and scarps pass by me, faceted in ice. A general blueness arrives, but even in twilight, the glaciers glow with hoarded glory.

The conductor says, "Wishram. Wishram."

We arrive in Portland in the morning, and the connection to the final leg of my journey—the Coast Starlight—goes smoothly, bringing me into my last roomette, identical to the others except for small variations in hooks and latches. Somewhere to the north: Cape Alava, where the sun last strikes America. My destination is San Francisco, and as we tremble southward, I watch the sun set above Chemult, Oregon, one of the many places I never thought I'd see, or, rather, I never thought about at all. I find it deficiently laced with snow. I enter the café car just in time to overhear a kerfuffle in Klamath Falls.

"Somebody tried to jump the train!" says a thirtyish redheaded woman in a kimono. Her hair is long on top but shaved on the sides, where it is dyed green; her also green kimono reveals a troupe of tattoos (not in their entirety). She is eating from a block of cheese. I ask if she is headed to San Francisco, and she informs me she is going back to her lover. "I made the wrong choice," she says, looking at the cheese. "I hope he can forgive me." Her description of him? A tattooed Taiwanese phlebotomist. "And you?"

I tell her I'm waiting for a sign.

She frowns and offers me some of her cheese. I think of a sociologist in the cold of a porch in Maine and I decline. I find myself thinking: *Can I live without cheese?* We descend in darkness from the snowy mountains and in the lamplight, she reads aloud news of a Prize for a literary career. I tell her I know the man.

And now I must report an intriguing pattern that, had I not been shocked by recent news, I should have noticed earlier:

A ruckus in Redding, over the California line: During our brief stop this morning, I watch as an Aztec-red rental car screeches into the parking lot. I pull my curtain closed as some bandit actually tries to board the train without a ticket and a stalwart attendant thwarts his plot directly outside my window. I watch the struggle in a shadow-puppet play until their silhouettes shift northward and our train rumbles south along the Sacramento River.

Mountain shapes appear in the morning light, then gradually pine trees are revealed, covering them like feathers, and in Chico, just as we are about to leave the station, what seems to be the same determined Jesse James from Redding tries to board again, this time too late even to bribe the conductor, and through complex reflections, I can just make out a figure from the movies: a man running after a caboose. Unfortunately for him, modern trains have no caboose. I assume he is left coughing in the dust.

From here until Sacramento, because of the constrictions of river and rock, the rail runs along the highway; I become convinced the same Aztec-red sedan is keeping rapid pace with us, at some point coming so close that I can almost see the driver, but the road pulls away and I have surely mistaken one car for another. It occurs to me we are nearing a pirating spot on the American River as well as the Hotel d'Amour. But then we pass, quite unexpectedly, into a fogbank; the Starlight floats across a land becalmed by whiteness. Not like snow, not like something falling or moving, tangible or evident, but a blindness. A hush upon the world; this must be what it feels like for the dead to haunt our world, for now it is the Starlight that floats through the dominion of ghosts. What ghosts? Aleut and Delaware, Spanish and Navajo, English and African, French, Hopi, Wampanoag, Dutch...and Walloon.

Wait—I see something, and before I can name it, I see it, starboard, suspended otherworldly in the cloud: a presence. Why, as the poet said, this sweet sensation of joy? Hovering in the mid-distance, an unfinished work on canvas, he turns and looks at me as well:

A moose.

Across the nothingness we stare at each other. Then he is gone.

The train slows. The Aztec-red sedan speeds off ahead, casting three-dimensional shadows in the fog, and vanishes.

Oh, fog of loneliness; oh, mystic moose of love; oh, Arthur Less.

My roomette trembles as we pull into Martinez, in whose parking lot the Aztec-red sedan has found a home. The river spreads wide everywhere and the fog is lifting, and on a bench someone has painted WELCOME TO THE MILD, MILD WEST. Another tremble and we move on toward San Francisco.

There is a knock on the door.

We could invent a time machine, my Walloon, and go back and never choose each other. We could go back further still and try it all over again with what we know; try to be young together and in love, the way hardly anybody gets to be. Young and foolish and happy. But I have an easier solution: Just take the ordinary time machine. And try to grow old. Old and foolish and happy.

Another knock. Someone from behind the door shouts:

"Ladder down! Ladder down!"

I look at the fogbound landscape one last time, then

stand up, open the door, and as for what wanderer is standing there, face whittled by worry, creased by a hopeful smile, a bright carnation blooming on the crest of each pale cheek, what prizewinner has raced across America to choose me, gasping in relief as he sees my face...

Well, reader, I will simply let you guess.

ABOUT THE AUTHOR

ANDREW SEAN GREER is the author of six works of fiction, including the bestsellers *The Confessions of Max Tivoli* and *Less*. Greer has taught at a number of universities, including the Iowa Writers' Workshop, and has been a *Today* show pick, a New York Public Library Cullman Center Fellow, a judge for the National Book Award, and a winner of the California Book Award and the New York Public Library Young Lions Fiction Award. He is the recipient of an NEA grant, a Guggenheim Fellowship, and the Pulitzer Prize for Fiction. He lives in San Francisco and Milan.